PARTICULAR PASSAGES 2

EAST WING

Dedication

Welcome, intrepid reader.

This book is for you.

Thank you for joining us…
for venturing down unknown
passages alongside us.

May your bravery bring you
that for which you search.

May your search be that
which brings you the most
pleasure.

And may your search be
never ending.

Table of Contents

Imperfectum

by
Dave D'Alessio

Imperfectum

Sonata: Exposition

*W*illiam Sebastian Ralts sat in his tiny, cluttered basement office, his chair cranked up as high as it would go. He hunched over the cheap keyboard unrolled across the student essays, piled three and four deep beneath it. He stroked the plastic keys; the tinny tones of the keyboard's tiny speaker could not disguise the power and grace of the composition.

Ignoring the scarf that hung from the coatrack and tickled his ear, and the mouse that darted across the desk to help itself to a bite of forgotten pastrami sandwich, Ralts played a sequence of chords, three, and then four, and then a full four bars' worth. He reached across the keyboard to tap his pad, correcting a note it had transcribed improperly.

In the doorway, Okajima cleared his throat.

Ralts played on, fingers running across the keys, lost in the music he was composing. Soon Okajima was as well; the two of them wafted away on the elegant melody.

The theme resolved. It concluded on the tonic, which Okajima found perhaps too conventional, but, when it was done, Ralts leaned back and looked up. "Ah, Rokuro," he said. He bit into the sandwich. "How lon 've oo enn ere?"

"Just a few minutes, sir," Okajima said. He bent his head toward the pad. "It sounds most excellent. An étude, perhaps? Or a rondo?"

Ralts beckoned his assistant forward to let him read the notes off the pad. "A symphony, Rokuro. A symphony for the ages. And I mean that most literally." He tapped the work's title on the screen.

Okajima read, "*Imperfectum.*" He sounded dubious. "You intend it to be flawed?"

"I intend it," Ralts said, "to be unending. I intend it to go on forever, never finished, always in performance, new passages to be added as they are written. An infinite work for the infinite future of Humanity." There was a gleam in his eye that made the hair on the back of Okajima's neck stand up.

Okajima said, "I liked what I heard. Is it for the sonata?" Traditionally a symphony opened with a sonata.

"Yes, the exposition." Ralts spun back to his keyboard. "It's going quickly. Now that I have the theme, the development and recapitulation follow logically." He stroked the keys quickly, a second theme developed from the original melody, the notes scrolling across the pad as they were transcribed.

Ralts played on as though Okajima were not there, fingers on the keys, eyes on the pad, watching to be sure the transcription was perfect. Okajima had to clear his throat again. "How long will you be working on that, sir?"

Perhaps the assistant meant, "How long will you be working on that today, because you have classes and tutorials," but Ralts answered the larger question. "For the rest of my life, of course."

Ralts quickly completed the first movement, the sonata. He created an adagio for the second movement, a piece that moved more slowly but with great intricacy, lasting almost thirty minutes on its own. For the third movement, he chose the scherzo form; the simple ABA structure lending itself to extension, ABABA, ABABABA, and so forth. Okajima saw the point: a work meant to be unendingly performed needed to be flexible in structure.

For the fourth movement, Ralts chose a rondo with intertwining melodic lines, one twisting through the other and around a third. It was here that his genius truly showed as he added a fourth and a fifth voice to the music. Okajima listened in awe as they chased each other up and down and around and around, Ralts eventually weaving all five together. He added yet a sixth voice, sending it in to dash back and forth across the cloth the first five themes formed. The rondo lasted, according to Okajima's phone, for two hours, and when the sixth voice came together with the other five in a final chorus, it was clear that the symphony did not, could not, would not possibly end there, after only four movements.

As to the next movement, "Perhaps a recapitulation of the sonata," Okajima said.

Ralts faced him, eyes pointed in his direction but focused a thousand miles away as he heard the music in his head. "Brilliant, Rokuro," he said. As the fourth movement, another sonata would have signaled the end of the symphony; as the fifth, it led the music yet further on. "Brilliant."

Sonata: Development

Fourteen movements of the *Imperfectum* were transcribed on the pad when the symphony's performance started. It was played in a small hall, one specially built on the second floor of a building near campus. As befitted the playing of a song that would never end, rooms surrounding the hall included cots, showers, and lockers for the musicians. A small kitchen provided sustenance, and a storeroom was well equipped with violin strings and clarinet reeds and any other knick-knacks that might be of use to the modern major orchestra. Listeners were shepherded to and from their seats by silent ushers in black leotards and slippers; phones were checked at the door. "Not allowed inside, I am most sorry, sir or madam."

Sir Sergei Godzich conducted the first eight hours, his handlebar mustache twitching in time with his baton; he cycled through the rondo twice and was seen to cry at each performance of it. At the end of his shift, he turned the dais over to Marion Powell, on loan from the New York Philharmonic, with a whispered, "It is magnificent!"

As Powell looked down at the score on her pad, she saw a fifteenth movement upload, this one a largo, long and slow, but as she scanned it, she saw it was no simple musical brick house but a cathedral of sound, constructed of strong, soaring arches; she signaled the orchestra to skip ahead to it and forever after Ralts' fifteenth movement was called The Twelfth.

Ralts wrote and the orchestra played. Not for hours or days or weeks, but for years, exactly as he had planned. Twenty movements, fifty, a hundred and more, and always there was someplace else for the music to go, always a new director with a favored movement or set of movements. There was always an audience, willing to sit and listen to old music constructed in new ways as conductors jumped from movement to movement, or to the simple *Imperfectum* from beginning to end, now a two-day event.

Through the years, Ralts did not live on deli sandwiches and Chinese take-away alone: he was wined and feted, accepting the accolades he was offered with gratitude and a distant look in his eye as he heard more music in his head. He grew stouter and his fringe of hair grew out white, and he stooped rather than hunched over his keyboard. It was a real keyboard now, specially manufactured with ivory keys recycled from an older age before people learned respect for their elephant brothers, but integrated with his pad by the most modern wireless connection.

Okajima, too, was recognized for his contributions to the symphony, and for his own compositions, a series of concertos that was said to "infuse Eastern instrumentation with Western sensibilities to give us a new way to hear what we have heard all our lives." Strands of gray streaked his black hair now, and he sometimes brought his grown children with him to watch Ralts at work, the maestro smiling and writing leitmotifs for each that were subsequently heard in the *Imperfectum*.

It was as inescapable as physics that they were growing old. Ralts especially: prostate cancer slowed his productivity for several months. He survived the big C, but wrote only one new movement in that time. By then conductors had over a hundred twenty to choose from, and there was lively betting in Las Vegas on which would be played next as the performance went on and on.

And through this Okajima could not shake his sense of disbelief. Despite Ralts' intentions, the *Imperfectum* would end. It had to end. When listeners believed they had heard it all, when conductors looked over the score and decided there was nothing new to be learned, the infinite symphony would become finite.

And then one day Okajima went to Ralts' office, now a fine, sunlit studio instead of the cramped basement he had started in, and found the old man lying across his keyboard, smiling with his eyes closed.

Ralts was already cold.

Okajima did not try to find a pulse. He did not bother 9-1-1; he simply called Campus Security. They handled everything.

Once Ralts was gone, Okajima was left alone with the expensive keyboard and the detritus of Ralts' life. Most of it would be his after the will was probated; the old man had died childless and had told Okajima, "Rokuro, it's yours. The books, the instruments ... The symphony is yours as well. It is endless. It is *Imperfectum*, Rokuro. It must go on."

Okajima did not want to be enslaved to one piece of music the way his mentor was. He had a life, a career of his own. He closed the keyboard, started to turn away.

The pad, Ralts' pad, began to play.

It was a minuet that danced and laughed and spun the listener around and around, and deep inside it Okajima heard a tiny echo of the original theme, the theme that had started the Sonata, buried in the minuet. He heard how the new movement echoed what had come before and suggested what would someday come after.

To Okajima's ear, the minuet cut off three bars and two beats early. It was the point Ralts had died at.

Okajima could hear it in his mind, hear how the minuet would end, could feel the notes in his bones and feel his fingers playing them on the keyboard. Eleven beats. Surely, he could do that much for his mentor?

He played through the notes he could hear, the notes that would resolve the movement, and tapped "Upload."

After the minuet, the next movement should be slower, an allegro perhaps. Okajima sat down at the keys, adjusting the height of the chair.

Adagio

Critics hailed the Okajima era in the *Imperfectum*. "A worthy pupil of the master, respecting what has come before while adding a new vision of the future." "A-plus, an eleven out of ten." "Double-plus good."

Okajima added nearly seventy movements to the symphony. Of them all, he was fondest of the first; the eleven notes he had added to what Ralts had written, for that was the one piece that was both of theirs and bigger than both of them.

He retired. It would have been clichéd to die at the keyboard, and unlike Ralts, he had family. But by the time he retired there were others.

Jacob N'Dede added African sounds, African instruments, African sensibilities to the *Imperfectum*. At first, they were played *en bloc* but later integrated into the whole, the sound of one man's legacy heard through another man's ears, and they were beautiful in themselves. So, too, Shenhua Chang. She took time from her composing to direct the orchestra, and showed rapt audiences how her allegro (Movement 302) followed from the ideas behind a lento from the fingers of Ralts himself (Movement 37), through Okajima's sublime Adagio (Movement 172). It was subtle and beautiful, and when she called N'Dede up from the audience to lead his version of the Sonata (Movement 212) with her, the standing ovation lasted for twenty minutes.

The orchestra played constantly, now in a new concert hall outside the city proper, an entire campus for the orchestra and guest musicians, and for the people it took to support a small city of that size: the cooks and hairdressers, the janitors and bartenders, the dishwashers and floor moppers and bottle washers.

As they played, all year, every year, Humanity spread through the Solar System, into Luna's tunnels and to a terraformed Mars, to the balloon cities bobbing in Venus' winds, and domed colonies on Ganymede and Ceres and Titan. With them they took the *Imperfectum*, the original transmitted by radio, local musicians and high school bands picking out two or three movements to add to their repertoires, closet composers in a dozen solar colonies delicately taking hold of one of Ralts' themes and twisting it and turning it, speeding it up or slowing it down, building in their spare hours one single movement, one tiny part of the ever-expanding whole, for upload. New conductors knitted them into the body of the symphony, sliding them in here, using them to counterpoint there, as if to say, "These are the thoughts of many writers, but on a single subject."

The Earth-killing asteroid, long predicted, arrived. Earth was abandoned, her billions of people evacuated, the orchestra transported to Marsport, the symphony to anywhere there were human beings prepared to sit and listen, to feel the music moving forward.

Sol System suffered invasion. The Zarn, green-scaled and taloned, came to seize the riches of the system, the gas giants Jupiter and Saturn; when Humanity protested, the Zarn slapped them down, ruined their cities, herded resisters into camps. Only those who bowed their heads were left alone while Zarn factory ships dipped into the fifth and sixth planets, converting them into products only the Zarn understood. And still the symphony went on, quiet rebels writing subversive movements to be played under the snouts of Zarn foot soldiers, the rhythms tapped out on the steel walls of corridors, a few notes drawn in Mars' sand or scratched into the rock of uninhabited asteroids, symbols of unity, and of hope.

And when Humanity rose up against its cruel masters, when its tiny suicide ships destroyed the great Zarn cruisers, when men and women and children threw themselves bare-handed on the foot soldiers and slew each and every one, wordless voices sang the simple theme of the *Imperfectum's* Sonata, the song that had come to mean all that it was to be human.

Liberated, Humanity celebrated its freedom with a fete like none held before. There were games and feasts, and a party that lasted a week. Flags were flown wherever there was atmosphere, and fireworks fired into space, and at the height of the celebration a new movement was revealed, a chorale that added words to Ralt's symphony for the first time. A chorus of school children in red and white robes sang of poor, dead Terra:

"Our mother's bright, clear skies
"Stand over her green, cool hills
"Ocean waves lap
"Sweet winds waft
"Great rivers her lakes refill…"

Scherzo

The Zarn died, but their machines did not. Humans took them and learned their secrets, the way the factory ships transmuted hydrogen into higher elements, the way their engines powered cruisers at hyperlight speeds. Humans took those secrets and improved them and made them their own, and used them to leap out of the Sol System and into the Milky Way. They brought with them human determination and human ingenuity, and a symphony that never ended, that grew daily and even hourly as the anthem of an entire people.

The galaxy was full, full of planets and full of life. Homo sapiens met friends among the stars, allies they could depend on; they met enemies, warrior races prepared to fight for any reason. A great human Federation formed, arching across thirty planets in a dozen systems. There was a golden age as Humanity grew rich through trade and invention, became the idol of older, slower, less clever races. Ralts' *Imperfectum* was the soundtrack of the age, swifter, more upbeat movements preferred in performance, played by an orchestra of over a thousand pieces organized at the capital.

The Federation lasted for three hundred years before it was torn apart, looted by jealous and greedy neighbors.

Desperate and poor again, religion made its way to the front of peoples' minds. A prophet came forth, eyes glowing in his fervor, and Humanity united behind him. They freed themselves of their oppressors and vowed to bring human gods to the unbelievers. New movements in new styles were added to the *Imperfectum*, psalms and hymns and chansons; certain of its verses were sanctioned and some proscribed, to be erased from all official files of the score.

The theocracy marched forward to convert, or conquer then convert. Again, Humanity expanded; again, its neighbors resisted violently; again, it was driven back, its planets bombarded and occupied, its temples defiled.

After a century of occupation, Humanity rose once more, united by a single strong woman who declared herself Empress as she stood before a crowd of a hundred thousand souls, screaming themselves hoarse, tears streaming down their faces, the martial strains of Movement 2317 welling up behind her. This time Humanity would conquer!

And humans took their ships and weapons, and with their *Imperfectum* as their anthem they fought, defeating twenty, fifty, a hundred alien systems. They took that globe of space by force and held it for a dozen generations, powerful, respected, feared. The *Imperfectum* took another martial turn with new movements added at march tempos and in major keys, with new lyrics containing words like "hail" and "victorious," but still it continued to grow, in length, in volume, in spectacle.

After those dozen generations, the Empire of Man fell. It was an old story: a weak ruler, ambitious usurpers ... it collapsed into squabbling sectors, each with its own warlord.

The fall of their empire was the end for Humanity. Too dangerous to be allowed to roam free, occupying planets enemies lusted after, they were fought and fought hard, no quarter taken and none given. Most stood and died, hunted down by races who had vowed never to allow humans to injure them again.

A few, a lucky few, found their way through cordon and blockade, and looked for new lives on new planets.

Separated, isolated, these pockets of Humanity clung to life as they knew it: they worked hard to survive, they kept their history alive, and they played the *Imperfectum*, a voice or two every generation finding another way to add yet another movement.

But slowly they disappeared: their colonies were found and exterminated; or died of despair; or were too small, too inbred, to survive. Or they evolved into new species, one that was almost hairless, one that had a back that would not go out when lifting a weight, one whose telomeres repaired themselves, giving them extraordinary lifespans in human terms that no longer applied.

The candle that was Humanity, burned low, sputtered ...

Coda

The planet was called "Nest" in the common language, and its predominant species had once been avian. They were too heavy to fly now; millennia upon millennia of making and using tools, using wingtips that evolved into deft, useful fingers, had built their muscle mass as a species so high they were no longer aerodynamic.

Now they were intelligent, and built great soaring cities, structures that were fixed in the soil but spread upward, pods made of light metals replacing nests woven of twig and fluff.

There was a menagerie on Nest. It was a proper menagerie, with enclosures meant to mimic open habitats and not cages. One whole wing contained their ancestors, some of them still able to fly, others grounded forever; another wing housed the great predators they had once flown from but by now had outthought and outfought for Nest.

And there was a third wing, more of a tail as the zoo was laid out, and in it were wonders from around the galaxy, endangered in the wild but cared for here by keepers who loved them and veterinarians who did their best to care for their alien metabolisms. There was a Blacksport wyrm, and a Thalaxian tingler, and prowling its cage, tasting the air with its sensory tendrils, was a declawed Franexx, fifteen feet high at least.

In that wing there was a human, a solitary human, so far as anyone knew the last human, and it was very, very old. It had good days and bad; on the good days it would stand at the edge of its enclosure— there was no need to lock it in—and twinkle its fingers at the immature fledglings hopping by. On bad days it stayed in its hut, humming a song no one but it knew. The song was simple, only a few bars long it seemed, but it hummed those bars over and over, all day until it finally dozed off.

The time came when the vets just looked at each other and shook their heads, their cranial feathers flat with sorrow.

It seemed to know as well. It lay down on the pads it slept on, breath growing short, and stared up, humming when it was not coughing. Its habitat was open to the skies when the weather was clear, and it stared up at the stars and wondered if any of them was Sol.

Its breaths grew short and rattled in its chest. It gasped for air. Its fingers flexed, its fists clenched, its toes curled as it fought to inhale one more time.

It forced itself to take one more breath.

It sang.

"Our mother's bright, clear ssss........"

Sonata: Recapitulation

The Woolalon might have been designed to be archeologists. They were motile and intelligent, but their bodies owed more to ferns than lions or orynx or thrawls. Their four upper limbs were stronger than they looked and tipped with sturdy pads. It was like having a brush at the tip of every finger.

There was an old star, a G2V in a quiet arm of the galaxy, that was about to expand into a red dwarf. It wasn't going to happen today or even during this orbit of the planet, but it was going to happen soon, and when it did the inner planets of its system would be scorched down to their mantles, destroying any signs of past civilization.

The closest planet to the star was nearly volcanic even as the star shined normally, and they decided not to waste time there. The second had some artifacts, but its atmosphere was brutally hot and savagely windy; it wasn't worth the risk, at least not yet. The third planet was barren. Tests showed it had once been habitable, but an asteroid strike had finished that.

The fourth planet, though, was loaded with artifacts. There were entire cities still intact after a fashion; the constant winds and scouring sands might have damaged them, but their outlines were still clear, and here and there artifacts could be recovered.

The inhabitants had mastered printing. Fragments of ancient writing were arranged horizontally and composed of a number of symbols so restricted that it suggested a phonetic language. Scholars labeled it "Linear X," and turned it over to the linguists.

Ona-Wool flicked her fingers across the sand, brushing the grains aside a layer at a time. There was something delicate below; the scanners had detected it. Now, bringing it to light required her delicate touch.

It was bound in stiff, heavy paper, the best kind from her standpoint, because the hard, heavy outside would protect lighter pages inside. She breathed across it, clearing the last dust away. There was writing on the outside. She sounded out the phonemes of Linear X: "Ee-mm-pp-urr-f-eck-tu-mm." The sounds meant nothing to her, but the subtitle, "Ralts' Unending Symphony," well, "Ralts' " was nonsense, "Unending" she thought she understood, and "Symphony" included "phon," which indicated sound.

She slid a tendril under the cover and carefully turned it over.

There was a whole new text inside, most of it clearly not in Linear X. For one thing, the characters were outlined on a graph or table of five horizontal lines; sets of them cascaded down the page. There were some markings in Linear X, but inside the grids was an entirely different text, a simplified notation of circles and lines.

She brushed her tendrils across it carefully. One day ... one day they'd be able to read this too, and when they did ... "We'll hear this," she said.

From the Author

Imperfectum was originally written to a prompt I can't remember any more, and originally appeared in Space Opera Libretti, edited by Jennifer Lee Rossman and Brian McNett. Like a lot of my stories, it's full of Easter Eggs, since I love them dearly. One is the obvious shoutout to Robert A. Heinlein, but one is more personal to me: The character of Rokuro Okajima is named after a character from the anime Black Lagoon, but patterned after a friend, Dr. Michael Ego. Michael unexpectedly passed away before publication and never got to see "himself" in print. I hope he would like "himself."

You can drop me a line and ask about some of the other Easter Eggs if you like.

About the Author

Dave D'Alessio is an ex-industrial chemist, ex-TV engineer, and ex-award-winning animator currently masquerading as a social scientist. His more than thirty published short stories have appeared in venues including Daily Science Fiction and Heroic Fantasy Quarterly; "The Twenty-Year Reich" was a finalist for the Sidewise Award in alternate history fiction. He lives near an Ikea, enjoys assembling furniture, and could really use an agent.

Free Pie

by
Matt J. McGee

Free Pie

*T*he first call came at 3:17am last Tuesday. I know most people don't have home phones anymore, but I do. I'm a 90's guy. I may have an iPhone but in some ways I still smell like teen spirit.

The ringing Panasonic cordless broke a lovely Ambien slumber four hours before the alarm. Unfortunately, the answering machine didn't pick up; the power had gone out Monday during a windstorm, and I hadn't reset it.

Ring.

I fumbled around the nightstand, found the phone, beeped the answer button, and pressed it to my ear.

"Hello."

"I want free pie!!!"

A stereo played in the background. A couple people talked casually. The guy didn't seem to be in any kind of a prankster hurry. Apparently, he just wanted pie.

"What?"

"Isn't this where I call to get free pie?"

"What? No. You woke me up. What's wrong with you?"

I plopped back on my pillow. The world had other plans. That would be the first of eight calls, the last coming at 7:18am.

"Hello?"

"Free pie guy!! I want my free pie!"

By now I had showered and was getting ready to go out the door. I was sitting on my bed buttoning my shirt. "Look man. I don't know anything about free pie. Stop calling."

"But—!"

I went to the answering machine, pressed a couple buttons and waited for the red RECORDING light.

"Hi this is Simon. If you have a message for us, leave it on the tape. If you're calling for free pie, I'm sorry. We're all out."

BEEP.

I came home that night to eight messages. For a guy without a possessive stalker girlfriend, that's a bit high.

Beep.

"Hi—my name's Bekka. I know you said there's no more pie, but do you know where I can get some? Marie Calenders sucks, and there aren't any good bakeries around that I know of. Call me back." Then this woman, who sounded around 30 and attractive in a haven't-got-too-many-cats kinda way, left her number. I wrote it down. She sounded like the kind of woman I could learn to bake for.

BEEeeeP.

"I want my free pie!!!"

That did it.

I went over to my laptop, opened Google, typed in "Free pie" and my city. Nothing. I added my name.

Bingo.

I work for Crane's, a high-end audio-video store. Last week I sold this guy a new big screen for his house. I gave Sylvester, that's the guy, my personal card and told him to call if he had any problems.

Not only did he have a problem with literally *everything*, he couldn't even program channels without calling us for detailed instructions. He called to ask what kind of batteries to put in the remote. Sometimes he'd call just to talk. His girlfriend, car trouble, Star Wars, blah blah.

After a couple days, I stopped taking his calls. There are limits to everything, and I draw the line at calling me while I'm trying to work the sales floor just to say, "I've decided red is no longer my favorite color. I think black is more neutral and less offensive to people, don't you think? I mean, everyone wants to be liked..."

I finally said, "Hey man I've got a customer, I gotta split."

"Oh, yeah, yeah. Go do your thing! Sorry to bug you."

"Thanks, talk to you later."

Bad choice of words. An hour later the desk phone rang again.

"Hey man, I was just going through the newspaper, and they've got these kickass deals on Sara Lee frozen dinners. There's all kinds. They've even got little desserts in the middle, like cornbread, and pie, and stuff. You feel like having one for dinner tonight? There's even one where—"

"Listen, Sylvester. I appreciate you're just trying to be friendly. But this is too much. I want you to stop calling."

"I—"

"No, listen man—don't fucking call me again or I'll slap you with a cease and desist so fast you won't know what hit you."

"You don't have to curse."

"Yeah, apparently I do, because you don't take a hint. I'm hanging up, Sylvester. Don't call again."

"I just thought you'd want some pie…"

I slammed the phone down.

And apparently that's where it started. Sylvester had my number, along with his very own Facebook and Yelp accounts. By doing a little tracing, I found a post on his page dated the previous Tuesday saying "call this guy for free pie!" and giving my home number. Who'd have thought a nutjob would have 807 online friends to do his bidding.

After a couple days the calls slowed down, and life got pretty much back to normal. I learned to shut the ringer off before bedtime. My calls for free pie were down to two a day. Sometimes no one called at all. I didn't miss it.

And Sylvester never called back, though that didn't stop me from calling my lawyer.

"These people usually forget about you. They're nuts and have other shiny objects to distract them. A cease and desist would just stir things. Don't kick a snake."

"You mean a sleeping dog."

"Exactly. Three months from now he'll be in jail or left town, moved on. Crazies always have a new target. They rarely recycle. They're constantly finding new battles to fight and never finish the ones they start. Makes life hell for us a little while but," he concluded, "eventually they just fall off."

"Like a wart."

"Or some other bad infection."

"Yep. So, meantime…"

I did what he said. I went to work like usual. One night, feeling good after having made a particularly big sale, I stopped by the bakery. I set the pink box on my kitchen counter and put away my things.

    I picked up Bekka's number.

    "Hello?"

    "Hi," I began. "I'm returning your call about the free pie."

From the Author

At the time I was having trouble with some people using encrypted software for 'spoofing,' where the caller mimics another phone number. I talked with a friend at the FCC who said the law hadn't caught up with the usage yet. About 40 miles away, Ashton Kutcher's haters were calling 911 to say there'd been a shooting at his house. Turned out that prank was a 12-year-old boy. The dateless losers calling me were in their 40s and apparently still own Jerky Boys CDs. They even used a similar voice. They stopped after I called one of them Sizzle Chest.

Then I took out my Blackberry and turned it into a story.

About the Author

Matt McGee writes short fiction in the Los Angeles area. In 2022 his work has appeared in Red Penguin, Sweetycat Press and Gypsum Tales. When not typing he drives around in rented cars and plays goalie in local hockey leagues.

Wicked Wellingham

by
Jason A. Wyckoff

Wicked Wellingham

"Refrigeration is what killed grave-robbing," the man said, and damned if he didn't use the same tone my great-grand-pappy the train engineer did when he talked about what the interstate highway system did to rail freight. "Late Nineteen-teens. Slowed the ticking clock of decay. By then the government had decided they had no particular obligation to keep the unclaimed poor from giving back to society one last time, which considerably upped the available supply for medical schools' demand, but the ability to cut into the same corpse, again and again, at your leisure, was the thing that really put an end to it."

He pursed his chapped lips as he stared off like he sure did miss that old tire swing hanging over the creek. "About the only time you'd want to dig up a grave now is to hide another body on top of the already-interred one. Nobody looks the one place you'd *expect* to find a corpse, even with the disturbed dirt."

Again, I was uncomfortable with the *familiarity* in his observation. I didn't want to ask him straight out, but he must have guessed what I was thinking because he chuckled. His voice was so low it sounded like the AC was rumbling.

"No, sir. Not a grave-robber. Just the opposite: grave-digger. But, same as any profession, you have to educate yourself about the competition. It brings to mind Oscar Wilde: 'You can always judge a man by the quality of his enemies.' What, I can't quote Wilde? Sure, I read. Lots of time to read: I've had my share of 'hurry up and wait' odd jobs over the years. But the one I did most consistently was grave-digging." He winced and muttered, "Don't ever say 'planting stiffs.' It's disrespectful."

How's this for dissonance? We weren't holed up near a low fire in a gothic castle while banshees rode tempest winds in the night; in fact, we were seated at the bar of a donut shack while the sun said 'how-do-you-do' to another gorgeous fall day in Michigan, and the closest thing to screaming going on was our server, half-tucked into the kitchen, cursing at her deadbeat baby-daddy on her cell phone.

I'd been holding on to a steady job, for once, at a natural food mart in Traverse City, when someone in the family tracked me down a couple days prior to tell me that Great Auntie Miran was losing to the big C in a big way, and, truth be told, I knew I was probably already too late to see her by the time I pulled out of the car rental agency. But, hard as it was to interact with my family at times, they were still family, and I owed it to Auntie Miran to see her off.

Maybe I'm too young to love a sour cream donut the way I do, but nothing else hits the spot four-plus hours into a drive. And of course I'm always up for friendly conversation. Now, if you said you were on your way to a funeral and the stranger next to you starts talking about grave-robbing, that would be pretty messed up. You know what's nuttier, though? When he starts in talking about it on his own accord. I never did say where I was bound.

"I can tell you about two exceptional things," the man continued, "and these are both first-hand accounts: the death of Jeffy Reebus, and the un-death of Parson Phillip Wellingham. The first led to the second, and the second led to my exit from that particular profession."

I admit he fit the mold. He was undeniably of Scandinavian descent, with gold-grey hair and beard, and ruddy, hollow cheeks. Even seated, he was a head taller than me. He looked like he might've used to participate in seal-throwing contests or whatever it is Danes do. And I told you about that voice. You put this feller in a cloak and hand him a scythe and anyone who saw him would say, 'Yeah, that's about right,' just before they turned and ran.

He said, "I was employed at a large cemetery with old and new sections on different hills, split by a county road. I was all-in-one caretaker, groundskeeper, and security. There wasn't anything more than a pizzeria and a one-screen theater within three counties back then, so I often stayed late in the visitor's center to chase off bored teenagers. The shack I was renting wasn't much worth going home to, anyway. This was outside of a small town you've never heard of, called Meadowlark, on the Ohio-Pennsylvania border."

He was surprised to hear I'd once dated a young lady from the western side of the divided town.

He rumble-chuckled again and said, "Well, that is a coincidence. A word of advice: don't go back. Me, I won't go within fifty miles of there ever again."

Naturally, I sized him up a second time, and of course I wondered what it was that could scare a frost giant who slept soundly in a graveyard. And then, right before he began on his narrative, our server, apparently concerned that we were listening while she harangued her man, nudged up the generic nu-country piping reverb-soaked twang from corner speakers.

Again, this isn't how these stories are supposed to be told, but there ain't anything I can do about the reality of the situation.

"I'd been living in Meadowlark for maybe ten years then. It was about the closest I'd ever been to putting down roots. I almost had a wife, and we almost had a child. But that was ancient history by the time I left. We'd had one desecration, a few years before: a couple of headstones got busted. If I tell you the names on them were Applebaum and Mendelsohn, then you probably get the idea. They caught the kids who did it and slapped them on the wrist. I heard one of them joined the marines later on, so maybe he straightened out and maybe he didn't. Crazily enough, this wasn't the first grave-robbing on my watch. At another cemetery back east, a distraught father took his daughter home three nights after her funeral. Set her up at the dining room table." He frowned and shook his head. "Sometimes love is an ugly business."

He took a slow sip on his coffee, which I'm sure, like mine, was long past needing a warm-up.

He went on, "You've heard the expression, 'a little bit of knowledge is a dangerous thing'? I guess Jeffy Reebus was the sort who should've stuck to his level of stupid. His co-conspirator told the police that Jeffy happened to read up on some local history—out of sheer boredom, one suspects—and got it in his head there was buried treasure in one of the outlying graves in the old cemetery; specifically in one that was part of a small cluster of graves which, strangely enough, lay *outside* the crumbling wrought-iron fence.

"Interred in this particular grave were the bodily remains of one Colonel Grover Crumb. Colonel Crumb fought for the Union, but he was no hero. Grant might've relied on marching an overwhelming force directly into the line of fire, and Sherman might've burnt every stick of tinder he laid eyes on, but both did what they did in service to the cause. Colonel Crumb's brigade of degenerates earned a reputation for robbing and raping their way up and down the river in the shadow of the second Army of the Mississippi, for no other reason than it suited them to do so. Crumb went from being a failed merchant before the war to landed gentry afterwards and never accounted for his good fortune, in life or in death.

"Well, Jeffy Reebus, cheat and thief that he was, intuited that the like-minded Colonel would've arranged for part of his fortune to be buried with him, so that he could keep a watchful eye on his ill-gotten gains.

"It was midnight or a little later. I thought I saw headlights up along the ridge, in the new part of the cemetery, where teenage boys liked to take their girls to park, hoping to scare them into not thinking straight. So I marched my way up. Moon was shining pretty good, so I left my flashlight off, figuring, 'they want a scare, I'll give them a scare.' Turned out I was wrong—no one was there. I was just about to turn back towards my bunk when I heard the explosion across the road.

"I could see smoke in the moonlight, and I heard screaming. So, I took off running down the hill. I turned my flashlight on right before I got to the road. It was already old back then—a big tin thing with a handle and a wide reflector cone; bright right in front of you, but with no range to it. I crossed the road, and I started up the other side. The screaming's turned down to a constant wailing by then. Outlined against where the moonlight hits this screen of smoke, I saw a man lumbering towards me, swaying. The way he was moving, even a reasonable soul would've thought it was a zombie come to life.

"I froze. I didn't know what the hell to do, and my legs decide not to work, anyway. I just held the light out a bit farther, like that would protect me. I didn't scream, but I know I made some kind of hellacious sound when Jeffy Reebus lurched into the light.

"His face looked like it had been torn open and pushed back to the sides of his skull. He was covered in sleek red blood wherever he wasn't scorched black. The tatters of his collar were still smoldering. One eye was bright, lidless white; the other wasn't there anymore. His wail shrank to a whimper, the last of which leaked out of him as he fell flat right in front of me, like he wanted nothing more than to kiss my boots but misjudged the distance by a few inches.

"I ran back to the visitor's center to phone for help, just because that's what you're supposed to do. I already knew Jeffy was beyond help.

"Jeffy's cohort was a guy named Mike-something. Cops picked him up on the way responding to my call. He told them they dug up Colonel Crumb because of Jeffy's wild theory. Crumb was buried a bit shallower than they were thinking, so when it came time to lift the lid, Jeffy jumped out of the hole and then lay down on his belly to reach in. They popped the lid and *ka-boom!*"

Out of the corner of my eye, I saw our server glance over, annoyed.

"Mike was scared shitless and didn't know what to do about Jeffy, so, brave soul that he was, he lit out of there. When the cops talked to me, they asked if there was any way there had been dynamite in the coffin. I told them, 'yup, there was that possibility.'

"Jeffy *had* found himself something damn unlikely when he dug up the Colonel. He'd bad-lucked himself face-first into a rather obscure bit of historical trivia: the coffin torpedo."

"Say again?" I prompted. I'd heard him just fine, but I liked the sound of it.

He nodded and grinned and drew it out for effect. "The coffin torpedo. A nasty defense against grave-robbing. An explosive or a projectile triggered to go off if the lid was tampered with. They were really more a fad of interest than of acquisition. Though a few contending models were patented and heavily advertised, probably very few were ever manufactured, and even fewer actually purchased.

"Even in digging up a grave from the narrow era where one *might* have been installed, for Jeffy to find one was a million-to-one against. To find what *must* have been the sole intact and functioning device more than a century later, well...it's almost a shame Jeffy didn't get the notoriety he paid for in blood."

I raised my white ceramic mug in salute. "For whatever it's worth."

"Hear, hear."

Our server misinterpreted the toast and finally came back to give us a refill.

After she retreated to the kitchen entryway, he went on, "Crumb had quite a charge loaded. Jeffy was *almost* lucky. The blast went mostly sideways. If he'd have pulled back from the other side or opened the casket from the bottom, maybe his piano-playing days would've been over, but he likely would've lived, and spared me some nightmare fuel.

"There was a mess of shattered and scattered bones and pine splinters where the Colonel used to lie, and a huge divot notched to the right of his final resting place—big enough to expose and damage part of his neighbor's casket."

"That'd be Parson Phillip Wellingham," I guessed.

He nodded, impressed. "You pay attention. That's a rare trait these days.

"Yup, Parson Wellingham—of whom I could have told you his birth and death dates and nothing else at the time of his unearthing. What followed was a couple days of excitement, as far as cemeteries go. County sheriff's deputies dallied there between calls. I don't blame them; the cemetery was a nice enough spot, and if they didn't have anywhere better to be, then why not?

"The Historical Society sent an archaeologist to sweep up the Colonel. He had to wait for a munitions and demolitions expert to come in and give the all clear. The demo guy had never heard of a coffin torpedo and seemed disinclined to believe what I told him. He thought there must've been unexploded ordinance buried there for some reason. And, he figured, as the coffin next door was already exposed, we'd better look inside it to make sure nothing else went boom—despite my assurances it was unlikely there was another working coffin torpedo in existence.

"I think he was just trying to bill the state for extra hours. Of course the archaeologist was up for more digging. And then when he saw the name on the tombstone, he got excited. I could read it plain as day on his face; his eyes got wide and he worked his lips over his gums. But he didn't say anything.

"The county balked at the demo guy's request to have his engineering firm contracted for an excavation. He made a big dramatic stink about how the government assumed liability, and he wasn't responsible for my safety. I said, 'Fine, I'll get the backhoe.' So, then he decided he'll just put a flexible scope through a crack in the casket. He didn't want the archaeologist— Rick was his name, by the way; skinny guy with glasses—he didn't want me and Rick staring over his shoulder at his laptop screen while he worked, but even from a short distance I could see there was something funny about the body, but I couldn't tell what.

"Then the demo guy gave the 'all clear.' He made a big show about taping off a twenty-yard perimeter and insisted Rick and a deputy by the name of Parcell, who happened to be there, get back behind the yellow tape. 'It's all yours', the demo guy told me, and his smile said, 'I hope you get blown to kingdom come' even though, by that point, I'm sure even he didn't believe that was going to happen.

"Which of course it didn't. I dug up a three-and-a-half-foot deep rectangle with edges that looked like they'd been cut with a scalpel. I left a sliver of sod on the top to make Rick feel useful.

"First, he sifted through Crumb's mess and put bits of bone and a buckle, and what might have been a medal, into a plastic tub. Having never seen such a thing done before, I wouldn't know, but I got the feeling he rushed the job, anxious to get into the Parson's casket. I couldn't blame him; there wasn't much of interest left to the Colonel. There sure as shit wasn't any buried treasure; sorry about that, Jeffy. Rick found a few scraps of scorched parchment, so maybe that had been something, but we'll never know.

"I had a coil of rope with me, which I threw on the ground by the graveside. I intended to slip it around the top and bottom of the casket to lift it out. If I was doing it nowadays, I would use ratchet straps and a lowering device—seriously, that's the creative name they gave those grave winches: 'lowering devices.' Anyway, Rick decided I didn't need to bring the casket out. Since it was damaged, and since the Colonel had excavated a nice big hole beside it, he preferred to work on it where it was.

"Rick brushed off the top of the Parson's casket. The demo guy checked again for 'wires', he said, before giving me the go-ahead to pop it open. The casket didn't have a 'lid'—it wasn't hinged to swing open—just a 'top', nailed shut. I pried around with a flat bar, loosening each nail carefully. It took a while. The nails were long, and there were a lot more of them than I might've expected. They were square, iron nails. And each one of them creaked like a screaming son of a bitch on the way out. Finally, I got the top to where it was propped a few inches up from the sides with the points just about all loose. The nails looked like prison bars.

"I got a weird feeling. I felt something was dead wrong. So much so that I stopped to ask Rick, 'You sure about this?' But I could see from the hunger in his eye what the answer was before he said it.

"So, I gave a quick yank with the flat bar on each side and the top came loose. I turned it over, nail side up. As I pushed it out of the way onto the grass, I heard Rick jump down in beside me, and I noticed the demo guy and Deputy Parcell crowding near. Rick said, 'Wow', and then the deputy said, 'That's crazy', and the demo guy said, 'The blast must've done that.'

"I looked down and a chill shot through me. Because, like I said, I read. And I know there weren't no way the blast turned the Parson over nice and neat like that. No, sir. He had to have been buried that way. He had to have been buried face down."

I asked him, "Face down?"

He nodded. "Facing Hell. Somebody seemed to think Parson Wellingham was not a man of God at all. Somebody thought he was a warlock. Now, what somebody happened to believe about him a century ago shouldn't count for anything, right? Especially *that* sort of nonsense. Sure, I knew that. Which is what kept me from suggesting we put the lid back on right away and rebury him as he was. But still I was creeped out. Couldn't tell you why. Definitely couldn't *explain* why to somebody else.

"Rick snapped me out of it when he said, 'Looks like some roots got in.' That would hardly have been a surprise; we were shaded by a big oak. But I saw what it was he was talking about, and I wasn't so sure. It looked like a cord tied around the Parson's arms and chest.

"When Rick bent over to cut it with a utility knife I actually said, 'Hold up a minute', but he didn't hear me. And then he cut the cord once and slipped it out from beneath the body. If it had been a root going into the ground, he would've had to have cut it in two places, minimum. Then he handed it to me, figuring it's just yard waste, and I saw that it was a dried-out vine, not a root. I was surprised it didn't crumble at the touch. Of course I couldn't be sure what kind of vine it was, but river grapes grew wild all around the area, and I guessed it was cut from one of those. I tossed the vine away and wiped my hands on my jeans.

"Rick said, 'Give me a hand with this', indicating we should turn him over. But I didn't want to touch him. So I said, 'I have to take a piss,' and I jumped out of the hole.

"The demo guy laughed because he thought I was skittish—which, right then, I was. Deputy Parcell, by now, was totally entranced, so he jumped in to help. I went over by the oak and pretended to do my business while they flipped him. Then I came back and looked.

"Wellingham was just bones and tatters. The skull was off from the neck bone. I didn't bother to point out there's no way everything could've got turned neatly together by the blast when the parts weren't even connected.

"I guess skulls always look malevolent, don't they? We're conditioned to see them like that. But the sight of that fleshless skull struck me worse than Jeffy's half-peeled one. I backed up, shaking my head, repulsed. I think the demo guy laughed at me again, but by then I was far past giving a shit what he thought.

"I sat on the backhoe and had a smoke while the archaeologist took some pictures. Deputy Parcell got a call for a domestic disturbance. The demo prick announced he was leaving like he'd achieved something meritorious, and I just waved to him like, 'shoo.'

"After he was gone, I went back over and asked Rick the archaeologist, 'So, are you going to put him in a tub, too?' He

35

laughed and said, 'No, he'll be reinterred. Because of the damage to the casket, I'll have to have the Commonwealth purchase him a new one.'

"I said, 'Doesn't seem like it would make much difference to him.' Rick said, 'No, there's rules.' I asked him if I should rebury the old casket until the new one arrived. He looked at me like maybe I was simpler than he'd originally took me for, and said, 'No, I'll just lay out a tarp to keep the rain off. It should only be a few days.'

"The thought of leaving those bones unburied for a few days did not sit well with me. I think I noticed about then that all my limbs were light and my head was buzzing. My body was reacting instinctively, pushing that fight-or-flight response. I tried to tell myself I was being stupid and superstitious, but it wasn't calming my nerves any.

"I said, 'You know something about this fella? I saw your face when you spied his name on the tombstone.'

"He smiled and said, 'Wicked Wellingham.'

"Well, that didn't calm my nerves any, either.

"He explained, 'Almost nothing is known about Phillip Wellingham directly. Historical records tell us he was born in Philadelphia and later moved to Pittsburgh to attend the Reformed Presbyterian Theological Seminary. He wasn't ordained in the Presbyterian Church, but he became Parson of a non-denominational country church on Grimmet Creek, about six miles outside of Meadowlark. Other than that, his name might have passed from history if one of Hearst's early scandal sheets hadn't published a sensational article based on the rumor of a notorious letter—without any journalist having read the letter itself. The letter was written by a professor at the seminary, and then forwarded by the seminary's President to the head of the General Assembly. It related the events surrounding Wellingham's death. It seems Wellingham sent what he considered to be an academic paper to his alma mater for review. Internally, the paper—a thesis on the nature of evil—was immediately condemned. None of the students ever read it; only a few of the faculty did. Concerned that Wellingham was actively propagating his theories—concerned for his sanity, as well—the

President of the seminary dispatched the professor to meet with Wellingham and to assess the situation.' "

The former grave-digger made a motion with his hand to interrupt the story. "The letter is real, apparently," he said. "Rick said he read it.

"So the professor goes to Wellingham's church. But by the time he got there, there wasn't any church anymore. Rick told me, 'It was burnt to the ground. The roof had fallen in and most of the charred timber had collapsed and shriveled to charcoal. The professor wrote, *The scent of smoke was prominent, and the ash was unsettled,'* indicating no rain had fallen on it yet, meaning the fire occurred after a round of storms passed through less than a week before. He noted that several nearby trees appeared to have been recently felled and removed, and that there was a circle of sand in the surrounding grass, as though someone had made an attempt to stop the spread of the fire, but not to put it out. Or maybe someone prepared for it beforehand. A building like that would have gone up quickly, though the professor also mentioned Grimmet Creek was running full.

"Of course, there might not have been enough people nearby to form a bucket chain at the time of the fire. The crazy thing was that the pulpit, though it was blackened with scorch-marks, was still standing. It looked like someone took an axe to it, but abandoned the assault after just few hacks. There was a small trail of blood leading away—which meant the attempt to destroy the pulpit must've occurred after the fire. The professor noticed something and brushed away the ash and soot behind the pulpit. He didn't describe the shape of what he saw, but he wrote that painted on the floorboards was a *'known occult symbol, the presence of which lent no doubt to the practice of fell paganism or diabolism, possibly even the heretical invocation of the Adversary as the Shadow Avatar of God Himself, as described in Mr. Wellingham's monstrous epistle.'* The professor went on to write, *'Upon inquiring as to Mr. Wellingham's home address, I was thereto guided by the town Constable, where I was unsurprised to find our errant alumnus hanging by the neck from the rafters of his upper room. The Constable immediately declared Mr. Wellingham's death a suicide and seemed relieved to have had a member of the clergy 'discover' the body. I did not aloud observe the peculiarity of Mr. Willingham's hands being tied behind his back...*

" *The Constable made arrangements for the internment of Mr. Wellingham's body the next day. By the time I arrived, fifteen minutes before the appointed hour, the casket was already buried. I offered a few choice prayers. Several people I took to be former parishioners were present, though none were dressed in mourning clothes, and none save the Constable would approach within speaking distance of the grave. I left the town directly thereafter; upon my cart was loaded the entirety of Mr. Wellingham's library, which I later secured far from our venerated halls until such time as a decision can be made as to its final disposition.'*

"'After the letter was forwarded, someone at the Presbytery must've blabbed to one of Hearst's boys. They were always hungry for something juicy and would pay. The story made several regional papers, and might have gone on to attract nationwide attention if an anarchist hadn't shot President McKinley and pushed everything else off of the front page.'

"As you might imagine, being on edge like I was already, I didn't care at all for what Rick told me about the individual we had exhumed, whatever his current condition. Disinclined as I was to touch those bones, I decided right then that I would replicate the conditions of his burial when I put him back in the dirt: face down, tied with grape vine, and hammered shut with the same square, iron nails—no matter what they sent to bury him in. And even if I was going to have to wait a couple of days until I could make it permanent, I would at least get him flipped and tied while I waited.

"It was getting late in the day. I asked Rick if he was going to finish up soon. And he said, yeah, why don't you help me get this tarp secured over the exposed graves? We laid the lid for the casket back down. I offered to nail it shut but Rick said don't worry about it. He pounded four stakes into the ground and ran a length of twine around them to cordon off the 'dig'—never mind that the demo guy hadn't bothered to take down his yellow safety tape. By the time we got the tarp secured, the sun was almost down. So I told him I'd better get the backhoe locked in the garage and I drove it away.

"It was supposed to be my excuse to hurry out of there, but I didn't think it through: it would've been a lot faster just to walk down the hill, cross the street and go up the embankment on the other side. To drive the backhoe out, I had to follow this winding course that ran the length of the cemetery more than twice over. By the time I got it back in the garage, the purple part of twilight has just about given out. There was a cool breeze moving, but I was sweating—still going on instinct. And more than once that breeze on the back of my sweaty neck turned me around like I'd been touched.

"I got ahold of a flashlight and some clippers from the tool shed, and I put my hammer through a belt loop. The cemetery was bordered by a run from the creek on one side—about as far from Wellingham's grave as you could get. I knew there were some river grape vines in the tangle on the embankment. There were snakes there, too, but I never saw a rattler or a copperhead, so I tromped straight through the brush in full dark except for my flashlight.

"It was too early for the moon yet. I didn't get bit but I did take a hard tumble once and came *this close* to splitting my scalp on a rock. But I found my vines. I cut a good length and rolled it palm-to-elbow like an extension cord. And then I hurried back out of there.

"Now, any reasonable person would say I had no cause to be scared, and maybe that was true. But I was scared, good reason or not, so I have to be a bit proud of myself for not hesitating one single second. I trudged right on past the garage and the visitor's center, on down the hill to the road, and across.

"Just about then the moon crept up over the treetops, jaundice-yellow, and big like it is when it's low and just about full, so I had some more light.

"I said there was a breeze, but there hadn't been any strong wind that blew through in the last hour, so there wasn't any accounting for that blue, vinyl tarp to be torn free from two of the stakes.

"I set the vine down on someone's cracked marker, and I got that hammer in my hand post-haste. I didn't see anything moving. Suddenly I thought he might be behind me—I'm *sure* by this point that Wellingham's bones are up and walking—so I spun around with the hammer out. If anyone *had* been behind me, I would've sent them to the dentist, but there was no one there. So, I crept closer to the hole. Like I said, I was already certain that grave was empty.

"But brother, nothing can prepare you for finding out you're right about that sort of thing."

The man closed his eyes as though forced to remember, much as his pained expression told me he didn't want to. I didn't breath or twitch a muscle until he spoke again.

"I shone my light down. The lid was knocked off to the side. There wasn't nothing in that box but some loose dirt and a few scraps of rotted cloth.

"So, I spun around again—and again; every time I took my light off of one area, I wanted to shine it back there again, like maybe something moved in the dark I left behind. I'll be honest; I was shaking. I tried to tell myself some asshole kids were pranking me, but I knew the kids around there, and none of them had the perspicacity for that kind of stunt. And I try to tell myself that there's no reason to be scared of a skeleton, anyway, that one good swing would smash it to pieces, but that wasn't any comfort, either, because skeletons ain't supposed to be up and walking around no matter how you look at it.

"And right when I start to wonder *how* it could be up and about—like, physically—even if it *was* animated by sorcery, I notice a couple of things I'd failed to notice before, because I was so keyed up. Namely, that the security tape was gone. And so was the twine rectangle Rick put around the graves. And I remembered the coil of rope I'd tossed aside—which I hadn't bothered to pick up before I lit out with the backhoe—and sure enough, it was gone, too.

"And then I heard a car horn blare, and tires squeal from a hard brake. I looked down at the road. It was way too far away for my flashlight, but, just before this car peeled out and sped off fast as it could, I saw a figure in the headlights.

"I don't know quite what to say about what I saw. It was a human figure, you know what I mean? It was six foot tall and bipedal. From that distance, seeing it only for a second, maybe that's all I should be willing to definitively say about it. But I knew what it was. I *know* what it was. That thing didn't stand right, didn't move right. It was too skinny, especially around the waist and the thighs. And I feel sure that in that split second, I saw with complete certainty the light from that car reflecting off of the yellow safety tape braided with the twine and rope holding that bundle of bones together, and off of the naked white skull on top.

"After the car was gone, there was only moonlight, but it was enough to see there was something there, even if the detail was lost. Enough to see it turn, like it was looking back up the hill at me.

"I ran. And since I couldn't cross back to the garage and the visitor's center without going past that thing, I ran the other way. I ran down a slope through a thick stand of trees. I must've spooked a deer because I heard something big move close by, and I nearly pissed myself. Then I came out into a fallow field. The mud was grabbing at my ankles, making me run slow, like in a nightmare. I was worn out halfway across, but I sure as hell kept on going. I found the road again. I looked too much a mess by that point to even try to hitch, and nobody passed by anyway, so I ended up going heel-toe all the way home. I locked everything that I could lock and dug out my shotgun. And I waited. I stayed awake as long as I could.

"I fell out of my chair onto the kitchen floor, and I was damn lucky I didn't blow my own head off. It was daylight. I opened my door to go out on my porch, and I saw the mesh on my screen door had been torn to shreds.

"I got a ride from a neighbor back to the cemetery. I was hoping maybe the Parson had to come back to rest during the day, like a vampire, but no dice. The busted casket was still empty. I went back to the visitor's center and waited for the archaeologist to come in yelling about where the hell did the skeleton go? After a couple of hours, when he hadn't shown, I turned on the radio. And I heard about how Deputy Parcell had been found hanging from a Catalpa tree about a quarter mile from his cruiser.

"There were only a couple of motels nearby back then; it wasn't hard to track down where Rick was staying. And then I came to learn that he checked out in the middle of the night. Told the night manager he suddenly remembered he had to get back to Wilkes-Barre by morning. Apparently, he didn't need his wardrobe, though, because he left without his suitcase.

"Well, that was enough for me. The day before, I had tried to stay as far from the Parson as I could, but it seemed it wasn't far enough. He'd paid a visit to all three of us overnight, and Deputy Parcell got the short end of the stick. I didn't know enough about the demo guy to warn him, other than I knew he wasn't local. It's not like he would've believed me anyway.

"So, I thought about it for five seconds, and I decided I didn't want to stay there another night. I buried the empty casket. None the wiser, right? And I packed everything I owned—which never was much—and I left there forever by sundown."

He set down his empty coffee mug.

I asked him, "You didn't try to contact Rick?"

He laughed. "That son of a bitch? That whole morning I spent waiting for him, he didn't check to see if I was alive, did he? I figure he got away just fine, and he probably figured I didn't, so to hell with him."

"So, you think fifty miles is a wide enough berth to keep away from Meadowlark?"

He shrugged. "Probably I'd be fine with less than that. My guess is the Parson went back to his church. What he's been up to since then, I don't care to guess. But if you're asking, do I feel safe? Christ, no."

He stood up and dug his wallet out of his jeans pocket. He flipped some bills on the counter.

"Let me put it to you this way," he said. "Even if Wicked Wellingham's ropes-and-bones corpse keeps to his neck of the woods, well, if there's something like *that* in the world, then what the hell *else* is out there lurking in the dark? Plus, like I mentioned, he and Crumb weren't the only ones buried on the other side of that cemetery fence—in unhallowed ground."

From the Author

Stories often bloom from simple ideas, and ideas often germinate from little tidbits gathered in idle web-surfing. Having discovered the coffin torpedo—a very real invention, albeit one without much commercial success—there could be no question I would put it in a story as soon as possible. But ideas are only one aspect of my writing process. I like to give myself a challenge, usually formal in nature, with which to wrestle. In the case of "Wicked Wellingham", as I was already dealing with levels of narrative—the author>the narrator>the one relating him the story—I decided it might be interesting to see how many levels deep I could go without it becoming too confusing. I hope I succeeded and the story entertains.

You can find links directing you to other works at jasonawyckoff.weebly.com

About the Author

Jason A. Wyckoff is the author of two short story collections published by Tartarus Press, *Black Horse and other Strange Stories* (2012) and *The Hidden Back Room* (2016). His work has appeared in anthologies from Haverhill House, Plutonian Press and Siren's Call Publications, as well as the journals *Nightscript*, *Weirdbook*, and *Turn to Ash*, among others. He is a graduate of The Ohio State University and lives in Columbus with his wife and too many cats.

The Loosing of havoc
by
Edward Ahern

The Loosing of havoc

*T*he foot trail guttered out at the ruins of an abandoned village, Thatch and pole roofs were collapsed inside wattle walls. Bare earth mounds were scattered about the open spaces, hinting that plague or battle had destroyed the hamlet.

Malame pursed his lips, then dismounted and let his horse drink from the brook that trickled downhill from the huts.

He wasn't lost, for he didn't know where he should be going. The runes he had cast had withheld purpose, and visions had failed him. He knew only that he couldn't return to the Old One without proving himself.

His master, as always, had been brusque. "I hold no future for a chela who cannot find his own direction. Go, and return only with proof that you have achieved goetic distinction without my guidance."

Malame knew his unleashing was a test, but he'd been trained like a choke-chained dog since early childhood, and he couldn't begin to savor his liberty.

He unsaddled the horse and let it graze freely. It was bound to him as he was bound to the Old One, and would not stray. There were few vermin left in the village, but Malame mind-lured four field rats in to him, enough meat for supper. He did so grudgingly, every exercise of magic drained water from a well of finite capacity. But it took only a sip of magic to feed him.

The rats were skinned and skewered on a stick in minutes. The cooking fire would alert anyone or anything nearby to his presence, but he sat next to it unconcernedly while nibbling around the little bones.

The ruined village was an apt place for what he would attempt. As the little fire was shifting from yellow to gray, Malame took the skewer and began tracing characters in the coals of wood and bone. The stick was gradually consumed in the writing, as was also fitting, for he was appealing to Chaos for purpose. When the scribing was complete, he tossed the stub into the fire and lay down beside the coals.

It was in the tremolos of false dawn that he was approached. His horse shied away as a darker blackness encroached.

Its voice was the grinding of stones. "I do not answer prayers, spell-caster."

"And yet you are here."

"Inchoate curiosity."

Malame stood and faced the fountainhead of other gods. Shifting odors of milky newborn and aged fetidness drifted into his nostrils. The shape half-formed body parts and then decomposed them into ichor.

"And I have no wish for another master. What may I call you?"

"The names are many and changing. Ymir will do. You petitioned us, magician. For what?"

"My vision fails in determining a meritorious quest. It may be that I can serve a purpose of yours while achieving a proper one of my own."

"Such layers of self-flattery. I can consume you like your fire stick and your Old One could do nothing."

"And lose an agent of your discord. You operate best through us, what better vehicle than a trained mage?"

"There is that. Wait."

Ymir's amorphous shape solidified into knobby obsidian, then, after several moments, re-loosened into swirling black festoons that Malame suspected would cut him like glass knives.

"There are no straight lines with me, apprentice."

"And what I achieve may not be what I wish, this I understand."

"Your paths will shift as you walk them. But are you really asking for a quest? Or are you seeking knowledge of my workings, greedy little sorcerer. You cannot ride the tip of an eagle talon. Do you still wish my agency?"

"I do, Ymir."

"So be it. Listen closely, for even as I enter into you my intentions shift."

Pain rushed into Malame's ears, making him gasp and briefly lose focus. Then, surmounting the pain, an obscene vision.

Malame shuddered as Ymir finished. "So many will die."

"And you might live and be restored to service. Ask yourself what will happen if you do not follow my course."

"And the cost?"

The laugh was the sound of shattering bones. "Your temporary bondage to me. And the deaths of many shriveled should-have-beens and ought-tos. What are several more for you?"

The blackness folded onto itself like a funeral cloth and disappeared. The village was empty. His horse had backed off a quarter-mile, but returned on command. Malame broke camp and rode toward Mylartha, a travel of two score days by horse and an equal measure by ship.

While traveling, Malame shooed off two robbers with threats, able to avoid having to spell them. He carried a crippled woman back to her village, who insisted on giving him a talisman that measured sexual attraction, and discovered a child with goetic potential who could be revisited in three or four years.

Poverty washed in surging ripples around the walled city of Mylartha, those furthest from the safety of the walls were the poorest and least able to protect themselves. A lone man on horseback was fair game for alms or theft, and clots of beggars edged toward Malame as he proceeded. Three men forced him to halt his horse.

"You may pass once you've provided your coin."

Malame was expressionless. "You choose your prey unwisely. Back off and I will not harm you. This is your singular warning."

The man closest to him removed a knife from under his tunic and held it so that only Malame could see its flash.

Malame studied the men, shrugged, then moved his lips inaudibly. The ulna in the man's right arm snapped, jagged bone pushing through flesh, the knife dropping to the ground. The man screamed and clutched his arm. Malame raised his right arm as if in blessing and the thieves backed off. Malame did not take pleasure in inflicting pain but knew that rumor of his malevolence would follow and help establish him.

The guards at the inner-city gate halted Malame as well, laughing when he asked for audience with Count Uhlstein. "The Count barely gives his own mother an audience, let alone a stranger."

Malame smiled benignly. Maiming guards would not earn him favor, so he took the extra minute to spell them into thinking he had important messages, and they waved him through. Once at the iron-clad oak doors of the keep he turned his horse over to a hostler and walked in.

Malame wore a coarse wool tunic and sandals and was malodorous. But he talked his way past a courtier's distain to learn the location of the Count's quarters, in the upper reaches of the keep.

He stepped into an empty bedroom, picked up an armload of bedclothes, and, bowing and scraping like an overworked servant, made his way upward. There was no mistaking Uhlstein's spaces, the double doors were faced with identical coats of arms depicting a rampant boar.

Malame dropped the linens on the flagstones, and fix-tranced the two guards as they glanced down at the sheets. He pushed open one of the doors and eased into the room. And, with an inner tingle, his luck turned, the first of what would be many unwanted gifts from Ymir. The Count wasn't alone. His mage, Dulong, held a scroll and faced Uhlstein.

Dulong needed to drop the scroll and turn toward Malame before incanting. Malame was able to complete his spell just before her, and as static electricity crackled through the chamber, confined her. Dulong, gaunt and wrinkled, could be seen but not heard, and despite her flailing, could do no harm.

The Count had yelled "Dulong, help me!" and drawn his sword. But he held his ground, perhaps doubting if he could get in a blow before being seared. The Baron had surpassed portly, his ornate belt sunk a full two inches into his ample belly. "Guards!" he yelled.

"I'm afraid they're bound up, Count." Malame sighed. "This is awkward. I'd hoped to speak to you privately, but your magus will hear everything we say. My apologies, sister, for my bluntness."

Dulong glared.

Malame turned to the Count. "Should we sit, my lord? The discussion could be long."

"I'm going to have you disemboweled."

Malame smiled. "Ah. Well, before that, perhaps we should chat."

They sat at opposite sides of a table, scrolls and books scattered between them.

"My lord, I am Malame, bound to Ishfrig,"

"Your master's unsavory reputation has reached us. Dulong knows of him."

"You will grant his proficiency, and by extension mine?"

The Count nodded slightly. "Continue."

"The performance of your servant, Dulong, although diligent, has been disappointing. You fear, rightly, that there are plots to unseat and assassinate you, and she has been unable to uncover them."

Dulong snarled unheard curses from inside her confinement.

Count Uhlstein, undoubtedly accustomed to tense negotiation, was expressionless. "You cannot know this."

Malame seamlessly lied. "I have a resource, a talisman, which permits me to sense some of what your courtiers are feeling. My words seem blunt, but they're not ill-intended, not even for Dulong."

He took the crippled woman's little talisman from his tunic and held it up. It was useless against treason, but even Dulong wouldn't know this without study. "With this most potent artifact I can identify and prove that many you now trust mean you ill."

Uhlstein smiled unpleasantly. "You are a probably diseased, unpleasant smelling stranger who I trust not at all. Why would I believe you rather than those who have followed me for years?"

"Belief isn't necessary. I'll confirm plots you have long suspected. What you do with the plotters is your concern."

"And you do this because you admire me so."

Malame's smile was disarming. "There's no need to provide reward until after I prove my worth."

Uhlstein stared at Malame as Dulong's containment vessel shuddered and vibrated, but held.

The Count glowered. "And what, charlatan, do you propose I do with her?"

"Dulong is not one of the plotters. And she is intimately familiar with the workings of your court. She is still of great value to you in ripping these vicious ticks from your flesh."

"Very well, tell me of these plots."

Malame smiled again. "Ah, the wiles of the nobility. First let's set terms. You must oath-take that if I speak truth you'll protect and reward me. Oh, and Dulong retains her position with you."

"You don't wish to replace her?"

"I have no desire for another master."

Malame turned toward Dulong. "If you give your oath not to harm me, I'll release you so you may counsel the Count during our discussions."

She studied him for several seconds, then nodded and hand-signed her oath. He broke the confinement and watched as Dulong approached.

"This plague-riddled offal is who he says he is, the journeyman assistant of Ishfrig. I would not trust him to carry out your slops bucket, but I suspect his bucket does carry knowledge."

Uhlstein's expression and posture had altered, perhaps emboldened by the company of his mage. "And what extortionate reward would you seek?"

"Gold is a heavy carry, and I travel light. Unmounted blue sapphires, to a weight of five Minas, would be appropriate."

"That would take weeks to assemble."

"And it will take weeks to exterminate your pests. If you wish, I can leave you both so Dulong may properly curse me in private."

Dulong flashed and repressed a hard smile. "My lord, you're aware that many in court are protected by amulets which prevent me from learning their intentions. If this mongrel has a way to circumvent this, it might be beneficial. There's no cost without result, although the price is high. We would also force him to swear that he would do you no harm."

Malame nodded. "This I so swear." Given Dulong's support, Malame thought the Count would agree. But he could sense Ymir again intervening, changing Uhlstein's mood.

Uhlstein stared sullenly at Malame. "Your help is not needed. Begone before I have you imprisoned."

"As you wish, my Lord." As Malame left the chamber he released the two guards from their trances. The spell had loosened bladders, an unfortunate side effect, and both had wet themselves. They spent several seconds deciding whether to desert their posts and change their leggings or check on the Baron while still wet. They entered the chamber and dripped on the Baron's tapestry carpet as he excoriated them.

Malame meanwhile was leaving the keep. He'd itched each time Ymir had provided his backhanded interference, a reminder that Ymir operated from a perch somewhere within him.

He found lodging inside the walled city and was able to bathe and eat. The mental flea bite he'd given the Baron would also itch until he talked again with Malame, and he settled in for the evening to wait for one of the Baron's retainers to locate him. But his first visitor was a surprise.

The gray cloaked and hooded woman entered without knocking. "Your door is unsecured. Not prudent considering your mission."

"I almost always welcome visitors." Malame sorted through possibilities and picked the most likely one. "Which faction do you represent?"

The woman removed her cloak, revealing a long gown suitable for court and nowhere else. She was almost as tall as Malame, with brown hair and eyes. She was well groomed and faintly scented of lupines.

"You may call me Gertrude. I speak for the Langfiefs, the most prominent vassalage to the Count."

Malame bowed slightly. "Credit is due your house. To reach me so quickly speaks well of your information sources and reactions. Please, sit." He pointed to one of two chairs in his room.

Gertrude smiled warmly at him. Malame assumed years of practice with men she despised. He discreetly took out the old woman's talisman and glanced at it. Its sullen gray told him that Gertrude would more readily maim him than fondle him. "Are you here to warn me or bribe me?"

The effervescent smile flattened. "Which would work best?"

"Neither, unfortunately. If the Count accepts my proposal, I'd work only for him. I would of course listen to arguments from all the houses."

Gertrude's apparent warmth and charm evaporated. "The balance among our factions is delicate. You must understand that the easiest solution to your presence is your death."

"I do, and assume you brought men to ensure that. Please don't send them in. They would die, and an attempted assassination would suggest your guilt."

"You couldn't move more quickly than their swords."

Malame raised his left hand and Gertrude stiffened, unable to move. "I don't need to move all that much. You might prefer to continue talking."

She tried to twist free but could only hunch her shoulders. "This game is childish. Release me."

"Of course." He finger gestured and she shook loose. "You're free to go. I won't mention your visit."

"Why not?"

"Because I would appreciate your insights into this complicated court. I'll measure your veiled comments against those of other groups and try and find the maggots of truth in the offal pile. When I return to court, may we talk?"

"Why not." She turned and left.

Malame barred his door and prepared his bed so it appeared he was in it, then clambered out the window to squat on the roof tiles and meditate. What he needed to achieve with Chaos would be difficult and perhaps deadly.

Some hours later, just before the door was broken loose, Ymir trembled within him. Three men ran in, knives drawn. They had reached the bed when Malame finished the spell that caused them to turn on each other. The smallest and quickest of the three, in close quarters and almost total darkness, was able to cripple and then kill the other two. But not before he'd been belly cut from rib to hip.

Malame was appreciative that he could interrogate one still living. He let the man bleed out a bit, then approached him.

He twisted the man's knife free and held the point to his right eye. "Don't move or your guts will spill out more. I'll know if you lie, and every lie costs you an eye. Who sent you?" The knife point pricked gently at the eyelid.

"You can die like me. I'm not telling you anything."

Malame looked down at the man's belly. "None of your organs appear to be cut. With quick treatment you might survive. If you tell me nothing, your death is guaranteed."

The man exhaled painfully. "What difference? I serve House Ratskrieg. I don't even know your name. We were only told to kill the man in this room. And to do it quickly, before we were hexed."

"And who gave you your orders?"

"The Baron of Ratskrieg's counselor, Bourlesh."

"And this Bourlesh, is he knight or magus?"

"Knight."

Malame smiled. Easier still. "Should you live long enough to report to him, tell him he should either speak with me or die like your comrades."

Malame fetched the innkeeper, who fetched the night watch, which carried the assassin out on a litter, and the dead men out in flour sacks. Malame braced the door and, avoiding the blood on the floor, waved aside the loose goose feathers on his bed and got in. He wondered if the woman from House Langfief was cunning enough to tip off House Ratskrieg as to his whereabouts and shift the blame. Then he slept.

Dulong arrived the next morning as Malame was eating gruel and ham hocks. Malame stood and bowed. Dulong was widely known and respected in their craft.

She sat at his table without asking. "That little trick of yours cost me years of credibility with the fat man."

"He looks like his sigil. You should find a better lord, or go out on your own."

"And eat insects while sitting on a dirt floor, like your master? No thank you. The beauty of a sinecure is creature comforts. I heard you had company last night."

Malame looked closely at her. The practice of dangerous magic is both physically and psychically draining, and every adept he'd ever met was gaunt. And Dulong, despite her comforts, was no exception. Her wrinkles jagged vertically down her face and into her neck, and excess skin hung from her arms.

"Their desire was unsatisfied. My hope, Dulong, is that we can cooperate rather than fight. What I did to you was unintended but unseemly, and I apologize and will provide you assistance to offset my insult."

Her expression was still stern. "Swear it, whelp."

Malame made a just audible oath. She nodded. "And how would you help?"

"You're bound by the court allegiances, but I can take radical action. As I uncover things, I'll bring them directly to you and the Count. You may discourage or encourage my findings depending on where you need to be with the houses. When I'm done you may discredit me and I'll leave in disgrace. With the sapphires, of course."

She allowed herself a grim smile. "You caught me by surprise once, it won't happen again. If I find you're playing a game against me, your master will lose a chela."

"Understood. The Count presumably allowed this meeting, which means he's interested. Are you agreeable to convincing him?"

"Perhaps. All noble houses plot, it's their nature. How many do you guess are threatening?"

"Two, perhaps three. The heads of the houses would have to be executed, and the families banished. Although I suspect the Count is a 'kill them all' type." Malame paused. "About those visitors. Unless there's a listener in the walls only you, I and the Baron know what was said. You would have merely tried to kill me yourself. That leaves the Count, who's perhaps less threatened by latent treachery than by overt extermination."

Dulong was silent. Then: "I regularly examine the walls and spaces around the Baron's quarters for eavesdropping. There's been none." She hesitated. "Long ago, your master and I were close associates. Because of that I caution you. This is your last opportunity to leave before the egg is cracked. You should take it."

"I should. But like you I have commitments."

She stood, the movement wickedly fast. Malame realized that Ymir had helped him bind up a quicker opponent, and reminded himself that not all chaos was ill luck.

"If the Baron agrees, he'll summon you. He believes in facades, so stop dressing like you're mucking out a stable." Then she turned and left.

As he was going out, Malame braced the innkeeper, who made a sign against the evil eye. "Here's coin, innkeeper. Tell anyone asking after me that I expect to be back here before the sun is overhead."

The innkeeper cowered, but reached out a hesitant hand to take the silver piece. "As you wish, sir."

Malame returned an hour later carrying what a merchant had assured him was proper court dress. Malame put on singlet and pantaloons more suited to a procurer than a courtier. The soldier who greeted him when he returned downstairs couldn't resist a sneer. "You're summoned."

"Lead away."

The stares that greeted Malame as he walked toward the keep made him want to return to mutilate the merchant, but realized that those who didn't take him seriously were more vulnerable, and smiled at the passersby.

The Count's stare, however, was insulting. "Looks like you're heading up an evening of debauchery."

"You summoned me, my lord."

Uhlstein nodded toward Dulong, who spoke. "Your terms are acceptable, and the Count will oath take to that effect. The specifics, please."

"Ah, the proper order, please. Count, your oathtaking?"

Dulong lead the Count through the oath, and Malame began.

"Thank you. It is probable that House Ratskrieg plots against you. I will assemble proofs against them and others. Meanwhile, please order your vassals to assemble in the ballroom in two weeks, telling them that I am going to expose traitors."

"That's ridiculous."

"They'll be afraid to decline, thinking that their absence proves their guilt. The innocent and the guilty will equally fear accusations from other houses, and will come prepared. Have your personal guard trebled for the evening, it may be that the guilty see assassination as their best escape."

Malame next sought out Gertrude.

"Bourlesh, what are his habits?"

Gertrude hesitated, examining Malame's bland expression. "You mean him harm."

"Does it matter to you?"

"No. Bourlesh is the Baron's blackmailer, he has proofs and records of many misdeeds. And it's common knowledge that Bourlesh rides most early mornings, and his horses is stabled here on the grounds."

"That almost suffices. What does Bourlesh look like?"

"Of average stature and weight. Balding, with leftover gray hair. A slight limp

caused by a war wound. He fights with his sinister hand."

"That does suffice, thank you. Your house should prepare to face accusations."

"And what might it take to dissuade you?"

That practiced halo warmth of hers had reemerged, and Malame admired her facility in donning it. "You're really very good. Your skills are wasted in a provincial house."

"But clearly not adequate. You should prepare for future attempts to silence you."

Malame's smile was thin lipped. "And you should be providing me with information about the other houses so that attention is diverted away from your lord."

Gertrude narrowed her eyes. "These are things best told in privacy, away from the keep."

"I'll await your telling me where and when."

Malame needed next to deal with Bourlesh. He entered the stable yard at night, and settled into an empty stall.

Early that next morning Malame listened as a stable hand prepared Bourlesh's horse Bourlesh limped in a half hour later, sword hanging off his right side.

Malame stepped out and said, "I am Malame, of whom you know. You have a choice, Sir Bourlesh. You can either die where you stand or provide me with the information I ask for."

Bourlesh hesitated, and for an instant Malame thought he could obtain what he needed. But then he felt the bulging pressure of Ymir, almost tangible and touchable.

Bourlesh's expression changed from fear to anger. "They should have killed you and I will." He yanked out his sword.

Malame sighed. He'd eventually have to deal with Ymir. But he needed no spells with Bourlesh. He ran forward, ducked under an awkward swing, and pushed Bourlesh onto the stable floor. He grabbed Bourlesh's fashionably long hair and his girdle and flipped him onto his stomach. Then he grabbed Bourlesh's sword arm and wrenched it so hard he heard the shoulder joint pop. The sword fell loose and Malame grabbed it.

"I have no wish to kill you, Bourlesh, but if you're not my informant you'll have to be my object lesson." But Ymir again roiled within Bourlesh.

Bourlesh, his mouth pressed against dirt and straw, gasped, "Rot from plague, conjurer."

Malame braced a foot on Bourlesh's back and shoved the sword just slightly into his anus. Bourlesh began to scream.

Malame's tone was cheery. "If I shove just a little further you won't be able to defecate properly for the rest of your life.

If I shove further in than that you'll painfully die. Let's avoid this grotesquerie, tell me how you plot against the Count."

Malame withdrew the sword and watched blood slowly stain Bourlesh's britches while Bourlesh spewed out words condemning the other houses.

"Where do you hide your proofs?"

"What proofs?"

Malame tapped Bourlesh's buttocks with the flat of the sword. "Another enema?"

"Stop! The fireplace in my chamber, on the right-hand side, waist height, behind a loose stone."

Malame bound and gagged Bourlesh, and went to get his souvenirs.

The other houses learned of Bourlesh's incident before the midday meal. Their responses were exemplary, and Malame spent days sifting through rumors, accusations and outright lies. Slander was rampant, and proof infrequent. But he was able to build many damning cases during that first week.

The same informants also secretly went to Dulong and Count Uhlstein to plead their case and attempt to discredit Malame should he accuse their house. But even the Count realized what they were doing, and waited for Malame's pronouncements.

Malame spent the second week devising how to extract Ymir without killing himself.

What he resolved to do was like dancing on a knife blade, but was the best he could concoct.

Gertrude came to visit once more during the second week. "You're dressed like a beggar-hermit again."

"Just think of me as a prophet surviving on honey and locusts."

"You're skinny, but too well muscled to be holy." She smiled again, this time looking as if she were laughing at herself. "I'll pay handsomely to know what you'll say about house Langfief. Not to change your judgement, just for advance information."

"A reasonable bribe, but I can't. One advice I'll give you without cost or favor—prepare your house to react to the unexpectedly dangerous."

Not quite two hundred courtiers were assembled in the ballroom that evening, clustered loosely by their houses. Gertrude stood in the first rank of house Langfief, as she should, for Malame had learned that she was the unwed daughter of the head of house. Bourlesh was there as well, standing stiffly next to his baron. Both their expressions were unreadable.

The Count, ringed by soldiers, sat in a slight elevation at the end of the room.

Malame had been granted two of the Count's servitors to provide evidence and written proofs to the Count when Malame indicated they should do so.

He and Dulong stood three steps down on the ballroom floor, he still clad in only a rough wool robe, bare legged and sandal shod. He noted that all of the men carried dress swords and daggers, and suspected many of the women sported pointed objects under their waist girdles. The mood was at best sullen, and the smell of fear overwhelmed the odors of perfumes. Malame bowed to the Count and turned to those assembled.

"My lords and ladies, we're assembled here to demonstrate the loyalty or treachery of those liege to Count Uhlstein. This I will prove by sworn parole, by written notes and documents of proven signature and writing style, and by certain damning objects. These items will be displayed to the Count as I progress, who can confirm the handwriting of many of his closest subjects. The Count will decide the disposition of each case. Any appeal of my findings must be taken up with Count Uhlstein directly before he passes sentence. Any interruption will be met by binding and gagging the offender."

The mutterings of the crowd swelled to shouts, but the Count waved for silence. "He acts under my provenance. Those of you who are innocent need fear nothing."

As Malame took up the first scroll he sensed Ymir chittering like a mad insect inside him, impatiently waiting to unleash himself. "The first house under issue is House Nahwust."

Malame held his voice calm and flat as he read the exonerations or accusals——House Nahwust found guilty of venality, and of the killing, perhaps through misadventure, of a woman from another House. Then House Furstfort, guilty of bribery of officials. The offenses gradually worsened as he progressed into the more powerful houses.

The assembled nobles grew unruly as they realized that Malame was including not only offenses against the Baron but crimes committed by them against other houses. The first murder occurred before he had even reached the houses of Ratskrieg and Langfief.

Malame sensed when Ymir left him and began hopping like a mad flea among the guests, enraging them. As soon as his tenant left, he began a complex spell, pausing briefly when a young knight unsheathed sword and struck down a noble who had dishonored a woman of his house. Blades of all sorts came out, and blood began to splatter formal dress.

Ymir ignited multiple melees, seemingly randomly. But Malame noticed that house Ratskrieg wasn't fighting with others, but instead lead an armed group toward the Count's throne.

Malame urgently needed to finish setting his trap for Ymir, but ran over to take position at Dulong's back. She glanced at him as she faced the approaching mob. "I need no help."

"Perhaps not, but the Old One would frown on my leaving you without it. And I suspect the Count will be appreciative."

Bourlesh was barely able to fight, but directed men to each side of Dulong and the Count's knights where they could better attack. Screams and curses and the clashing of steel on iron filled the chamber. Malame desperately continued chanting a spell of confinement while fending off sword swingers trying to breach the Count's wall of knights and slice open Dulong before she crippled them with spells.

Ymir, despite being in full blood lust, sensed that Malame had changed his lair, and reentered him. Once there the fly trap that Malame had spun closed about him. The more Ymir struggled the tighter the trap squeezed. The meninges that protected Malame's being was scorched and scoured, but held.

"Release me!" Ymir ordered.

"I am yours and now you are mine."

"Fool, I'll just have you killed and go free."

"Look more closely. If I die with you within, you rot inside my damnation."

Malame parried a blade as Ymir said, "Little chela, look what you've done. Very well, release me and I will release you."

"For each goetic pleasure there is a price. Yours you can already sense."

Ymir cursed in an eldritch tongue Malame had only heard of. "Very well, I agree. Release me so I can rejoin the party."

Bourlesh meanwhile had noticed Malame's distraction and edged closer. He slashed Malame's thigh with the same sword he'd been abused with and raised his arm for a more killing stroke. "He's my parting gift," Ymir said, and left.

But house Langfief had also chosen sides, and moved in to help defend the Baron. Gertrude ran over and stabbed Bourlesh in the back of the neck.

Malame lay where he'd fallen until the fighting finally subsided. He was dizzy from blood loss, but sensed he was being placed on a litter and carried off. His first clear image, the next day, was of Dulong's gutter-wrinkled face. Ymir was gone.

Dulong was smiling. "What a mess you've made of things. Four houses destroyed, lands reallocated."

"The Count lives?"

"And is busy killing people and seizing property."

"And Dulong is once again in favor."

"Indeed. You're in the quarters of house Langfief. Lady Gertrude asked to tend you and no one else wanted to."

"Bourlesh?"

"Quite dead. As is his Baron, and most of their knights."

"Ah. Are we now adversaries or associates?"

"Associates unless you do something else stupid. Will you tell me what this was really about?"

"No. Survive in comfort, Dulong."

"And you in discomfort, Malame."

Gertrude visited that afternoon. "Your leg will have a scar to add to your collection."

"And every time I see it, I'll think of your rescue."

Her frizzante smile was almost overwhelming. Malame glanced over at the little talisman that had been removed from his robe and placed on the bedside table. It showed streaks of rose. His convalescence might prove interesting.

Two moon cycles later he reentered the yurt of the Old One. Ishfrig did not rise. "Tell me."

"There is a boy a week's ride from here with promise. If he survives, he would be ready for training in another two or three years."

The Old One snorted.

"Your associate Dulong has been restored to favor with Count Uhlstein. Here is the reward for our saving the Count." Malame placed a large doeskin bag filled with sapphires in front of him.

The Old One waved an impatient hand. "Any competent street magician could have accomplished it. Is that all you were able to achieve?"

"No. Chaos will come thrice to my beckoning."

"Impossible."

"Look within me and see that I speak truth."

The Old One did, and an almost never seen smile creased his lips. "You are perhaps salvageable."

As Malame was leaving the yurt the Old One raised his head. "Tell me of Dulong."

"Healthy. Snake quick and puissant. And wrinkled like dried fruit."

"We gave each other those wrinkles."

From the Author

"The Loosing of Havoc" is the fourth and latest short story about Malame, journeyman sorcerer. His name is a combination of two French words which mean bad soul. I've tried to show Malame's progression, not into dehumanization, but into a mystic being increasingly alien to we humans. I've tried to avoid the usual misconceptions about dark magic and describe some of its grittier aspects... Hope you enjoyed the read.

About the Author

Ed Ahern resumed writing after forty odd years in foreign intelligence and international sales. He's had over three hundred stories and poems published so far, and six books. Ed works the other side of writing at Bewildering Stories, where he sits on the review board and manages a posse of nine review editors.

https://www.twitter.com/bottomstripper
https://www.facebook.com/EdAhern73
https://www.instagram.com/edwardahern1860/

Until Next Time
by
Mike Wyant Jr.

Until Next Time

I tuck her in.

It's a well-practiced moment. One worn down by infinite repetition.

But it's special. A thing between me and her. A moment where we leave behind all the worries of the world and simply be.

A moment when I get a reprieve from this reality.

I stroke dark hair from brown eyes and say things that make her smile. It always works. Always brings that same half-grin from the day we met in Rome. It's the same one captured in the wedding holograms, half-remembered blurs that flash on the barely rendered cabinet behind me.

I set a glass of water on the bedside table almost hidden amongst the machines beeping their discordant symphony. The water in the glass is an unnatural aquamarine in the false, yellow light of the room instead of its typical sulfur-sheen.

That's the signal. It's time.

A knife of panic shoves into my spine.

Time for what?

But the memory doesn't slow just because I do. I grab the glass and wrack my brain. She takes it from me right on cue, warm fingers lingering on mine. Smiling like always. And she drinks deeply.

She knows what's dissolved in the glass. It's her idea.

That almost breaks me. I savor these fleeting moments as I have thousands of times before. I breathe her in, a mix of sick sweat and sweet lavender.

She passes the glass back to me. It tinks as I put it back, and the slash of blue-green liquid catches my attention again.

What am I supposed to do? Why can't I remember?

I let out a sharp laugh that isn't supposed to be here, in this memory prison. I can't remember because I've done this for too long, but it was unavoidable.

We needed to give her time.

Frustration rises, sharp in my throat. Time for what?

My face gets hot as my beloved looks up at me, curiosity furrowing her brow. It's so hard to think in here, especially right here, with her, but it's the only place with enough emotion the AI can't track me. Especially with the hacks I uploaded before I was arrested. We told them they shouldn't connect the Prison AI to the Internet.

My breath is ragged as I try to remember. Try to piece together why that's important.

Her face, and the room around us, flickers like a buffering video file. I feel my will dragged into place as the Prison AI forces me back into well-worn patterns, through the electrodes lodged in my brain, a million miles away.

The thought, and recognition, flitters away...and I lean in slowly, her scent filling my nostrils.

I kiss her forehead.

Reaching over the edge of the aged mattress, I tweak the terminal behind the bed to start the transfer process. That's important, but I'm not sure why. Then I grab her favorite book and hand it over reverently, pulling a turquoise bookmark from pages worn with tender hands. Her eyes close and her breathing steadies, so I set the book down on her chest. It's open, ready to be picked up and read.

In case she wakes, I always tell myself.

Something about that tickles my memory, but it's swept away in a wave of nausea. My stomach spins, and I kiss her forehead again; quivering lips meeting her warm skin one last time, her nearly perpetual fever only now starting to fade.

"Until next time," I whisper with a small smile, and I step away to the slowing breath of one who never wakes.

The door leading out of the room slides open, and I step through, ignoring the screaming machines behind me. The acrid scent of the prison wafts into my nose; a heady mix of antiseptic and despair that clings to the chill, flat-walled cell the AI has crafted for me.

For the briefest of moments, I have my mind back...and I wish I didn't. An ache I can't stop scrapes and tears across my chest and up my neck. A rift tears my stomach in two. I fall to my knees. A wail echoes against the flat gray walls. It takes me a moment to realize it's coming from me.

You'd think I'd be used to it by now.

Through eyes blurred with tears, I tear off my clothes and throw them into the corner. The pair of drab ashen fleece pants, and worn blue t-shirt, smell of sweat and shame. The pounding in my chest radiates into the room. Heavy, hot, and booming. An unnatural crimson flashing off featureless surfaces.

That stops me in my tracks. There's something I'm supposed to be thinking about right now. Something urgent...

The water.

It takes everything I have to stop the shuddering sobs wracking my body, but I do.

None of this is real. Not my wife; not me. Not this cell. Not really. My jail sentence is something new. It's based off the work my wife and I did on managing artificial environments with AI. I coded the backend; she crafted the personality. At least, she did until the sickness made her too feeble. Then I took over.

We made it to heal. To provide closure. And it's used that way the world over.

Then we licensed it to Unified Penitentiary Incorporated.

My jailer uses it to punish. One Hundred Million Repetitions is my sentence. That isn't possible in a lifetime, but when your brain can force you to relive a moment once per second?

That's only four years, including processing. A great way to clear the prison system of "non-violent offenders."

Mercy, they called it in the original sales pitch.

Then I helped my wife die peacefully.

Mercy for whom?

There's a harsh snap like a whip crack.

The ticker in the corner incrementally records another sliver of my sentence.

I don't have much time now. I need to remember what to do in there or it'll be over. Meaningless. I'll be stuck here for another million memories before they send me out onto the street.

Alone.

It'd be better to stay in that moment forever. Then I can be with her. Sometimes, despite the push from the AI, all I want to do is sit back down on the bed and read to her as she passes...

My breath catches and, as I wipe tears from my face, the screech of a klaxon freezes me in place.

The clothes reappear on my body, their weight settling on my shoulders like a hair shirt: itchy and heavy. Acrid, nervous sweat fills my nostrils, almost washing away the stink of the prison. Behind me, the simulation winds back to life with a squeal like rewinding audio.

Ninety-nine million times I've said those three words. Until next time. A million more and I'll never see her again.

It doesn't get easier. Each session is a reminder I, not the cancer, killed my wife. Every trip into this damned machine layers more guilt. Guilt I know I'll carry to the end of my days...whenever that is. I sometimes wish we'd never created it.

My beloved may be gone, but the curse of her death follows me. The way her skin smelled that day. The beeps of the machines, and the glass of water in the yellow light of the side lamp.

Her final, rattling breath as the door closed behind me.

But it's not the memory I can't stand.

It's walking out of that room and remembering she's gone. Feeling the loss of the most beautiful person in my life. Knowing her smile and laugh are missing, forgotten by a world that doesn't even know it needs them.

This is the only place she exists now.

The door opens behind me with a creak. From beyond it, my beloved asks for a glass of water.

My heart melts and I smile. I know what I need to do.

We go through the motions: I tuck her in, kiss her forehead, hand her the water. My heart pounds through it all, but what I need to do runs through the back of my mind, unfiltered and undetected.

And now it's time. I lean in, heart hammering, breath short. I kiss her feverish forehead and whisper four new words. "Come back to me."

I hold my breath for a long moment, staring at her placid face as it succumbs to the poison, the machines ticking away their countdown.

This should've worked.

"Come back to me." There's panic in my voice.

She's not breathing anymore.

Everything skips a few frames as the AI redirects focus to me. My mind scatters trying to figure out what I did wrong, but this is it. The passphrase should have done it. Did they find the snippet, and its payload, buried in the behavioral analytics? I knew I couldn't do it, despite her faith in me. I'm not the programmer she was. I'm not good enough.

Some force grabs my limbs and pulls me to the door.

"No!" I scream, grabbing her cooling body in a fierce embrace. "No!"

But I don't have strength to fight it off, and I'm torn away, her body disappearing as I'm spun around and thrown through the exit.

I hit the ground in a crooked roll, limbs flailing. When I stop, I don't get up. There's no point. I had one chance and I failed.

It's over. She's gone.

I close my eyes and wait for the ticker.

But the crack of the whip never comes.

Instead, warmth suffuses my body, and I hear the distinct sound of my wife clearing her throat. I look toward the still-open doorway, tears trickling from my eyes as I choke out a laugh.

It worked. She's leaning against the doorframe in the green sweater and jeans she wore when we first met, a nearly blinding, white light shining from behind her.

"Well, are you coming?" she asks, grinning and extending a hand.

I climb to my feet unsteadily and take it.

It worked. The copy of her consciousness I grabbed as she lay dying, uploaded correctly into the AI.

Overwriting the old code with the mind of my beloved.

With a sure step, she turns and steps into the light. In that glow, I swear I see a million branching pathways, each leading farther away from this place. This prison.

If I follow her, I'll leave my body behind. Turn into a series of 1s and 0s just like her. Disappear into the ether.

I should be worried, but I'm not. Instead, I smile and step into the light.

I've kept her waiting long enough.

From the Author

"Until Next Time" was the result of a rather horrible thought experiment where I imagined how my world would change if my spouse passed away. My immediate next thought was, "Well, if I had the technology, I'd do absolutely whatever it took to bring her back." This story sprouted from that seed.

About the Author

When not being crawled over by his Writing Cat, Einie, Mike Wyant Jr. writes science fiction with a focus on exploring mental illness and its repercussions. Once upon a time, he was a Sys Admin, Network Administrator, and do-it-all tech drone. He's left those days behind. Mostly.

Mike is also the Editor and sometimes Producer/Director of *The Storyteller Series* Podcast, a full-cast short fiction audiobook podcast.

His science fiction series, the Anisian Convergence, will be published by Chris Kennedy Publishing and Theogony Books in the summer of 2022, beginning with the near future climate sci-fi, *Last Bid for a Dying Earth*.

To find out more about Mike or his other shenanigans, visit https://www.mikewyantjr.com. You can also find him on Facebook, Twitter, Patreon, and Instagram @mikewyantjr.

Slipping Away

by
Martin L. Shoemaker

Slipping Away

*H*arry Timms barely noticed the lights going out across the office as he sat in his cubicle, fiddling with one more spreadsheet. He sat in a window row, but it was only a window row when considering the small bit of glass barely visible down at the far end, in Christine's cube, and all *that* window looked out upon was the building across the way. So, Harry's only indication of the passage of time was the office lights. But the guards had long ago put his row on a different cycle because they knew how late Harry would be working.

When he finally had his spreadsheet straightened out, Harry checked his work item list to see what was next. *Damn,* he was hoping, after an eleven-hour day, that anything there could wait until tomorrow; but he saw three emails from Leeanne that needed an answer, and also a government safety audit that needed his input. All of these were due first thing tomorrow. He only needed another couple of hours—he checked the clock—and that put him home well after 9:00.

Lisa and Kenny would be asleep, and Tia would be annoyed or pretending that she wasn't. But it had to be done. They needed this job. They needed the money.

So, Harry flipped over to his other screen, to pull up his email. That was a mistake; he shouldn't have looked. Not the email, just the background on the screen, before he popped the email up; the picture of the four of them on the beach last summer.

Wait, was it last summer? No, in the picture, Lisa was still in diapers. That had to be *two* summers ago. They hadn't even gotten to the beach at all last year, had they?

It was still summer. There was still time. He could make it. Certainly not tonight. Not this weekend, judging by his backlog. And then he remembered the trade show coming up in three weeks, and how everyone had to put in extra effort to be ready for that.

Harry wasn't the only one putting in the long hours, just the only one here, at this point in time. Sometimes, the whole team was here, but this week had been just Harry.

He clicked the icon to bring up the email. He felt a tug at his heart as the picture disappeared behind the list of messages, but then, he had no time for regrets. While he had been busy, two more must-read emails had come in from Leeanne and from her boss, Mike. Harry started reading through them and answering them. He had to give credit to Mike and Leeanne: they were both still hard at work, both replying to his answers almost instantly.

Soon Harry knew the spreadsheet he had just finished wasn't finished at all. It needed a total revision, with all these new figures and assumptions. He sighed and opened the spreadsheet back up and went back to work.

Despite himself, his pace slowed as he went. He was starting to fade out, his mind slipping off to daydreams, unable to focus on the work at hand. He kept telling himself to give up and go home, but every time he shook himself alert, he remembered the looming deadlines, and he forced himself to concentrate on the work again.

Harry barely noticed when he melted into his chair. It wasn't that different from the daydream sessions he'd been fighting all night. But this time it wasn't just his brain that slipped away: his body started to sag in the middle, and his head fell upon his chest. While Harry's imagination had him chasing a rubber ball with duck feet, his head slowly continued to sink into his chest and spread out. His arms drooped on the chair, and his legs stretched like taffy, from the knees, until soon he was a puddle of ooze.

Harry noticed only when he started to seep through the space between the chair back and the seat; and by that time, it was too late. The thick, tacky blob that had been his head, slid down, following the rest of him through the crack and joining with his feet.

Harry had liquefied, clothes and all, into a sludge that pooled on the floor. He wondered why he didn't panic, but it felt so...inevitable. Maybe not peaceful, but something told him there was no sense fighting. He was done. He was a puddle of ooze. What could he do?

He could look around. His eyes seemed to have that much integrity left, though everything around him was distorted. His glasses, he realized, were still in the chair. He could see one of the bows hanging from the seat. The prescription probably wasn't right for his eyes now. Harry tried to stretch for it anyway, but he had no control left in this gelatinous form.

If he could call somebody, maybe a cellphone... No, if his cellphone was with him, like his pants, then it was sludge. If it wasn't sludge, it surely was still up in the chair, out of reach, with the glasses.

He wished he could call Tia, beg her to help him. But what could she do? She probably wouldn't even believe his story. She had accused him, more than once, of having another woman he visited instead of staying at work. *Or perhaps*, she said, *he was having an affair with Leeanne.*

Neither was true. He loved Tia and the kids so much. And besides, if he could never find time for them, where would he find time for anyone else?

Then Harry experienced a strange sensation—as if being ooze wasn't strange enough. He felt part of him stretching, expanding, and just the slightest bit of sinking. He realized his perspective was lowering, but only as his eyes sank into the carpet did he realize he was soaking through it. The stretching feeling was some part of him dripping away. He could feel himself stretch right through a crack in the floor and drip onto the ceiling tiles of the floor below. And he must be growing thinner as he dripped because the pace picked up.

Soon all of Harry was dripping into the entryway on the ground floor. His eyes didn't survive falling through such a thin crack, and then through the pores of the ceiling tile.

Harry pooled up on the tile floor of the entry. He was now much less differentiated, impossible to tell one bit from another, nor where they had been in Harry's original body. But he found that, in this form, eyes were unnecessary. He was just *aware* of his surroundings, aware of what he touched, and aware of vibrations in it as things moved around him. He sensed sounds in the air, and variations in the light. He didn't have eyes, but he was aware of shapes, and, if he really concentrated, even colors and details.

Harry was still experimenting with his new visual sense when a massive black boot sole came smashing down upon where his senses were currently concentrated. Harry shouted.

And he *moved!* Only a small ripple, but it was more than just the squish of the boot. Harry's shout shifted his center slightly to the side. He looked up just as Officer Gardner was bending down, his head looming like a giant, distorted in Harry's vision.

"What the hell is this?"

Gardner reached down a finger, and Harry was worried the officer would get Harry all over him. Harry tried to muster his energy again, to shout or move before Officer Gardner could touch him. But that brief burst of power was gone. Harry was still.

At the last instant, the guard pulled his finger away, before it reached Harry. "I don't know what it is, but it smells awful, and I ain't touching it."

Everything about Gardner was huge and distorted. It took a second for Harry to recognize what the man pulled from his belt was a radio.

Gardner pushed a button and called, "Maintenance, patrol."

Another voice came on. Harry recognized it as Brad somebody, one of the night maintenance crew who usually stopped to talk to him. "This is maintenance, what do you need?"

"We've had some sort of spill here in the lobby."

"Spill? What do you mean?"

Officer Gardner wiped some of Harry off his boot and onto a clean spot on the tile. "There's a mess spreading all across the floor. I think somebody better mop it up before the bigwigs show up and see it."

"What is it?"

"I don't know. It smells bad. It's, I don't know, sewage? Come check it out."

Brad paused. "Is it hazardous? Do you see any containers nearby?"

"No containers. Probably somebody had something in a bag and set it down, and then it leaked, and no one noticed."

"All right. I'll be down there. Try to find where it came from."

Harry was almost amused watching Officer Gardner search around for a bucket, or a bottle, or a can, or anything, but never once looking up. If he had, Gardner would've seen where the sludge came from. Even Harry with his weak and distorted vision could still see the last few drops of himself coming from the ceiling. And, as each drop separated from the tile and fell, he could just barely feel the drop stretching, letting go, and falling. Soon there wasn't enough left to form drops and fall, which was okay with Harry. Whatever might be left up there, he clearly didn't need it.

Did he need *anything* at this point?

Before Harry could ponder that, Brad showed up with a shop vac and a mop bucket. "Eww, that *is* awful."

"Be careful," Gardner said. "It might be toxic or something."

Brad did what Gardner hadn't: he crouched down, stuck a finger into the puddle that was Harry, and brought it to his nose. Harry felt a slight stretch and snap as a bit of ooze pulled away, but the little bit of film on Brad's finger wasn't enough to really worry about.

"Ugh," Brad said. "It's like ground meat and sewage."

Gardner frowned. "That might be toxic."

"No, no, let's not worry about that." Before Gardner could object, Brad pressed on. "Look, whatever it is, if we make a big deal out of it, we're both going to end up in trouble. How many times have you been through here tonight and not noticed it?"

"Three."

"And I've been through twice," Brad continued. "They'll ask us why we didn't take care of it then. Why we didn't report it. And who knows, if we even mention hazards, or if they just think of it on their own, then it's a hazmat incident. Neither one of us will get any of our reports done. It'll probably get us both fired."

Gardner took a step back, staring down at Harry. "What are you going to do?"

"I'm going to spray it, vacuum it up, mop the floor, and dump it down the drain."

"You can't do that. You're not supposed to dump stuff in the drain when we don't know what it is."

"Look around." Brad gestured, and Gardner looked. "Whatever this is, there's not enough of it to worry about. This isn't a major spill. This is barely more than somebody taking a dump."

"Whatever," Gardner said. "I was never here, okay?" He walked away.

When Brad brought out the hose and started spraying the puddle that was Harry, it was another new sensation. The spatters of the water would've felt like nothing more than a light shower to Harry in his human form. But now...

It didn't hurt. Pain seemed to be something Harry had given up in this form, at least he had that in his favor. But the water spattered him, spread him, thinned him, diluted him. He was less gelatinous now, more liquid, and his senses grew thinner and more dispersed. At some point, Brad must have been satisfied that he had thinned the ooze out enough, so he started up the shop vac and began sucking Harry up.

Suddenly, Harry's vision and hearing improved. As whatever he was became more concentrated, back together within the vacuum bucket, he started feeling more aware, more in control of himself. Not able to move yet, though maybe if he were a little more solid, he might. But his hearing and sight vastly improved. Not that it did a lot of good. All he could see was the darkened interior of the shop vac, and all he could hear was the motor.

Soon Harry could tell he was all inside the shop vac bucket. Well, he had left behind little drips and wisps on the floor above and on the ceiling tile, maybe even still a touch on Brad's finger. But what was missing was not an essential part of him any more than his sideburns had been back when he was human. For all that mattered, Harry was entirely in the bucket.

And he reveled in it. His sense of self was suddenly restored. He could think again, and wonder.

But he could also worry. Though he was aware once more, he realized that, as a practical matter, he was dead. Tia and Lisa and Kenny had lost their husband and father. What would they do without him, without his income?

Well, that was covered to a degree. He had good insurance. Tia had insisted on that. She had always been more sensible than him when it came to finances.

But kids growing up without a dad, Tia without him... If it had been possible in this form, Harry would have wept. Instead, he was simply terrified again, realizing he was powerless against this bizarre change, and he was lost, never to see his family again. His mind flashed back to his screen saver, to the beach—to Lisa and Kenny and Tia. He would never see his family again. He knew that now.

No. He couldn't accept that. While he was all together, while he had fear, and family, to motivate him, he was going to fight back. He would make someone notice him for once. He *would* see his family again!

What could he do? He had shouted before, and he had moved. If he had enough power, if he had enough energy... If he gathered his power and conserved it and got ready, he would *make* someone hear him.

This plan gave Harry focus. Instead of idly pooling in the bucket, he planned, he thought. He felt his strength gathering. He was very careful not to try to move, not to do anything to waste these energies. He might have only one shot.

He didn't know how much later it was that he felt the shop vac bucket shake. Something had jostled it. His time was coming.

And then came the sound of something scraping, and suddenly it was lighter inside. The janitor had removed the lid. This was Harry's one chance. He took all his gathered strength...and the bucket jostled more and lifted and tilted. *Oh, he's pouring the water out!*

With his last burst of strength, Harry shouted just two words: "Help me!" A large bubble rose, but the thin vibrations it contained were lost in the sound of water sloshing into a big drain.

Harry felt himself spattering against the cold concrete—parts of him sloshing through the metal grate, while others splashed around the tub basin, waiting for their turn to descend into the sewer pipes. Soon all that was Harry, was down the drain.

The pipes were rough, unclean. Harry felt and tasted all the bits of dirt and sludge that had passed through these pipes before him. As he stretched further and further, thinner and thinner, eventually Harry poured into a larger pipe, where parts of him were already hundreds of yards away. This pipe was totally dark, which was just as well. From the taste, the smell, and the touch, Harry could well imagine what it would look like, and he'd rather not see.

The water was slower moving here, wending its way toward...toward... Harry couldn't imagine where it was wending, if he'd ever known.

At intervals, more sludge splashed in from different sources along the way. Harry grew more dispersed and less clean with every turn of the pipe.

Then, suddenly, part of him was dropping, a part far away from where his mind lived; but he could still feel it, dropping into some larger body of sludge. He felt himself expanding yet more. Eventually, all of Harry fell into what felt like some large, round tank full of water, but none of it moving. Slowly Harry and the surrounding waste came to rest.

Harry began trying to pull his scattered self back together. With great effort, several times he created an area of almost pure Harry, but it never lasted. From time to time, more sludge fell in, and waves rippled across the tank and broke Harry up again, into his component pieces.

Harry wondered, should he just give up, accept this? Accept that he would never again see... those people on the beach...

Tia! Lisa and Kenny! For a moment, they had slipped his mind. Should he just let them go?

Before Harry could reach an answer, there was a sudden rushing sound, and Harry, and all the water around him, was swept through a drain in the bottom of the tank. It surged into another tank, and this one had something new in it. He couldn't say what, but it tingled, like the water was electrified, and he could feel bits of himself falling away. Non-essential bits that were not Harry the person, just little bits that had latched onto him through the years. At one point, he realized he could no longer remember how to balance a spreadsheet. And then, as more of the charge passed through him, he couldn't remember what a spreadsheet was. And then he couldn't remember the word.

Slowly Harry slipped through another valve and out of the shallow, tingling tank. He had trouble remembering words now. His distant pieces were still there, but faint. He clung to what he could—the beach, Tia, Lisa, and K—

It started with a K... K... Then he remembered: *Kenny!*

Time became impossible for him to track. How long he had passed through these pipes, he didn't know. He didn't care. He had his memories of his family, and peace of a sort, as he flowed to where he did not know.

Then Harry realized: he was not alone! Something was in this water—in *him*. Something alive. Alive!

Harry remembered being alive. He remembered the fear of being lonely, of being alone. Here, now, he had companions. Tiny,

tiny little companions, so small that had he had eyes, Harry could not have seen them. But he felt them. They were all in him and through him. Good little living things. "Stay with me. Keep me company," Harry thought.

Then to his horror he realized they were devouring him! They were chewing away at all the impurities that he still carried. All the things that might live again, if given a chance. But now they never would. The little organisms were eating him alive!

Harry tried to scream, but there was so little left of him, spread so thin, he couldn't even raise a bubble. But in his mind he screamed as bits of him were snatched away. His childhood home. His third-grade teacher. His father's name.

His name! He strained to hold onto that, but he hadn't the will left. He could hold the three people in his memory, or... He let go of his name.

Then he was in motion once more, his essence growing distant and thin, flowing somewhere new. All he had left was... All he had left...

All that he had was gone. *This* was all he had left, flowing through these pipes, very clean. He knew they were clean, but he couldn't remember what he had to compare them with. And light ahead. And moving air.

And then he poured out into the bright sunlight, across the sand, and into a larger body, more water than he could ever imagine, his tiniest little pieces spreading far across the waves. There was a word for this, he could dimly remember. This pleasant place, where he belonged. This... beach...

He was at peace at last as he lapped against the feet of the sad woman and the two children who slowly walked through the surf.

From the Author

I like to say that some stories are autometaphorical. If an autobiography is a biography you write about yourself, then an autometaphor is a metaphor you tell about yourself. It's not literally true, but it's truth. This is an autometaphorical story. As a programmer, I've spent many late nights in a darkened office, with my only company the security guards and maintenance personnel who passed through on their rounds. Sometimes it felt like I was becoming part of the furniture. And one dark drive home, I dictated that story.

About the Author

Martin L. Shoemaker is a programmer who writes on the side...or maybe it's the other way around. He told stories to imaginary friends and learned to type on his brother's manual typewriter even though he couldn't reach the keys. (He types with the keyboard in his lap still today.) He couldn't imagine any career but writing fiction...until his algebra teacher said, "This is a program. You should write one of these."

Fast forward 30 years of programming, writing, and teaching. He was named an MVP by Microsoft for his work with the developer community. He wrote fiction, but he gave up on submitting until his brother-in-law read a chapter and said, "That's not a chapter. That's a story. Send it in." It won second place in the Baen Memorial Writing Contest and earned him lunch with Buzz Aldrin. Programming never did that!

Martin hasn't stopped writing (or programming) since. His work has appeared in Analog Science Fiction & Fact, Galaxy's Edge, Digital Science Fiction, Forever Magazine, Writers of the Future, and numerous anthologies including Year's Best Military and Adventure SF 4, Man-Kzin Wars XV, The Jim Baen Memorial Award: The First Decade, Little Green Men—Attack!, More Human Than Human: Stories of Androids, Robots, and Manufactured Humanity, Avatar Dreams, and Weird World War

III. His Nebula-nominated Clarkesworld story "Today I Am Paul" explores the logical consequences of a medical care android with empathy, able to understand how its actions affect its patient's emotional state. It appeared in four different year's best anthologies and eight international editions. He expanded that story into his debut novel, Today I Am Carey (published by Baen Books in March 2019), in which the android learns more about humanity through life with its human family. His novel The Last Dance was published by 47North in November 2019, and the sequel, The Last Campaign was published in October 2020.

You can find more about Martin's writing at http://Shoemaker.Space. You can find him on Facebook as Martin L. Shoemaker.

The Valorous Deed
by
Emily Martha Sorensen

The Valorous Deed

As dawn appeared over the horizon, a rumbling sound came from deep in the mountainside, emerging from a dark, mysterious cave. For a long time, all was still; the snoring of the dragon was unmolested.

Clank!

The Knight arrived at the top of the hill, wiping his brow with exhaustion. The trek had been longer than he had anticipated, and his heavy chain mail had only increased the arduous climb.

Clank!

He panted for a moment, wishing he had something to lean on. His sword would do. He almost yelled for his squire to bring it to him.

But then he paused. No; the sword was not meant for leaning on. The King had not bequeathed it to him for that.

And what would Ambrosia think of him if he did?

Just as he was thinking of his lady fair, she appeared from behind him. "Why didst thou not wait?" she demanded, hands on her hips as he turned to face her. "Thou knowest I meant to come with thee."

The Knight tried not to groan at the sight of her. It wasn't fitting for women to see spectacles like the death of foul wyrms; he'd explained that to her numerous times, but she had perfected the art of turning to deaf ear to anything she didn't want to hear.

"This quest I must fulfil on my own. Thou shalt return to the camp below."

The Lady's smile had a hint of smugness in it. "Then thou wilt not have a sword."

He stared at her blankly. "Where is my squire?" He turned, searching the mountain behind him for the elusive knave. The boy had not followed him when he began the trek, but the Knight had been certain the boy would follow when he awoke, hastening to reach the top of the mountain before his enraged master began to head downwards again.

The smug look became a full-fledged smirk. "Gone, my lord."

"Gone!" He repeated the word, stunned.

"Yea."

"Where?" he demanded, anger boiling in him. "Where did the slothful rogue make off to? Where wouldst he dare be now?"

"Still in the alehouse, I would presume."

The Knight's face grew red. "When the wretch is beneath my fingers, then wilt he comprehend my rage at those who take my orders for naught—"

Ambrosia appeared unimpressed. That was, the Knight had to admit, her greatest failing; she had trouble understanding the magnitude of important situations. She let him rage for a minute or two before reaching behind her to disclose a heavy sword. "Is this the object of thy tirade?" she asked sweetly.

"Where didst thou get that?" he demanded, abruptly ceasing his diatribe. "Why hast thou my sword?"

"Thy squire," she said tartly. "While he was in the alehouse, I caused a large rock to connect with his head. I will come and see this spectacle which is not meant for women's eyes."

The Knight glared at her, but her stubborn gaze refused to relent. She lifted the sword into the air again, with some difficulty.

"Are we not near a cliff?" she pointed out. "And have I not the strength to heft this instrument of destruction over its edge if I so choose?"

He grumbled, "Ambrosia, thou knowest thou wert meant to stay with the camp below—"

"I did not come with the camp to stay below," she snorted.

"Thou wert not meant to come with the camp in the first place!"

The smirk appeared again. "But thou wilt allow me to watch the death of the wyrm, my lord, or thou wilt not succeed."

His eyes narrowed, but he didn't see what he could do. She did have his sword, and for all he knew, she might even know how to use it. She seemed to know far too many skills for a noble-born maiden. If not for the extent of her dowry, he might have been hesitant to agree to a betrothal. But her title and dowry were desirable to him. He sighed loudly.

"Thou must stay far from harm," he warned her.

Ambrosia gave him a look of disgust. "I hardly plan to stray in the way of a wyrm's breath, my lord."

The clanking of iron continued upwards as the Knight searched for the legendary cave of the dreadful wyrm. It was not until Ambrosia returned to the path they had taken before and pointed out a crevasse he had failed to notice that he discovered the opening of the cave. Then, and only then, would she relinquish the sword.

"Its weight is pleasing unto me, my lord."

Frustrated, the Knight understood her intent; he would have no chance to send her away if she continued to grasp his sword. He failed to press the issue, however; the armor alone was heavy enough to make him almost grateful to have the Lady stubbornly clinging to it.

For a brief moment, the Knight was certain it was the lack of light in the inner cave that caused the creature to appear so immense. The image failed to shrink as his eyes adjusted to the darkness. With rising dismay, he stared at the titanic head. His gaze moved along the vast body of the creature, ending with the prodigious tail.

Looking back, the Knight saw his Lady standing too far inside of the cave for him to be assured of her safety.

"Retreat farther!" he instructed.

"Nay," was the stubborn reply. "Did I not climb to this lair with thee to behold the death of the foul creature? I intend to witness the whole of it, whether it is suitable for women's eyes or not."

That was her other greatest failing, the Knight reflected. Ambrosia had never learned to cease being obstinate when an inappropriate idea entered her head. This was not something he had realized when he had agreed to the betrothal.

"Do not venture from thy current position, then," the Knight sighed, "save it be backwards, to preserve thy safety."

Her look was scornful. "Dost thou take me for a fool?"

The Knight took a deep breath and turned his attention to the dragon. His courage faltered slightly as he took in the immensity of the wyrm, but he held the sword steady. Was he not a knight of the king? Did he not have a quest to fulfill?

He had heard that the underbelly of the dragon was most vulnerable, but as the dragon was sleeping on its stomach, the knowledge did him little good.

"Why dost thou not attack?" the Lady called from the mouth of the cave.

The Knight winced, glancing nervously in the direction of the sleeping dragon. "Perhaps," he suggested, "silence would be advisable."

"His snores are louder than my father's. I would hear nothing if my night-noises were as deafening."

The Knight tried to curb his annoyance. It was only natural that a Lady would know nothing about wyrms; he should not allow her ignorance to cause him vexation.

He turned back to the dragon, hesitating again. Every part of the dragon seemed to be covered in scales—scales with thickness exceeding that of his chain mail. The Knight began to doubt the sword's strength; even a sword bequeathed by the King could not penetrate as deeply as would be needful.

The Lady decided to advise him again. "Why dost thou not hack at the tail, if thou must hack at something?"

The Knight turned back to her, distinctly irritated. "The tail hath a covering of exceedingly thick scales."

"The dragon hath a covering of exceedingly thick scales. Wast thy sword not created for the purpose of penetration? Or perhaps the King hath granted it unto thee for the purpose of mere observation."

She was mocking him. She had no right to mock him!

"Thou knowest nothing of the wyrms! I have spent extensive years of my life studying their choicest paths to mortality."

The Lady remained unimpressed. "Then why dost thou not attack? My knowledge may indeed have severe limitations, but the creature will hardly fall dead from thy stare. It might even awaken—and what wouldst thou do then?"

She was mocking him again. The Knight felt indignation.

"It would be possible—and hardly difficult—for one of my extensive study to slay the dragon during his period of wakefulness," the Knight retorted, defensive. "But the wyrm is slumbering and would likely be—cranky if it were to be awakened at this time. I had not planned a confrontation to take place during its hours of sleep."

"All dragons sleep during the time that the sun dwells in the sky," she answered scornfully. "Thou didst plan for it to be asleep by coming here in the day."

"Only because I sleep during contrary hours!" the Knight cried, frustration building in him. "And thy observation is not true for all dragons, my lady. Few wyrms there are that slumber at times which may be predicted by men. The foul creature would surely be lying dead at thy feet now, if thou didst not persist in interrupting my concentration!"

"Then glad am I to have chosen to make my interruptions. The reek of a wyrm's carcass at my feet would be unpleasant indeed."

The Knight turned back to the dragon, clutching his sword and clenching his teeth. Had he not told the Lady her senses would be repulsed by the hideous creature? Had he not warned her that her delicate stomach would fail her if she were to see its death? The sight of the dragon's cadaver would drive her away soon enough— even the blood spurting from multiple slices through its belly ought to be enough to cause her to flee in disgust—

Though the Lady knew nothing about wyrms, her suggestion contained limited merit. The tail was certainly the thinnest part of the dragon—could it also be a place of weakness, like the underbelly? Truly, his years of study had never raised the question.

Perhaps no dragonslayer had yet attempted to solve the riddle that would not have occurred to them. Or perhaps a few had, but failed to mention the true reason for victory, convinced it would seem ridiculous in contrast with heroic epics of dragonslaying of earlier times.

If the latter was the case, the Knight was determined to fail to join the ranks of fools who chose to do so. The effectiveness of the art of dragonslaying depended on the truthfulness of its members.

He hefted the sword into the air. The tail was thin enough, if the width of three humans at the base could be considered thin. He cast a doubtful glance at the sword and headed for the center of the tail; at the very least, the Knight figured, bringing the sword down in a powerful blow, he ought to wake the dragon and force it to expose its weak belly to him.

The sword struck the scales with a deafening bong! echoing around the cave and making the sword reverberate so fiercely in the hands of the Knight that it nearly shook out of his grip.

When the Knight was finally able to turn his attention back to the tail of the dragon, he discovered—with some dismay—its lack of alteration. The sword had only glanced across a few of its scales, though all his might had been behind the blow.

The dragon stirred slightly, the tail flicking the Knight across the cave and flinging him against the rock wall.

He heard Ambrosia gasp. "What hast befallen thee? Why didst thou not strike back where the wyrm would be most vulnerable?"

He didn't hear her rush to his side.

Perhaps she was keeping her word—not venturing forth if danger could be incurred upon her. Prudence, he told himself, was a virtue she had a need to gain—he should rejoice at this hopeful beginning.

The Knight made a valiant effort to arise. His legs felt broken—but behold, he could yet stand! The chain mail, blessed by a priest before he made his voyage, must be protecting him from the great evil of the monstrous dragon.

The Lady was watching him from her position just outside of the cave. "My lord, art thou—unharmed?"

He rose to his full height, ignoring the pain that shot through his back. The pain would vanish soon—and if it did not, it could not be said that he did not gain it valorously.

The dragon's tail, shifted slightly, no longer seemed a desirable target. The tail, he decided, was far too well protected.

The head, on the other hand . . .

All living creatures would die once their heads were detached; the same law could not help but apply to a treacherous wyrm. Had he not seen many paintings and heard many epics of noble warriors with the head of a dragon as proof of their valor?

The head, he decided, must be the true weak point.

The neck, rather. He examined it carefully. The neck was hardly thinner than the tail, but it seemed to have fewer scales—likely, to allow the monster to move its head with ease. He raised his sword, aiming with more care than he had when he attempted to slice through the tail.

Again, a ringing sound filled the cavern, leaving the scales undisturbed. The Knight, wary lest the beast should awaken, stood in a stance of preparation, attempting to ignore his sword's determination to shake from his grip.

The dragon's eyes remained closed, its snoring scarcely disturbed. It seemed the wyrm was oblivious of the Knight's attempts on his life.

"Die, foul wyrm!" the Knight cried, a hint of desperation in his voice. He stood defiantly before one of the creature's nostrils. "Arise and meet thy doom!"

The dragon snorted slightly, still slumbering; a small burst of flame darted through the air, frying the Knight.

This time, it took much longer for the Knight to recover from the difficulty of being flung against the wall; had it not been for the Lady's cries, he might not have revived at all.

A knight must always respond to a lady in distress. The Knight opened a weary eye. She might manage to awaken the wyrm with that wretched noise, exposing him in dangerous condition. Why had he not sent her away when he had had the chance? Surely her ceaseless distractions had been the true cause of his previous failures to slay the dragon.

She still had not rushed to his aid, he noticed dimly. But he should not have expected her to—had he not strictly prohibited it?

"I am unhurt," he managed, stumbling again to his feet. "The wyrm hath caused me no anguish, my lady, as is plain to see. The sword is well. The armor is well." He gestured at himself.

"The armor is black!" she shouted.

"It hath been blessed by a priest," the Knight reassured her.

"Its color bodes ill for the blessing!"

The Knight frowned, disliking the turn their conversation had taken. "Hast thou a recommendation for the final destruction of the monster?"

"Thou hast tried twice, and failed, my lord. Perhaps thou couldst find a smaller dragon to slay—that would seem wisdom indeed."

The Knight colored. "My earlier endeavors were merely attempts to gauge the wyrm's strength. Had I meant to destroy it from the first, it would have already be slain."

The Lady gave him a look of disgust. "Perhaps thou wert right, my lord, when thou saidst this scene was not meant for ladies' eyes. I expected to see a battle of great courage and honor, and instead I see a dragon defeating thee without even awakening. I see now why ladies are not meant to watch such battles; they could not have the stomach to see their lords made into fools."

"Enough!" the Knight raged, forgetting the dragon. "I shall slay the wyrm, and thou shalt respect my efforts!"

"Efforts? Thy efforts have profited thee very little, my lord. The dragon hath not even awakened!"

The Knight drew himself up to his full height, ignoring the shooting pain across his back as the singed chain mail links pressed against his skin. "My lady, thou mayest stay, if thou hast the wish. But if thou choosest this course, thou must refrain from mocking the arts of which thou knowest nothing."

Ambrosia let out an exaggerated sigh and sat by the mouth of the cave. "I will watch this tedious display of thy valor, my lord."

The Knight nodded curtly.

Now, it would be best to focus on the dragon and not his lady fair. The underbelly must indeed be its weak point, as other dragonslayers had foretold—he should have remembered his learning, and not attempted to go against the knowledge imparted to him through previous study. The lady should not have made distracting recommendations to him. Had it not been for her, this task would be completed already.

"Thou art taking quite a long time, my lord," the Lady called from the cavern entrance.

The Knight whirled and glared at her. "Silence," he hissed, and then turned back to the dragon.

His task would have been simpler if the wyrm had not been laying on its belly, but he was confident that a firm sword thrust beneath the slumbering creature would slice it open and eliminate its threat.

The greatest difficulty lay, he discovered, in the weight of the dragon's side. He had a laborious chore ahead, attempting to wedge the sword between the wyrm and cavern floor. After much poking and prodding, he succeeded in lifting the side up very slightly. It would have to be a large enough gap to fit the sword; the Knight doubted he could manage to wrest a larger space.

The Knight shoved the blade as far into the chink of space as it would go, though it was barely enough to admit the tip. Despite the Knight's fierce struggles, the blade would penetrate no further. Frustrated, the Knight pulled at the sword, preparing to try somewhere else.

The sword would not budge. The Knight pulled harder, dismay growing in him. If he could not retrieve his sword, he would never be able to complete his quest!

The jarring seemed to bother the dragon a little. It shifted onto its side, crushing the Knight beneath.

Ambrosia leapt to her feet, crying out, and stood for a moment, horrified. Then she sat again, slowly and thoughtfully. She had always wondered if knights who claimed to be able to successfully slay dragons had been lying, and now she knew they had.

She glanced at the dragon and sighed. This knight might have made a decent husband, but she could probably find another one somewhere else. Her father would find someone, she was certain of that. And so, bowing to the dragon for revealing her knight's lack of valor, she turned and headed down the mountain again.

Her father would, no doubt, not be pleased.

The Dragon woke as dusk approached. He yawned a little and stretched—jarring something uncomfortable by his side. He stood, looking to see what the lump was.

Another of those man-things, he noted, with the characteristic artificial protection that, he surmised, was meant to take the place of scales. He flipped the man-thing over, not seeing anything different about this one. A little flatter, perhaps—they weren't often this two-dimensional when their artificial scales had been roasted. But still recognizable as a man-thing.

Why did those man-things keep returning to his mountain, anyway? Their presence was little more than a nuisance, but even a nuisance could be frustrating.

Ah, well. Mysteries were mysteries, and some things defied explanation. In his six thousand years of life, he had at least learned that much.

Well, the dragon was hungry, and the man-thing was available. It wasn't enough to make much of a meal, but it would do for a start.

From the Author

I wrote this short story when I was in high school. My brother is a huge fan of dragons, and he was complaining about how very stupid it was that knights were supposed to be able to slay dragons, which are way more powerful, and usually way older, too.

So we laughed about the idea of a knight trying to slay a dragon, and it going . . . not at all the way he was hoping it would.

I wrote the first draft of this short story a few days later. I refined it several times over the years. While I think I'm a much better writer now than I was twenty years ago, this short story still holds a place in my heart because the whole plot concept makes me giggle.

About the Author

Emily Martha Sorensen writes fantasy and science fiction books with realistic paths to a happy ending. She considers all her books clean, with zero swearing and not much violence, but the romance between married couples can be PG-13.

She likes clever characters with unique personalities who charge straight through her plot and spend it spinning wildly off the rails. (Those brats.)

She likes magic systems with strict rules and intriguing limitations.

She likes romance after the happily ever after. That's where the relationship begins!

She likes plot twists that will make your jaw drop.

She likes hope and fun and humor.

She likes darkness that exists only to help characters grow towards greater light.

She likes—

Wait, where did those uncooperative protagonists put the plot this time? They just ran off with it, cackling maniacally!

Well, she hopes they'll leave you grinning.

You can find her books at

http://www.emilymarthasorensen.com.

Back in Time

by
Katie Kent

Back in Time

*M*y name is Alexandra," I said, my hands shaking. I concentrated intently on the notebook the spotty boy opposite me held on his lap. "You can call me Alex. I have OCD." I finally looked up. A room of ten other teens, plus the adult staff member leading the group, smiled at me encouragingly. Some of the butterflies that had been gathering in my stomach fluttered out of my body and I felt calmer. "My main compulsion is time travel."

I took a deep breath, glad to have got it out. I'd been dreading this moment for days.

Someone sniggered out loud. Others were trying their best not to laugh, while some just looked at me blankly.

Jeremy, the adult staff member, pretended not to be fazed, but I had seen his mouth twitch upwards along with many of the kids'.

"Welcome, Alex." His smile didn't seem to be quite genuine. "We've never had a time traveller here before." He coughed, and I swore it was to cover up a laugh.

In my head, I cursed myself, feeling the anxiety start to build in my stomach. So much for being honest. I should never have revealed this so early on, before anyone had got to know me.

It wasn't like I was the only time traveller, but there were few enough of us that most, if not all, of the people there had probably never met one before. There was still so much prejudice about us, and some people didn't even believe we could travel in time—they thought we were just delusional loonies.

I braced myself for all the usual questions. *When did you realise you could time travel?* (When I was 10, and my birthday party had been so much fun that I thought really hard about reliving the day, and found that I was suddenly right back at the beginning of the party.) *Were your parents time travellers too?* (No, they have no special abilities.) *What's to stop you travelling back and picking the winning lottery numbers?* (The time travel guardians, who monitor the time stream, enforce the relevant laws, and take action against anyone found to be abusing their power.)

I didn't really blame the others for laughing at me. Who had ever heard of a time traveller with OCD?

"That's just weird," the girl next to me said, finally. "I don't get how time travel could be a compulsion? This isn't a joke, you know. There are people here with real problems." As she stroked her long, blonde hair, and I looked into her striking blue eyes, I got a funny feeling in my stomach. Just my luck to have alienated someone so pretty.

I needed to fix this. My anxiety was getting more intense, until I could barely concentrate on anything else. I felt jittery, and the voice in my head was telling me to travel back in time. I shook my head, trying to block it out, but I couldn't tolerate the extreme panic coursing through my body. I knew I would have to give in. *Just this once*, I tried to reassure myself. There was no point starting the support group on the back foot, with everyone thinking I was odd. I had come here for help, after all—not judgement.

I shut my eyes tightly and concentrated on the moment I wanted to go back to. There was a whoosh in my ears—travelling through time felt kind of like when you change altitude in an aeroplane and your ears pop—and I opened my eyes to find myself back at the start of the group. As always, the relief I felt was immense. That's how the doctor had known it was OCD. Anxiety, check. Obsession, check. Compulsion, check. Relief, check.

"Are you okay?" I looked up to find the cute girl next to me staring at me with concern. "Your nose is bleeding." As she handed me a tissue, our hands touched. I felt a spark, and from the way she was looking at me, I could tell that she felt it too.

I felt myself blush as I dabbed my nose. Nose bleeds happened sometimes when I travelled. "Thank you."

She smiled at me, and I knew travelling back had been the right thing to do. I wouldn't have wanted to jeopardise anything with her, or the group, before it had even had a chance. Plus, I couldn't be cured immediately, right? I wasn't even in therapy yet. If I had been able to stop my compulsions just like that, I wouldn't have OCD. I was bound to slip up sometimes. I'd try harder next time.

I zoned out whilst the people before me said their names and why they were there; I'd heard it all before. When it got to me, I kept it vague. "My name is Alexandra," I said. "You can call me Alex. I'm new here, I've just been diagnosed with OCD, but I'm not quite ready to talk about it yet." This time my words were met with sympathetic smiles rather than scornful giggling, and I began to relax.

I paid more attention when the girl next to me began to speak.

"I'm Erin," she said. She had a pretty name; it suited her. "Most of you will already know me. I've been coming here for a few months now, and I've made good progress with some of my compulsions. However, I still have things to work on." She paused to clear her throat. "I have the stereotypical germ obsession. I used to wash my hands all the time, I had to open door handles with gloves, stuff like that.

"Last week, my sister got a stomach bug and it really stressed me out. My head was telling me I needed to go round the house with disinfectant. And I did clean the bathroom thoroughly after she was sick. But when she was crying, I went and comforted her. And I didn't wash my hands afterwards." There was pride in her voice.

"Wow, Erin, that's amazing! Well done." Jeremy gave her a smile, warmer than the one he had given me on my first attempt. "You've really come on since you started in this group. We all see the change in you."

I didn't participate much in the session. One of the boys said he obsessed over feeling that things needed to be perfect, and I said that I felt that urge too. But I left out the part about time travel. The discussion was helpful, though, and over the next week I resisted time travelling as much as I could.

As I arrived at the group the week after, I felt hopeful, and opened up a bit without being too specific. "I did do some compulsions," I said, "but I managed to resist a few times, too. When I felt the urge to fix things because they weren't perfect, I told myself that nothing in life is perfect, and although I felt the anxiety really strongly, I was able to stop myself doing the compulsions sometimes." I earned some encouraging words.

"Alex?"

As I gathered my things together at the end of the group, I looked up to see Erin standing in front of me.

"Hey, Erin." Butterflies beat their wings in my stomach as I spoke to her. She really was beautiful, her hair up in a bun this time, and wearing a neon pink vest top and blue denim shorts. "What's up?"

"Err, well, I wondered…." She twisted her silver ring around her finger self-consciously. "Do you want to go out with me sometime?" A blush was spreading across her face.

"Oh." I was momentarily stunned. She had taken me by surprise—I hadn't expected her to be so forward quite so soon.

"Don't worry about it. Forget I asked." The smile slipped from her face and her voice cracked; I had clearly embarrassed her, and as she turned to walk away, I started to feel light-headed.

The anxiety was bubbling up inside me. "Resist, resist," I mumbled to myself. The fingers on my right hand tapped my left arm, getting faster and faster. I tried to take deep breaths, but as I saw Erin outside, through the window, walking with her head down, a voice in my head said: *You've blown your chance. You'll lose her if you don't start this over again.* She might even stop coming to the group—when I hadn't said yes, she'd barely been able to look at me. I sighed as I concentrated on the moment just before Erin asked me out; I couldn't fight it this time.

"Err, well, I wondered…" She was just as nervous the second time, but then of course she would be. As far as she was concerned, this was the first time she was asking me out. "Do you want to go out with me sometime?"

"I'd love to." I answered immediately this time, my eyes focused on her face.

"You would?" Her eyes lit up. She pulled out her phone and handed it to me. "Here, put your number in it, and I'll call you."

That weekend I stood outside the café where we had arranged to meet, my palms sweaty as I scrolled through Twitter to pass the time. This was the first date I had ever been on. Unless you counted the time I went to the cinema with Michael Johnson, but I didn't. I wasn't nervous then—I just wished he wasn't a boy. Erin I actually liked. I didn't want to screw this up. I *couldn't* screw it up. Things had to be perfect.

"Hi, Alex." I jumped as I heard Erin's voice in my ear. I had been so preoccupied with worrying I'd ruin things that I hadn't realised she had arrived. "You look nice."

"Thanks. Want to go inside?"

"Sure." She bit her lip.

I flexed my fingers, trying to banish the nerves.

As I followed her in through the door, I realised I should probably have said something about how *she* looked. She'd obviously made an effort; at the group she dressed casually, but today she was wearing a dress, black with white polka dots, she had make-up on, and her hair had been styled.

I looked so drab next to her in my jeans and top, my mousy-brown hair hanging lankly down as usual. A voice wormed itself into my brain. *You should have said she looks nice. She might think you don't like her. You're messing this date up, stupid!* I tried to fight the anxiety I could feel in my stomach, but I was so afraid of doing this wrong. I shut my eyes tight and focused.

"Hi, Alex."

I gave her the biggest smile I could manage. "Erin, you look beautiful."

Her cheeks flushed. "Thank you. You don't look bad yourself."

I was so glad I had changed my clothes this time around—I was now wearing a skirt, my hair tied up.

Inside, I ordered a bacon butty. I had skipped breakfast due to nerves, and my stomach was starting to rumble. "They smell so good," I commented, catching a waft of crispy bacon as a waitress walked past with one for someone else. "Are you going to have one?"

"Not for me, thanks. I'm a vegetarian."

Shit. She was bound to disapprove of my choice of food and think we had nothing in common. I shut my eyes.

"I'll have the blueberry pancakes please," I told the waiter, the second time around, trying to ignore my mouth watering at the smell of the bacon.

"Ooh, they sound amazing. Same for me, please."

"So," she said, after the waiter had brought me a coffee and her an orange juice, "how are you feeling? I'm intrigued by your OCD. You haven't actually said what your compulsions are."

I took a deep breath, followed by a long sip of coffee. I swiped the foam from my top lip as I debated what to say.

"I'm sorry," she said, reaching across to touch my arm. "You don't have to tell me. I didn't mean to pressure you."

"No, it's cool, honestly. It's just a bit weird, that's all." I thought back to her response when I had first gone to the group.

"Tell me about weird." She rolled her eyes. "I'm sure I can raise you. This one time, I was at the station waiting for a train, and I had to keep going back into the toilets to wash my hands. People were looking at me, they must have thought I had the smallest bladder in the world."

I laughed. "Okay, I'll tell you about mine." I didn't want to start our date off by not being honest. "I'm obsessed with things being perfect. If I feel they're not, I have to time travel back and do things differently."

She narrowed her eyes at me, her hand around her glass of juice. "Are you having a laugh?"

The anxiety was back. *What had I done?* "No, I swear. I'm a time traveller."

"So, wait. Have you travelled back during this date?" She fixed her stare upon me, and I felt myself begin to sweat.

I looked down, unable to meet her eyes. I didn't want to lie to her.

"Wow." She shook her head. "That's really messed up. You're playing with me." There was bitterness in her voice. "This isn't a game, you know. I've only just come to terms with the fact that I'm gay. This is serious to me."

"It's not like that!" I had no idea how to get out of this mess, so I travelled back.

Erin was looking at me expectantly, having just told her anecdote about her OCD.

I laughed, as casually as I could manage. "Okay, you win. I guess mine isn't really that weird. I'm just obsessed with perfection, and after every conversation I have, I go over and over it in my mind thinking about what I should have said and done differently." It wasn't a million miles from the truth, at least. I just left out the bit where I travelled back in time to have the whole conversation over again.

"Hey, that's not weird at all! That sounds like a pretty normal OCD thing to me." She paused, compassion shining in her eyes. "I'm really sorry you have to go through that, though. I know what it's like to not be able to let something go. When I was at my worst, my mum kept telling me I didn't need to wash my hands for as long as I did. But it's that feeling of complete panic, isn't it? Like you *have* to do something, right now, or the feeling is intolerable. You feel like there is no alternative."

I smiled. I liked this conversation much better than the first time around. "It's nice being with someone who gets it."

"I know what you mean." She reached for my hand.

The waiter arrived with our pancakes, and Erin let go of my hand. I picked up my cutlery and tucked in immediately. Erin, however, didn't. She was looking at the plate suspiciously.

"Are you alright?" I asked her, between mouthfuls.

She shrugged. "I'm just being paranoid. I thought the waiter's hands looked a bit dirty. I'm a bit scared to eat the food in case it makes me sick."

I frowned. This was the first time I had experienced Erin's OCD first-hand. In the group, she had said that she was much better. Maybe she was nervous about the date, like I was, and that was affecting her mind. It was certainly causing *my* compulsions to come out.

"Hey, they're good," I said, cutting a piece of a pancake and some blueberries and shoving them into my mouth. Blueberry syrup dribbled down my chin, and I wiped it away with a napkin.

She tried to smile, but I could tell she was preoccupied with what was going on in her head. She cut a tiny piece of pancake and put it in her mouth, then swallowed. "Yeah, it tastes good." She picked up her napkin and wiped her hands carefully. Her eyes were darting all over the place, like she was looking out for germs everywhere.

"Anything I can do to help?"

She shook her head. "Nah, I'm okay. But thank you."

We spent the next few minutes in silence while we ate. When I'd finished, I leaned forward and said: "So, anything you want to know about me?"

"Uh…" She chewed her lip self-consciously. She looked so cute at that moment, I just wanted to lean across and kiss her. "Have you done this a lot?"

"Done what a lot?"

"This. Going on dates."

"Ah. No, actually." I took another sip of coffee and then confided in her: "You're my first girlfriend."

"Woah." She raised her eyebrows and leaned back against the back of her chair. "Steady on, this is only our first date. I don't think I'm quite ready to put labels on it. I haven't even properly come out yet."

I swallowed and shook my head, trying to banish the voice that was whispering to me. *You've really messed up! You should have played it cool.*

"Shut up." The words were out of my mouth before I realised what I was saying. I looked across to Erin, whose eyes had gone wide. "Erin, I wasn't talking to you. I mean… shit." I shut my eyes and travelled back.

"So, have you done this a lot?"

"Going on dates? No, actually. This is my first one. But I'm hoping there might be others." I gave her a sly look.

"Others? With other people?"

I noticed the twinkle in her eyes a bit too late as I jumped back in time again. She had clearly meant it as a joke. I was so jumpy, my nerves on edge. The urge to do the compulsions was stronger than I'd ever felt before. I felt powerless to resist them; I wanted to have the perfect date.

"Going on dates? No, actually. This is my first one. But I'm hoping there might be others. With you, I mean." I took a deep breath and looked across at her. She was smiling again. I relaxed, just a little.

As I walked home from the date, about an hour later

(although it was longer with all the do-overs), I felt exhausted. My legs buckled underneath me, and I had to sit down on a bench and catch my breath. I wiped my nose with my hand as I felt blood trickle down my face.

"Time travel isn't supposed to be like this," my doctor had told me when I had first been to see him about this. "This isn't normal. I think you might have OCD. I'll put you on the waiting list for therapy, but in the meantime, I recommend you attend a support group for teens with OCD. What you're doing is dangerous and could lead to serious problems both for you and other people. And if the time travel guardians catch onto what you're doing, you could be in big trouble."

I sighed and put my head in my hands. I wanted to be over this, but I felt like I wasn't in control of my actions.

Erin wasn't at the group when I arrived the next week, which was unusual—she was usually early. As the rest of us took our seats, she came in the doors. I caught her eye, and we grinned at each other. We'd been texting non-stop since our date, and I had barely stopped thinking about her.

She sat down and crossed her hands in her lap. I couldn't stop myself gasping. They were red and cracked. She saw me looking and quickly dropped them to her sides. I tutted to myself inside my head. I shouldn't have been staring, she was obviously self-conscious. I travelled back as soon as I started to feel anxious, almost without thinking. It had become like an automatic reaction.

This time I was sure not to focus on her hands.

"So," she said, when it was her turn. "It's probably obvious that my OCD has got worse." She shifted in her seat, and her voice was quiet. "I can't stop imagining germs everywhere, and the urge to keep washing my hands is so strong I can't resist it."

"I'm so sorry to hear that, Erin. Has something happened in your life to bring this on?" Jeremy asked. "Stress can often make OCD worse."

She frowned. "I can't think of anything. Things are pretty

115

good in my life right now. Apart from the OCD, of course."

I felt warm inside at the dreamy smile on her face, but a stab of guilt pierced my gut. Maybe this was my fault?

"Well, our thoughts are with you," Jeremy said. "Try and remember what you did before. You'd got so good at resisting the compulsions. Okay, Alex, how are you this week?"

"Things are good with me. My OCD isn't too bad at the moment," I lied. I wanted to support Erin, and what use would I be to her if she thought I was falling apart too?

"I'm sorry your OCD is playing up," I told Erin that weekend as we sat on a bench in the park during our second date. She'd put a plastic bag on the seat before she sat down and pulled a pack of anti-bacterial hand wipes out of her bag.

She shrugged. "It's cool, don't worry. I can get better, I know I can. I was making such great progress. This is just a setback." She sounded determined, and my heart lifted. Maybe things would work out after all.

A lock of her hair blew across her face. I leant closer to her and carefully moved it out of the way with my hand. As she swallowed, her eyes flickered onto my lips. My heart was hammering in my chest as we both leaned forward until our mouths were touching. Slowly, our lips met, and we began to kiss.

It would have been the perfect kiss. Except my head kept telling me I hadn't done it right. I knew that she had kissed a girl before. This was my first kiss, and as we pulled apart, I couldn't stop thinking about what I could have done better. Maybe I should have been more gentle, or perhaps more passionate. Should I have used more or less tongue? The thoughts began to swirl around in my head, and my heart was racing.

"What's the matter?" she asked, the smile on her face being replaced with a frown. *Maybe she thinks you didn't enjoy it,* my head said.

Ugh, this felt all wrong. I concentrated and turned back time to just before the kiss. Then I tried again. And again. And again. Kissing Erin was one of the best moments of my life, but each time we kissed I got more and more preoccupied by the thoughts in my head, and actually enjoyed it less. By the time I forced myself to stop the compulsions, we'd had our first kiss ten times, and none of them had matched up to the very first one.

"Well, that was nice." She gave me a shy look after she'd pulled away.

"Yeah," I said, as another stab of guilt pierced my stomach.

The next time I saw Erin at the park, her OCD had got worse. When I leant in to kiss her, she backed off.

"I'm sorry." There were tears in her eyes, and I could tell that she wasn't herself. "I can't."

I chewed my thumbnail. "Hey, what's wrong? Have I done something to upset you?"

"No!" She sighed. "I really want to kiss you—you have no idea how badly—but I can't. When I look at your lips, I think about all the things you've eaten and drunk, and I picture all these germs crawling across your lips." She shuddered as she spoke.

"What if I wash my face?" I asked. "You can even watch me do it."

She shook her head. "It's not enough." She looked down at her cracked hands. "I understand if you want to break up with me," she mumbled.

"Hey, no! Erin, that's not going to happen. I want to help you through this."

She looked up. "But I'm such a mess. And you're so strong. You seem to have got a handle on your compulsions. I'm just holding you back. I don't want to affect your recovery."

"You may think that, but you're wrong. I'm doing compulsions all the time. You just don't see them." I wanted to be honest with her for a change.

She gave me a puzzled look. "But you said at the group that you were much better." She narrowed her eyebrows. "Are you trying to say you been lying to me?"

Shit. I travelled back immediately.

"But I'm such a mess. And you're so strong. You seem to

117

have got a handle on your compulsions. I'm just holding you back. I don't want to affect your recovery."

"You're not," I said. "I want to help you. Just because things are better with me doesn't mean I don't know what you're going through." I took a deep breath, and said, "I think I'm falling for you." The anxiety rose in my stomach as I poised myself to travel back.

She managed to smile through her tears. "I feel the exact same way about you."

I felt my body relax.

"So how have things been since we last met?" the doctor asked me a few days later. I had decided it was about time I went back to see him.

"Not so great." I told him everything that happened, about Erin and about all the time travelling I had been doing.

His face turned serious. "Oh, Alex." He took his glasses off and put them on the desk in front of him. "I don't think I need to tell you how bad this all is."

"Do you think…." I took a deep breath. "Do you think I could be making Erin's health worse?"

He spoke softly but firmly. "It's a definite possibility. You know that constant time travel can have serious consequences. Time was not made to be messed with like this. Time travellers are supposed to use their gifts for good. To right wrongs. Not to keep reliving moments of their lives until they're perfect. Life isn't like that."

I rubbed my eyes. "So, what do I do?"

He typed on his keyboard as he spoke. "You know, as doctors we have a responsibility to act if we think people are a danger to themselves or to other people. I'm going to have to refer you to the guardians."

"No." I felt a stab of terror run through me. "You can't." The guardians took it very seriously when someone was found to be manipulating the laws.

"You're not going to be punished," he reassured me. "I'll

explain everything in my referral. They'll do a mental health assessment and then most likely refer you to a psychiatrist. This isn't your fault, but you really need to get help sooner rather than later." He paused. "To be honest, you might already be on their radar. They do monitor the time stream, after all. I'm just accelerating the process."

"What about Erin? They might stop me seeing her."

The doctor sighed. "If you really like her, you'll see that this is for the best. It sounds like she's getting really sick."

I squeezed my eyes together. I heard the doctor say "Alex, no!" as I concentrated on the moment before I went into his office.

At the door of the doctors', I turned around and went back home.

I still had time to fix this. I just needed to try harder to resist my compulsions. I could get better, and I could help Erin get better too.

"You seem preoccupied," she told me, the next time I saw her, just before the group started.

"Look, I need to tell you something," I began.

"Evening everyone!" I cursed to myself as Jeremy entered the room, prompt as always. I had got here early, hoping to be able to talk to Erin first, but she had only just arrived. I had been on the verge of texting her so many times, but I kept chickening out.

Erin gave me a quizzical look.

I shrugged. She'd find out soon enough, anyway.

"I'm really struggling right now," I admitted, when it got to my turn. "And I've been trying to hide it. I'm trying to be the strong one. But I got myself into a mess, and the only way out of it is by resisting compulsions. But that is so hard. I feel constantly anxious, and I want to give in. I know how to make myself feel better, but I know I need to stop the compulsions. Because it's starting to affect other people too." I felt a tear run down my cheek, and I sniffed and wiped it away.

Jeremy gave me a sympathetic smile. "Thanks for being so honest, Alex."

I looked over to Erin, but her face was steely.

I cornered her as she was about to leave. "Erin." I reached towards her, only remembering at the last minute how anxious that would make her feel, with her OCD worsening. Instead, I let my arm drop uselessly to my side.

She turned. "You've been lying to me."

"I'm sorry. I wanted to be strong to support you. I didn't want you to have to deal with my problems as well as your own."

She shook her head. "I don't need protecting. How are we supposed to be in a relationship if we can't be honest with each other?"

"I'll be honest from now on, I promise."

She raised her eyebrows. "Okay. Let's start by you telling me what exactly your compulsions are. You've always been vague before. If we're going to help each other, we know what to look out for."

My heart starting racing. I knew that if I told her the truth, we'd get into an argument. It had happened before, after all. But she'd be angry with me if I didn't tell her. The anxiety was building up inside me. I balled my hands into fists as I struggled to resist the urge to time travel.

"I told you," I said, sounding much calmer than I felt. "It's all about perfection. I have to keep redoing things."

"How, exactly?"

"I…" I scratched my neck. "Uh…"

"Forget it." She turned to leave. "You clearly don't trust me."

"Erin, don't go. I love you." I was pleading like a little kid who wanted attention.

She looked back, and I felt hope rise inside me. But then she shook her head. "I'm sorry, but I can't do this. I'm not well enough to deal with relationship drama as well as the OCD. We're over."

"No." A strangled cry escaped my mouth. But she was gone.

I sat down on the floor, shaking, my head in my hands. The inevitability of the compulsion I was about to perform hit me. There was no way I couldn't do it. Despite my best intentions, I couldn't resist this time. I didn't want to lose Erin, and this was the only way.

I shut my eyes and focused on starting the session over. I had thought that being honest was what I needed to do, but I couldn't do it at the expense of my relationship.

I opened my eyes, gasping with exhaustion, and wiped my bloody nose on a tissue. I looked across to Erin's seat, but it was empty.

Dread built up in my stomach. "Where's Erin?"

Jeremy pushed his glasses further up onto his nose. "Erin's mum called in a few minutes ago. Unfortunately, Erin has taken a turn for the worse. I'm afraid her OCD has got so bad that she's now unable to leave the house."

There were gasps. I felt numb as he continued. "I know that many of you were close to her and will want to wish her well. I'll be buying a card for you all to sign and bringing it along to next week's group, so she knows that we're all thinking of her."

When it got to my turn, I passed. There didn't seem much point saying anything now. What was happening to Erin was all my fault, and I wasn't sure how to make it right.

"Hello?" A tall woman with blonde hair opened the door. The resemblance to Erin clearly identified her as her mum. I'd tried ringing Erin after the group, but she didn't answer, so I had immediately gone round to her house.

"Is Erin up to visitors?" I asked, really hoping that she'd see me. "My name is Alex." I knew she wouldn't have mentioned me as a girlfriend; she hadn't yet come out to her family. "I'm a friend. From the support group."

Her mum shook her head. "I'm sorry, she's really not well. But I'll be sure to let her know that you popped around. Alex, was it?"

"Yes." I felt tears drop down my face. "Please tell her I'm

sorry." I turned around and walked away quickly.

When I got around the corner I sank to my knees and cried like I'd never cried before. Loud sobs wracked my body. A man looked across at me, obviously wondering if he should come and help me. I shut my eyes and prepared to travel back for the last time. There was no anxiety this time. I was doing what had to be done. I just hoped that this would fix things for good and not make them even worse.

"Are you okay?"

I'd never travelled back so far before, and it had left me doubled over in pain.

I pulled myself up, forcing myself to smile. "I'm good, thanks."

"You must be new. Are you coming in?"

I turned and looked into Erin's eyes. I couldn't remember the last time I had seen her smile like that. She looked happy and healthy, her hands soft and the light back in her eyes.

I felt a twinge in my heart as the pain hit me. "No, I'm just passing by."

"Okay, no problem." As she opened the door and walked into the group, I turned away and headed for the doctor's surgery.

"Back again so soon?" the doctor asked as I sat down in his office.

"Actually, it's been longer than you think." I chewed my thumbnail. "I've really messed up, and I need help. Please refer me to the time travel guardians."

From the Author

"Back in Time" combines two of my writing interests—time travel and mental illness. The story came to me one day whilst on a YA Writing evening class. Being an OCD sufferer myself, I know how difficult the disorder makes everyday life, but the beauty of writing fiction about it is that the sufferer can become obsessed with literally anything, which makes for great stories. I thought, why would a time traveller not become obsessed with their ability? I knew that I wanted the story to feature a romance, and that it would ultimately end sadly.

I originally saw it as a novel, but soon realised that sustaining the story for a whole book would probably be a bit much. I started the story and then, like many others, it sat part-finished on my laptop until I saw a call for a time travel anthology, which spurred me on to finish the story. The anthology didn't take the story (it did take another one of mine, though), but I sent it to the quarterly Writers of the Future competition, where it was awarded an Honorable Mention. I'm very pleased that it has now found a home.

About the Author

Katie Kent wanted to be a writer from an early age. Life and mental illness got in the way but starting a career in Publishing was a way for her to rediscover her love of books, even though she ultimately ended up in journals publishing.

When a colleague started a writing group at her workplace, Katie remembered the joy of writing and hasn't looked back since, even though a year of rejections ate away at her self-esteem. She almost cried when she got her first acceptance from *Youth Imagination*, and here she is now with about 20 published short stories to her name. Her stories are mostly for a YA audience and are particularly about LGTBQ characters, mental illness, time travel and the future—sometimes all in the same story! She's proud to have featured in a number of anthologies including *The Trouble with Time Travel*, *Summer of Speculation: Catastrophe*, *Growth* and *My Heart to Yours*. Her non-fiction, mostly mental health-related, has been published in *The Mighty*, *You & Me Magazine*, *Ailment*, *OC87 Recovery Diaries* and *Feels Zine*.

Now working part time, Katie spends her Tuesdays writing on her laptop in bed with her cat, Haribo, curled up next to her. As well as short stories, she's also working on a few novels. She also lives with her wife, Sam, and long-haired sausage dog, Maverick, who is as naughty as he is cute.

You can visit her website at:
https://www.katiekentwriter.com/
and follow her on Twitter @uniKH80

Children of Things

by
CJ Erick

Children of Things

*D*ane found her in their small washroom, in front of the vintage one-sink vanity. She was staring at something in her fingers, her brown hair hiding most of her frown. Her voice was the whisper of a dying smoker. "There must be something wrong with me."

She thrust the object at him like a shiv. He could just make out the negative sign in the pregnancy test's window.

Her normally bright eyes were hollow and dark, with a desperate look that frightened him.

"The doctor said you're fine. It must be me." He felt like he'd punched himself in the gut.

"But he said you're fine, too. So, there's something wrong with *us*." She exhaled the last word and tossed the sensor into the wastebasket, where it clattered like a spray of gunshots.

"You're right. We're fine. The doctor tested both of us."

"Then what, Dane? We've been trying for three years. All the timing and the pills. Waiting between . . . you know."

He knew.

She said, "I think we need to go back to the clinic."

He felt his jaw tighten, but he tried to smile and nodded. "OK, set up an appointment."

"I already did. This afternoon at five."

He sighed, nodded. Another golf night bit the dust. But she hadn't given up, even if the haunted look in her eyes scared him.

On the way out of the building, Dane stopped at their landlady's apartment to drop off their rent check.

He knocked, and then listened for the dependable sound of her slow steps over the creaking floor before she pulled the door inward.

"Hello, Mrs. B. Another month gone already."

She chuckled. "Any news on the baby front?"

He shook his head. "No. Robin's been patient, but it's getting to her."

Mrs. B clucked her tongue and eyed him long enough to make him uncomfortable. "And what about you? How are you feeling about it? You came from the same background, foster care, right?"

"I'm just fine."

He'd thought he was fine, but his words sounded hollow.

"Chin up, Dane. I trust things will start happening for you two *very* soon." Her smile was small but seemed to come from a place deep inside. "I think of Robin as a daughter, the one I never had. And that would make you almost my son-in-law."

Her eyes sparked with intrigue, as if she'd just told him a joke with a punch line that meant more than it seemed.

He said at last, "Thanks for your support, Mrs. B. I'd better get moving."

"Yes. By the way, you may be getting a new neighbor soon. A very nice woman may rent one of the vacant apartments upstairs. Meanwhile, tell Robin to keep her head and spirits high. The Lord works on his own timetable, and always with good reason."

Dane worked late and drove home in the dark on quiet roads. As he mounted the narrow stairs to the second floor, he heard dull banging above, like someone working on the roof. He paused to listen for a minute before entering the apartment.

Robin stood in front of the stove, the fragrant smell filling the kitchen. Dane encircled her waist with his arms. She hummed and melted into him, and he savored her warmth. She seemed better, humming a little.

He took the plate she handed him and sat at their small table.

He said, "What's all the noise upstairs?"

"Our new neighbor. Mrs. B said there would be a new tenant renting 333."

"Yeah, Mrs. B told me. What's she doing? Expanding the kitchen?"

Robin shrugged. "Probably hanging pictures. Women don't feel like they're moved in until they have the towels put away and the curtains hung. Men can throw a six-pack in the refrigerator and a sleeping bag on the floor and call it home."

"Right on, woman. You meet her?"

"In passing, on the stairs. Didn't say much, but she seemed nice. Her name's Tina. Pleasant face. I offered for you to help her carry things up."

"How old is she? Living on her own?"

"Mid-thirties? By herself, as far as I know."

"Well, I hope she's not going to be banging around up there for long. I've got to go in early tomorrow."

Quiet hours for the building began at 10 p.m., and the dull banging and scraping ceased exactly on time, just as Dane's head hit the pillow. He barely remembered another early rise and the bleary day, but when he returned that evening, the racket was there again, just enough to annoy. It ended at precisely 10 p.m.

The next day, and the next, the noise continued, but two days later, when Dane came home, Robin grabbed him immediately.

"I'm worried about our neighbor. I haven't seen her for two days, and her car is still parked out front. I tapped on the door, but no one answered."

"Maybe she walked to the bus station?"

"I would have heard her leave. Should we call the police?"

"Maybe, did you ask Mrs. B about it?"

"She hasn't been home all day."

"I guess we should check if she's fallen or something...let's take a quick look."

"You mean break in?"

"We'll knock, but if she doesn't answer, I can pop the lock in three seconds."

"You've wanted to sneak a look in there."

"Yep. And now I have an excuse." He scrabbled in the kitchen's utility drawer for his locksmith's set.

"What if she comes home while we're in there?"

"The truth. We were worried about her and checked her apartment. No crime in that."

"I'll come with you." He started to protest, but she looked terrified.

The stairs creaked with each step. Dane ignored the noise, but at the upstairs door, he hesitated. He'd opened several apartments in the building, when residents had forgotten keys, but something held him back at Apartment 333.

He rapped the door loudly, waited. No response. No sound of movement, footsteps, or even a weak call from the other side of the door. He knocked again, then pressed his ear against the door. Nothing.

He glanced at Robin. She still looked frightened but made no effort to stop him. He opened his toolset and slid out the flat hook-shaped metal strap that had worked so effectively on the neighbors' doors. Before sliding the metal between the edge of the door and the doorjamb, he gripped the doorknob. It turned with a click and the door pressed inward. Unlocked.

With one last look at Robin, he eased the door open. It swung with a grating, creaking in the dead silence of the apartment. From inside, there was only quiet.

Dane squeezed through, and Robin followed on his heels. The apartment was as he remembered it from dinners with the Randolphs, who'd moved to Minnesota months earlier. A short entryway led into several larger rooms. Light filtered in from the living area, just enough to see.

In the entry, two pictures had been hung, accounting for some of the pounding. The apartment's stillness pressed upon Dane, and Robin's cold hands gripped his arm. The air smelled faintly of dust and freshly cut wood.

"Anyone home?"

No response.

For no reason, they stepped lightly, mindful of the creaking boards in the old wooden floor. In the room's library quiet, his heartbeat pounded in his ears.

Robin whispered, "I don't remember that door."

She pointed towards two doors, set in the long wall to their right. They looked identical, covered in aged brown stain, darkened to cola color, the doorknobs and hinges fashioned from the same tarnished brass.

"Are you sure?"

She nodded. "There was only one closet door here before. The one on the left is new."

Dane eased over and opened the right-hand door. Behind it was what he expected: a shallow coat closet. Inside hung a brown wool sweater and a mid-length coat; the 1950's uniforms of a middle-aged spinster.

Robin, on tiptoe, looked over his shoulder and met his eyes. He shrugged, stepped back, and pushed the door closed, then opened the other one. Beyond, rather than another closet, was a narrow corridor leading away into darkness.

"What the hell?"

Robin met his eyes. She shook her head in wonderment.

The passageway's walls were painted dull gray or beige, and it looked old, as if the color had once been brighter and happier. Dane could see no turns or doors, and the only light was from the open door. Warm air flowed outward past his face, then reversed and flowed back in.

He asked, "Should I try it?"

Robin shook her head.

Something compelled him to ignore her, but before he could, she gripped his arm and tugged him back. The draft washed outward again, dry and tepid.

He pushed the door shut and ventured further into the apartment. Robin tapped his shoulder and pointed at a door set in the wall to their left. She shook her head.

The door was the same as the others, old in appearance, but apparently new in existence. Dane opened it and revealed the same crazy thing: a straight corridor of pale walls, disappearing into darkness. Like the other doorway, a warm congestive draft moved in and out, carrying the smells of wood, plaster, and an odor he still couldn't identify.

Robin stood nearly on his heels, fingers touching him lightly on the back. She whispered, "This is creepy. Let's go."

He pushed the door closed. "Anyone home?" he yelled, again to no response. "We have to check the other rooms. Make sure she's not unconscious."

They went to the kitchen, where two identical doors were set side by side, each with ivory paint, now yellowed, their knobs and hinges the same tarnished brass, with blue-green rust on the edges. One opened on the pantry. The other revealed another corridor into darkness, with the same fetid draft.

Dane whispered, "That's impossible."

"Why?" Her hand, on his arm, trembled.

"Behind that pantry is the wall of the outer hallway to Apartment 305. This passageway would cut right through the other hallway."

Robin frowned. "Maybe it's an illusion."

"No. I can visualize the layout. This hallway can't be here."

"I think we should go."

"Not until I understand what's going on."

"Please, let's just check the bedroom and get out of here. This is scaring me."

In the bedroom, one identical to theirs, they found another door where one wasn't before. The passageway it opened upon was no longer a surprise.

He said, "We have to find out where these go."

"I'm freaked. We need to get out."

Robin's eyes held a desperation he'd never seen. Truthfully, he was freaked-out as well. He pushed the door closed with a click, sealing in the eerie draft.

When Dane returned from work the next day, Robin told him Tina had greeted her on the stairs, as if her absence wasn't unusual. But there was still no sign of Mrs. B and no word of where she could be reached.

"And I've got to show you something," Robin said.

She led him down the stairs and out into a small children's play area he'd forgotten was even there. It had stood unused for the four years they'd lived here. In the autumn breeze, dull metal swings swayed uneasily on rusty chains, and paint peeled off the slide and teeter-totter.

It reminded Dane of the last scene from the film *On the Beach*; a playground abandoned in the deadly fallout from a nuclear war.

"They're over here."

Dane followed Robin to a child-sized wooden picnic table near the swings. The red and yellow paint had long since blistered and faded.

"What do you think about them?"

She pointed to an object on the old table—a tiny picnic table, a model of the larger one. It looked to be built of folded paper or cardboard, weighted at the edges with paper clips. Four figurines of children sat at the table, two on each side. They appeared to be made of loose cloth and string, with vague facial features, small bumps for ears, colored beads of powder blue and pink for eyes, and hair formed from felt, or tinted modeling clay, in orange and guacamole green. The tiny figures were unlike anything he'd ever seen. Dour, surreal, unsettling.

Dane shrugged. "They seem harmless. Creepy-looking, though. You think *she* made them?"

"I don't know. They're just bizarre."

"When did you last see *her*?"

"On the stairs, at three, coming in with two giant paper bags, just like usual. If she's suspicious of me meeting her there every day, she doesn't show it. She just smiled like we have some bond or secret in common, said 'hello,' and went up the stairs."

Dane thought a moment. "Tomorrow's Sunday, so she may not leave. But watch her on Monday and see if her schedule's the same. If so, I'm going back up on Tuesday and following one of the hallways she built."

"I'm afraid."

"She doesn't seem dangerous, but I think we have to find out what she's doing. It looks like we're the only ones to do it. Mrs. B hasn't come back, and," Dane lowered his voice, "have you seen any of the other residents recently?"

Robin frowned. "No. The Fishers were going to Orlando, and Tamara and Charles disappear for days at a time... but I haven't seen *anyone*."

"Hmm."

Dane picked up one of the figurines. The design was rough, but the piece was solid, a tight bundle of fibers, knotted and bound by thin silver threads, clearly a young girl with long blue hair and a white skirt. He raised one of its arms in a wave and then placed it back into its seat at the table.

The arms and legs apparently held wire bones since they held their position when moved. But in a trick of the failing light, the figurine seemed to settle back into its original pose.

Puzzled, Dane lifted it from its seat again and examined it more closely. He felt it move and nearly dropped it.

As he watched, the crude figurine changed from a tiny caricature of a child into something impossibly alive. The tiny mouth opened and stretched grotesquely, a gap with no lips or teeth, like a sock puppet. No sound came out. The tiny pink beaded eyes blinked twice, opened with focus and awareness, and looked about. The limbs moved in Dane's grasp, flexing and stretching but making no effort to escape.

Its eyes fell on the tiny tea set on the table, and its hands reached out toward it. Dane set the tiny child in its seat. As he watched, Robin gripping his arm and staring in horror, his hand, seemingly moving of its own accord, lifted another of the dolls.

This one, a boy with short olive black hair, also stirred and flexed its limbs. It stretched, yawned, and examined the surroundings. It pointed at the tea set and the first doll, which was pouring invisible tea into the four tiny cups. Dane set the second doll back in its place.

The sensible part of his mind urged him to grab Robin by the arm and pull her away, but some deeper part, controlling his body, guided his hand to the third doll, another boy, judging from its short green hair. He lifted it with two fingers and watched, stunned, as it came alive, yawning, stretching, reaching for the small table.

He set it back and lifted the last of them, a small girl doll with orange hair and a tan frock, held it gingerly until it breathed with life, and then set it with the others.

Now all four dolls sat sipping imaginary tea at the table, moving their arms and hands and mouths in a Lilliputian tea party.

Robin and Dane stared, mesmerized. The dolls soon spoke in titters and chirps, oblivious to the two giants staring open-mouthed at them. Dane realized he'd stopped breathing and gasped, then gripped Robin's arm and dragged her away to the safety of the lighted apartment building.

He didn't remember climbing the stairs or pulling the bourbon from the liquor cabinet, but he came to his senses sitting at the kitchen table with a nearly empty tumbler in front of him. Robin sat with her own glass and stared into space.

Robin finally broke the silence. "My god, Dane, what's going on? What did we just do?"

He shook his head. "I don't know." He caught himself staring at his own hands. They seemed foreign to him.

Work was a blur. At the end of the day Dane found Robin sitting at their small table, focused on her electronic tablet. She smiled when he came in, much of the anxiety gone from her face.

"Your dinner's in the oven. It should be hot."

"Did she go out today?"

Robin replied without looking up. "Yes. But I don't think you should go up there."

"Why not?"

"Something funny happened today. I went to the picnic table. I had to check on those children. They're different now, Dane. They aren't freakish dolls anymore."

He stopped picking at dinner and studied the back of her head. "Are they still there? Doing tea?"

"Yes. But they're different. Larger now, like they're growing. And they don't look like dolls. They look like children. They still have funny-colored skin and hair, but now they have real ears and lips, and even fingers. And something else happened."

She spoke matter-of-factly, unaffected by the enormity of what she believed she'd observed. Sudden anxiety gnawed at the edges of Dane's mind.

"One of them waved at me. And then they all turned and waved."

"What did you do?"

"Well, I was stunned at first. But I waved back. And then they just went back to their party. It was unbelievable."

When Robin turned around to explore his reaction, there was a glow about her face he hadn't seen in months. It was the look she'd had when she'd held their friends' one-week-old baby girl.

They'd always agreed they'd have children, but until the moment she held that baby, he never really appreciated the depth of her need, perhaps a product of growing up in a group home. Early in their dating days, when he'd asked about her parents, she'd evaded the inquiries, saying only she was told she was abandoned.

He'd never known his own parents either. Was their history, and the stress of their failure to conceive getting to both of them?

But he'd seen the dolls come alive, move, play.

"I have to find out where the hallways go, Robin. We have to understand what we're dealing with here."

"Okay."

He could tell her mind was out at the picnic table, having tea with animated dolls that acted like children.

Early next morning, Dane left as usual, but didn't go to work. Instead, he parked three blocks away, and camped out at a nearby coffee shop.

A few minutes after 1 p.m., their neighbor's tan sedan drove by. As the car passed, the driver looked directly at Dane as he peaked around a newspaper. Then she continued up the street.

Dane paid his bill, stole out of the diner, and crossed the four-lane boulevard on foot, fighting the urge to run to the apartment house. When he got there, Robin was waiting.

"I've got to show you something."

"No time."

"They're different, Dane. They talk to me now."

The look in her eyes wasn't terror. It was the sparkle of wonder. Dane shuddered. "Watch the stairs and text me if she comes in."

He grabbed his tools and headed for 333, taking the stairs two at a time. He paused at the door to allow his pulse to slow. As before, the door wasn't locked.

In the entry, he had to decide which of the new doors to try. The one in the pantry, the door with the hallway that cut impossibly through the center of the building, drew him.

He went to it, took a deep breath, and gripped the handle. It turned with a noticeable catch in the mechanism, like it hadn't been operated in months, even though he'd opened it himself days earlier. Beyond was what he expected but couldn't comprehend—the corridor leading straight into darkness.

Air flowed past him. The wood smell was weak, but the other odor jarred him. It wasn't a plant smell, or paint or varnish, or any chemical he recognized. He shook his head to clear it.

He pulled a large metal flashlight from his belt and pointed the beam down the corridor. It illuminated only several feet ahead. Beyond, the darkness remained.

Dane stepped forward fully into the passage, sweeping the light from side to side and up and down. It revealed only more of the same; dim painted walls and a dull wooden floor, both faded and worn, as if the tunnel had been there for ages.

He eased forward at first, striding faster when no openings or doors appeared on either side, and nothing jumped out at him. The light of the doorway fell away behind.

The passageway couldn't exist. It defied logic. But, in the flashlight beam, it continued straight onward, into the space that should have been the hallway to Apartment 305.

Minutes later, he felt the way turning downward and to the right. He paused to look back. The open doorway into the apartment was no longer visible.

For a moment, he felt the walls closing in on him, and his chest tightened. He fought the sensation and carried on, telling himself that the tunnel must lead to something.

He went on for five minutes more, then ten, then what seemed an hour. The flashlight beam dimmed, and he regretted not bringing extra batteries. Another panic attack lurked in the shadows.

Something more than gravity drew him on, like a magnetic current compelling him forward. There was no going back without finding what lay at the end of the tunnel. The answers to all the strangeness would be there.

The tunnel coiled downward, and he began to question his earlier confidence. The urge to keep going clashed with the logical side of his brain telling him to turn back and run. Inertia won the battle and propelled his feet forward.

Eventually the corridor began to rise again, and with it his spirits. It had to be leading somewhere, or why would the strange resident of Apartment 333 have built it?

What it came to was a closed door, abruptly, so that he squeaked and nearly ran into it.

The flashlight revealed seasoned, painted wood, with rectangular panels. The knob wasn't just tarnished, but old; old in design and style, shiny with the wear of many hands, with the last residue of black paint visible only in its seams.

Just as when he'd grasped the child-dolls, his body took over where his mind refused to move. His hand reached into the flashlight beam, took the knob, and turned it. Metal ground metal in a creaking slippage like ancient fault lines, and the door pressed inward, opening yellow cracks of light around the edges, just bright enough to cast the corridor in a wan translucence.

He pushed it open and stepped through.

It was another dining room.

He paused just inside the door, listening for movement, hearing nothing.

The room was very different from the one he'd just left; this was a place filled with antiques and heirlooms. Furniture was placed in almost exactly the same locations, but it was different; older style, but not old.

The air smelled strongly of the unknown scent, mixed with burnt soot, coal, or heating oil, and it made him a little sick and a little lightheaded.

He tiptoed through the dwelling; a small apartment in what appeared to be a boarding house. In each room there were two doors, each the same aged design. In the kitchen, one door revealed a pantry, stocked with boxes of food, sacks of flour and sugar, and metal containers, all old, but not, like vintage props.

The second door revealed another featureless corridor, and the urge to follow this one surprised him and sent a chill up his back. He closed it quickly.

His sense of time passing, and danger, grew, and he knew he must find something, anything to explain what was happening. He'd about given up when he spotted something that stood out. In the kitchen, in front of the fireplace, a large stoneware pot, sitting on a metal stand, drew him.

In it were pieces of fibers, cloth, yarn, beads, colored clay, and odd things. And then there were things he recognized. A patch of cloth that matched a blue and gray flannel shirt he'd discarded months earlier. An old hairbrush, like one Robin had trashed at about the same time.

He felt an electric shock, and remnants of his rational mind screamed that he didn't belong, and must run for his doorway, return to his world.

He became aware of a hum, a vibration coming up from the floor, through the bottoms of his feet, through his skin from the air all around him. He'd felt it before, through his fingers as he held the dolls' flesh.

The hum calmed him, and that should have terrified him. He let himself feel it and breathe the dry, cracked breath of the place, but was soon struck by an impulse to choose another random doorway and follow it, follow any of them, follow them all.

Before he could act on that impulse, his hand reached out and settled among the tokens, his fingers stirring them, feeling the textures, the softness of the cloth. He lingered over the rasp of fibers on his fingertips. The fragrance filled his head; he felt a touch of dizziness.

He felt himself drifting loose from his body, his senses, his place. He should have felt terror, but he wanted to laugh, to dance.

When he returned to his own head, he was walking down a passageway. Time had passed. He couldn't remember entering a passageway, or which one he had taken. He'd been gone for hours. Robin would be petrified.

His feet moved, one in front of the other, on the wooden floor of the passageway.

He could only hope he'd taken his own passage. If so, the neighbor would be waiting for him. He would tell her the truth. He suspected her of something bizarre and evil. He found her tunnels and the other house. He found the fetishes, the dry cauldron full of...things.

Fair to say, she would have ways of dealing with him, but he was surprised that fear didn't grip him. At least he might get answers.

The tunnel coiled upward, out of the depths. After what seemed like days and hundreds of miles, the way became level and straight, and the rectangular light of an open doorway appeared.

He expected a silhouette to fill the doorframe at any time, but no one blocked his way, and he stepped into the empty kitchen of Apartment 333.

Robin was sitting at the living room window, with its clear view of the play area. She turned a surprised frown on Dane.

"Did you change your mind?"

Dane paused, his mouth suddenly dry, and his voice frozen, his mind a jumble of images. He pushed himself toward the kitchen, and she rose and followed. He returned the flashlight to the utility drawer. At the sink, he splashed water on his face, and drank enough to ease his clamped throat. "What do you mean?"

"You're back so soon."

"How long was I gone?"

"Less than ten minutes."

"It seemed like hours."

He told her about the second house with its own bizarre passageways. He described the crucible, his trance, finding his way back.

She nodded as if it made perfect sense.

His mind felt numb, the hum of the old house still vibrating through his head. "This is something beyond weird. I don't know what we do next."

Robin seemed not to have heard. She sat down at the kitchen table and began working on some craft project—a cardboard box with holes cut along the bottom and plastic garbage bags taped over the surface.

"This is for the children. It's supposed to be raining and windy tonight, and I want them to have some shelter."

She flashed him a small smile that chilled him more than anything he'd experienced over the last few days.

She asked, "Will you help me take it down there?"

Dane carried the box and followed Robin down the steps. He would have to take her out of this place, leave town like the others. If she resisted, he would insist. She needed help. He'd call Alex and

Anna, set up house in South Plains temporarily, and ask them to recommend a therapist.

"See?" Robin pointed.

A new miniature picnic table lay where they'd found the paper one. This one was larger and made of wood, built of toy logs. The dolls sitting at the table were different as well, larger and more refined, like miniature people. Their hair and skin were still bright colors, but their eyes were no longer plastic beads. They were mirrors of Robin's and his own.

The dolls sat at the table and poured tea. They spoke in words now, possibly English, but the speech was too high-pitched and fast for Dane to understand. They saw Robin and waved, and she waved back. When they paused and waved cautiously at Dane, his hand lifted and mimicked them.

Robin broke his paralysis. "Set the box on the table, Dane."

Robin adjusted the box and smiled with satisfaction, before leading him back to the apartment.

On the way, his sense of time and space fractured.

Dane remembered sleeping a lot, and Robin prodding him to eat. He woke once to hear her talking on the phone, telling someone he wasn't well and would not be in to work.

Days later, he revived enough to return to work. Robin was like a different person. She rose early, and the sounds and smells of cooking came to him as he showered. In the kitchen, she handed him an insulated coffee mug and a lunch sack heavy with food.

"Have a wonderful day!"

She gripped his shoulder and leaned in to kiss him on the cheek. On the counter behind her, next to the cutting board and knife rack, was a small china plate. On it were thin wafers of meat and bread cut into one-inch squares. Sandwiches.

Dane avoided the picnic table on his way out and drove to work in a fog. His head cleared sometime in the afternoon.

If his trip to work had been in a fog, his return was in crystal-fine resolution. He saw buildings, signs, and trees in intense detail, as if driving the streets for the first time. As he walked up the sidewalk to the main door to their building, the chilly air was eerily quiet. He could see the silhouettes of the playground toys and table, and he thought of tiny dolls tucked inside a cardboard box.

The house creaked and whispered around him as he moved through it. The handrails and wooden steps showed their age, worn and faded by many hands and feet sliding over them. He would ask Mrs. B for an allowance on the rent to buy stain and urethane finish to repair the woodwork. It would take him several weekends, but she wouldn't push him. The front door and walls in the entry needed paint, but that could wait until spring. The women could negotiate over the colors.

And then his mind halted. Robin and he weren't going to be there in the spring. They were leaving, and not soon enough.

In front of the apartment door, he found a wicker basket, its white paint worn from handling. A bright red kerchief lay over the top. It was lighter than he expected, as if filled with packing paper. He fitted the key in the lock and pushed the door open with his hip, and carried the basket in.

Robin worked at the table, her small sewing kit laid open next to her. He'd forgotten she owned one. He dropped into the chair opposite her, suddenly exhausted, and set the basket on the table.

She smiled and nodded at the basket. "What's that?"

"Dunno. It was in front of the door. I think Mrs. B, or someone, left us a care package."

Robin frowned, but her eyes and hands stayed focused on her work, hand-stitching scraps of cloth together. "I haven't seen anyone. And her car is still gone."

"What are you making?"

"Blankets. The children have outgrown their beds already. It's amazing how fast they're growing."

"They're not children, Robin."

She stopped then and laid the stitchwork down. She folded her hands together on the table. When her sky-blue eyes met his, their directness confronted him, another new thing for her. "Then what are they, Dane?"

"I don't know."

He remembered the disturbing sensations as he'd held the figurines. Their limbs had moved, their sock mouths had opened and gasped, and ice had slid down his spine.

She said, "Well, I do. They're children. I don't know how or why, but that's what they are. They play and they talk to each other, and they grow every day."

Dane shook his head. "You're crazy. We're both crazy."

The tunnels and the other house, what were they about? What was their significance? He had seen them, touched the walls of the corridor, smelled the cut wood. The crucible of tokens. Hallucinations? Robin said he'd been gone only a few minutes. Perhaps he'd been drugged?

"They're dolls, Robin. Just dolls. We've both been caught up in trying to have children. We've lost it."

"They told me their names today." She laid her head on her hand, her elbow on the table propping her up. Her serene smile made his heart suddenly pound again, like it had when he'd returned to Apartment 333. "The tall girl with blue hair is Marta. The shorter one with the black hair and green eyes is Tanya. The two boys are Christian and Stephan. I helped them build some stairs out of blocks so they can climb up and down from the table on their own."

"Crazy."

She pushed herself back from the table and stood, gently pushing the chair back into place before grabbing her jacket. "Come on. I want to check on them before bedtime."

He fought away the fog that threatened to take him again, put on his own jacket, and followed her. He carried the "blankets," and they followed the flashlight beam across the wet grass to the picnic table. The cardboard box was there, but now a stack of wooden blocks and a toy metal ladder led from the ground to the bench seat, and from there to the tabletop.

"Hey, kids! We brought blankets!"

Robin rapped the flashlight on the table, and then traded Dane the flashlight for the cloths and laid them on the table next to the box.

A tiny flap on the side of the box swung aside, and a sharp metal spike came out the opening, point first, followed by the thing holding it—a girl-child, about eight inches tall. Except for the odd colors of her hair and eyes, and the unnaturally warm color of her skin, this doll bore no resemblance to the one he'd held, the finger-long larva that had twisted in his hand, opening its featureless mouth in a silent scream of birth.

The girl-child twittered and waved the spiked weapon.

Robin nodded. "I'll take care of it if it comes back." She turned to Dane and gestured toward the doll-child's weapon. "We had a cat scare this afternoon, so I gave them the olive picks in case it came back. I'm getting a trap tomorrow morning."

Another figure joined the girl, a boy, not as tall, with hair the color of motor oil and eyes a devilish red. He pointed at Dane and spoke in a higher pitch than the girl, the voice of a finch.

Robin laid her hand upon Dane's shoulder. "This is my husband, who I told you about. His name is Dane. He woke you up."

The two child-things tilted their heads at an identical angle, eyeing him. The boy gestured in Dane's direction and twittered rapidly.

Robin answered, "Yes, he's very strong and fast, and he doesn't like cats either. Here are the extra blankets, kids. You'll need them tonight. It's going to freeze. Keep the door shut, and pad around the bottom to keep the draft out. I'll check on you in the morning. Good night!"

The tiny, odd-colored children chirped, gathered the stitched cloths in their arms, and went back into the box. Robin took the flashlight and led the way back into the house.

Inside the entryway, as they were taking off their jackets, Dane heard himself speak. "Shouldn't we bring them inside where it's warm?"

"No. I asked. They like it where they are. But I'd like to give them your Taser in case that damn cat comes back."

Later, they sat again at their small table, Robin humming and working with glue and paper and tongue depressors. A table and chairs were taking shape in her hands, larger than the ones the child-beings were using.

Dane became fascinated, watching the skill in her handiwork, something he'd never seen before. How could he have known her for so long, nearly six years, and still not know she could do things like this?

There were always secrets, like an old house with corridors hidden in the walls.

What else didn't he know about her? She'd grown up in a group home, she'd told him, and had never known her parents. She assumed she was abandoned, and the pain of that was a strong incentive now, an incentive to raise children in a real home, as she called it.

He searched his own memories. His childhood in foster homes held no images of his parents either.

Without looking up, she nodded toward the wicker basket. "May I see what's in there?"

With effort, he pulled his eyes from her work. The old basket challenged him, like a sinister piñata. He knew it wasn't a care package. It would be something inexplicable and frightening, like everything that had happened since the woman upstairs arrived.

"We should burn this," he said.

"Nonsense. Push it to me, please."

From beneath the cloth she removed odd things, or perhaps not nearly as odd as they once would have seemed. She laid them in piles near the basket. Small stacks of heavy threads, like carpet fibers. A spool of string, random scraps of felt. Tiny stick pins with heads painted in rainbow colors. A child's watercolor paint set.

Dane shook his head.

Gray fibers, like soft fiberglass filter material, clung together in loose mats. Robin pulled them apart into lengths about four inches long. They looked strangely familiar to Dane.

She took one wad and flattened it, then split it apart at one end. On the opposite end, her fingers pulled strands out to the sides at right angles. She turned the bundle upside down, bunched the end opposite into a round knob, and pinched the fiber at the base of the knob together into a constrained spot—a neck.

It was then Dane realized what she was doing.

"Stop, Robin. Don't."

"It's okay, Dane. Really it is."

Her fingers continued to work.

He watched, fascinated by her craft, terrified of it, like a recurring bad dream. He knew where this was leading but couldn't make her stop.

From the pile, she selected a piece of kelly-green felt, ripped off a corner, and wrapped it over the tip of the doll's head. Black felt formed shoes, and two stickpins became eyes, one lavender and one blue. She laid the doll on the table, pulled another bundle of fibers from the matting, and split out legs, arms, and a head.

This time, bright yellow felt covered the crown of the head and fell down the doll's back. She stuck orange and blue stickpins above its cheeks, and pressed yellow felt to its feet, like the hair. She separated a piece of red cloth and wrapped it around the doll's lower body and legs, for a skirt, and then squeezed a piece of yellow cloth around the torso to form a blouse.

Robin said, "There's a paintbrush in the drawer by the refrigerator."

With the watercolors, she painted thin red lines across the bottoms of the dolls' heads. Lying side by side, they looked like artifacts from a fair-skinned pre-Colombian civilization. She picked up the female and straightened the felt hair.

"Here." She handed the doll to him.

Almost immediately, he felt the fibers stir. The face twitched, and the mouth parted in a silent cry, just as the others had. The creature stretched and kicked weakly.

Robin nodded at the basket. "Put the handkerchief in there and lay her on it."

Still holding the little person in his fingers, as he might have held a wriggling crawfish as a young boy, he spread the cloth out on the bottom of the basket and lay the new girl-child gently on it.

Robin said, "Now the boy."

He could find nothing right about what was happening, but he couldn't simply blame mutual insanity. Too much of the experience was real. He knew if he crept up to Apartment 333 again and followed one of the passages, it would lead him to some place unimaginable, perhaps with another house where frightening bird-voiced children played in the yard. All of those things he'd seen and smelled and felt. There was no drug in the breath from old house. These things were not hallucinations.

"It's okay, Dane. Wake the boy up." Robin was as placid as someone seated in a lotus position, listening to New Age music. Her whole face smiled and glowed, and her eyes glinted with hidden color in the wan kitchen lighting.

Dane picked up the remaining doll and stroked it with his fingers. It remained a lifeless, loosely bound bundle of fibers. He glanced over the edge of the basket, checking to see if the girl was indeed awake. As he watched, she turned her head from side to side and grasped her tiny felt feet by the toes.

He examined the male doll again. Perhaps she'd made it wrong. Something was off-balance. He removed and straightened the hairpiece and the eye-pins and shoes. On a whim, he pinched the sides of the head to form crude ear bumps.

There was still no activity from the boy-doll despite his touching and massaging it. Had he used up his tiny reserve of magic? He pushed the doll's chest several times, playing doctor, performing CPR.

He laughed at his idiocy, but then took a deep breath anyway and blew it out into the doll's face. Nothing happened at first, but then he felt the tiniest of movements. The arms pressed against the pads of his fingers and the feet kicked, and then the doll drew a breath, the yawn of an earthworm. He held the boy-child until it began blinking, then laid it in the basket next to the girl. They promptly ignored each other.

Robin was still watching, entranced, giving Dane a look he remembered. The same look she gave him when he canceled a fishing trip with friends to walk with her in a cancer benefit.

The look of love.

He heard his voice speaking, not sure what part of his brain was controlling it, because the rational part wanted to run from the apartment, from the house, from the city.

"Do you need to give them food or anything tonight?"

She shook her head, tossing her hair. "I think they'll be okay. I'll check on them later." Her look turned devilish. "The calendar says tonight is a 'go' night."

Two days later, the tan sedan disappeared, along with its driver, and Mrs. B's white Subaru returned.

Dane tapped on Mrs. B's door. Mrs. B peeked around the door, then seeing him, smiled and swung it open.

"Dane, good evening. How may I help you?"

"I need to talk to you about … what's being going on here."

"Oh, you mean the lady upstairs. Come on in."

He felt rocked back. What did she know? Numbly, he followed her in.

Mrs. B said, "Sad, but the new tenant has lost her job here, and must move back to... Oh, where was she from? No matter.

"Maybe you and Robin will want to move up there. It's much bigger than it appears, with the extra bedroom, and the views are better. You can see the city skyline."

She smiled tightly, her eyes regarding him.

"You know, Dane, I've been thinking for some time that when I go, this building would pass on to you and Robin. I have no other family, and I can't imagine anyone else I would rather have care for the place. It's become part of me, like part of my own body. I want someone who will cherish it, as I have."

As she spoke, Dane noticed a photograph on top of her desk. The photo was cracked, and the colors faded. A young woman leaned against a pale sedan, an early '50's model, probably a Ford.

Below, a stack of mail lay on the corner of the desk, just inside where the flexible top would roll down. The addressee caught his eye.

Mrs. *Tina* Boranski.

From the Author

My wife, Cee, is heavily into crafting, particularly paper crafting. I can only guess this is what led to the intense, detailed, fully realized dream which became "Children of Things." I remember the sensations, the smells, the colors, and the horror of the dream, and I hope I've rendered them all in this story.

The story isn't just about where we come from as human beings, but the nature of reality and our perceptions. News headlines are full of speculation about the nature of the universe, its creation, and how we perceive it. Is this a simulation? Are we really physical beings of flesh and bone, brains and brawn, born of male and female parents? Or are we by our very natures otherworldly and brought into existence in ways we don't know or understand? I see "Children of Things" as a small molecule of these open-ended questions.

About the Author

CJ Erick's stories have appeared in anthologies from WMG Publishing, WordFire Press, and others. He won the FenCon short story competition in 2015. He writes in multiple genres, publishes novels in a space fantasy series, and dabbles in poetry. He's an MFA student in creative writing at Lindenwood University, and an editorial assistant for the Lindenwood Review. He lives in Dallas area with his wife and their rescue superhero dog Saber-Girl, calls his sourdough bread starter "Ursula" (K. Le Guin), and cooks crazy-good Cajun food for a Midwest Yankee.

Tell Your True Name

by
Eric Fritz

Tell Your True Name

*T*he city was dark and the alley in front of Circe's Bar was empty save for a lone figure in a coat. Cars and groups on foot passed occasionally, but none turned down the alley. Most people saw the cracked pavement and flickering lights and kept moving, which made Circe's a perfect gathering spot for the city's more interesting citizens.

The lone man exhaled a lungful of smoke straight up into the dark awning over the door and hugged his duster tighter around himself. "The new cloves just aren't as good."

Above him, eight red eyes shone in the darkness below the awning. "They still smell divine." The raspy voice that drifted down sounded unfamiliar with the shape of English words.

"It's not the same." He blew another puff of smoke straight up.

The spider let out a contented sigh. "I still find them delightful." A hairy arm, longer than a human's, descended to swirl the smoke around in the air. "You need to enjoy the little things in life."

"Easy for you to say." He dropped the filter on the sidewalk and crushed it out with a boot heel. "To you, everything is little."

"Have you time for another?" the voice asked. "I find I cannot get enough."

"Maybe after a drink." He reached up to make sure the necklace was still tucked into his shirt and then pushed the door open, leaving the spider where it always stayed.

Circe's was still mostly empty. Three men had their heads together at one end of the bar, and lone patrons occupied a few different tables in the back. The woman behind the bar was not the bartender he had known years ago, but Circe had a habit of picking up strays. The new bartender had black hair pulled back into a ponytail of tiny braids, and a riot of piercings around the top of both ears. Her smile gleamed when she talked to everyone else, but right now she was glaring at him.

"Not thinking about skipping out on your tab, are you?"

"Not hardly." He folded his coat in half and dropped it over one of the many empty stools, then reached into his pocket. His hand came back with several crumpled dollars, a lira, five pounds, and a few gold coins bearing a woman with three eyes. He selected one of these and jammed the rest back into his pocket. "That should cover it."

Her glare relaxed as soon as she picked it up. "Well then. What else can I get you?"

"Two fingers of bourbon, the good stuff. No ice." He sat down and dropped his elbows onto the bar, his hat going on top of the coat beside him. "What did you say your name was?"

"I didn't." She placed a glass in front of him and tipped a dusty green bottle over it. "But it's Maddy."

"Short for something?"

"Short for lots of things." She smiled. "And you?"

"You can call me Mort." He took a long drink from the glass. "Not bad."

"Aye! You Mort McArthur?" a new voice called.

The three men sitting at the end of the bar were getting to their feet. They were all tall and gaunt, almost too tall, and wearing mismatched athletic clothing. One wore a red baseball cap, one a blue trapper hat, and one a black knit winter hat. It was odd clothing for New England in the fall. Mort picked up his whiskey with an exaggerated gesture while the other hand crept under his shirt towards the gun at his hip.

"Might be." He tilted his glass towards them. "Who's asking?"

The closest one, the one with the red cap, stepped forwards. "You'd better come with us." The handful of other people in the bar all appeared to be suddenly fascinated with the tops of their drinks.

"You three need another drink?" Maddy called over. "Maybe one for the road?"

Without taking his eyes from Mort, Red-cap tossed a handful of coins onto the bar. Most of them bounced off, onto the floor. "Take that, and mind your business. We gotta have a word with him."

Mort waved his whiskey glass again. "Sorry to put you gentlemen out, but my only business tonight is with this drink."

"Duke wants a word with you." Red-cap sneered. "Seems you might have something that belongs to him."

If the rest of the bar had been quiet before, they were silent as a graveyard now. The fae had a complex political system, but the Duke of each city was a de facto god unless a Monarch troubled themselves to get involved. The last time anyone knew of that happening was over a hundred years ago, and the resulting fire was still making everyone think twice.

Mort pushed himself to his feet. "I doubt that very much."

"You better listen to us." Red-cap said, "You wouldn't want to get on his bad side. He knows someone's moving a Heartstone through here, which means it now belongs to the Duke. You know the rules."

Mort did know the rules, which meant if they found the stone, he was going to have questions to answer. He resisted reaching up to make sure his necklace was still tucked away. "Good luck finding it."

"We heard it was with someone looking like you. And answering to your name." His two friends were moving to block the door as he spoke.

Mort had only seen the Duke of this city once, but low-level thugs in a bar didn't seem like his style. Especially not a group who seemed this out of place. He looked between the three again then settled his gaze on Red-cap. "I didn't know Duke Reginald employed a lot of elves."

Their posture changed immediately. "What do you mean?" Red-cap kept his voice calm, but his tension was obvious.

Mort took a slow step forwards. "Well for starters, your friend's got one ear poking out." He nodded towards the one in the blue trapper hat with white fur covering his ears.

"What?" The other two turned to stare as he clapped both hands against his head. "I do not."

"Yeah." Mort nodded. "But the thing is, a human wouldn't have bothered to check."

"You idiot." Red-cap glared at him.

"Don't be too hard on him." Mort stepped closer. "You blend in well, but your ears are a little too sharp, and your eyes are a little too bright. You're what, third generation?"

Red-cap turned back to Mort with a snarl. "It doesn't matter. You're coming with us. The only question is how roughed up you want to get first."

"I don't think so." Mort put his face right up to the elf who had just spoken. "I'm not going anywhere with a bunch of knife-eared bastards."

Red-cap's mouth flattened into a line. "We don't have to bring you in unharmed. I might just rough you up anyway."

They were getting mad, but not mad enough. He leaned in, lowering his voice, and the elf leaned even closer. "If you think I couldn't recognize your beady little goblin eyes the second you walked in, you're dumber than you look."

"You watch your fuckin' mouth!" He shoved Mort back with both hands.

Mort let it carry him backwards, grabbing one of the bar stools and bringing it down with him as he tumbled to the floor. He rolled, came up into a crouch, and heaved the stool towards the three of them. It caught Red-cap on the shoulder and sent him reeling. As he dropped, Mort stood and drew the revolver.

The elves were faster than he'd given them credit for. Blue-hat already had a pistol trained on him. Knit-hat was hefting the stool as his boss stood up and drew a small semi-automatic.

"Don't try it, McArthur." Red-cap motioned with the barrel of his pistol. His hat had fallen off, revealing tousled blonde hair. "You're not going to stop three of us with that thing."

Mort smiled. "With iron bullets I might. Try me."

That made all three of them stop. Mort could probably take out two of them and jump behind the bar before the third got his gun out, but it would be close.

"Three against one." Red-cap sneered. "You'll never get all of us."

"I'll get you though." Mort narrowed his gaze. "Even if one of your guys takes me out, do you really want to taste iron?"

Red-cap's face tightened. "You think you can shoot before I do?"

Mort was pretty sure he could, but it wasn't a bet he wanted to take if he could talk his way out. Luckily, Maddy didn't seem interested either.

The sound of a shotgun racking echoed in the sudden silence. From behind the bar Maddie pointed a sawed-off pump action piece at the three elves. "No guns in the bar." She swung it in Mort's direction. "You too, tough guy."

One of the elves had moved to aim at her, and the other was looking at their leader. Mort had a feeling that if he ever wanted to drink here again, he needed to nip this in the bud.

"Easy, easy." He held his gun out to the side, careful not to move too fast. "No one needs to shoot anyone. I'll have a talk with you three right here."

The elf nodded towards his gun. "Get rid of it."

Maddy held her gun up higher. "You all get rid of them."

"No problem." Mort kept his other hand out in a friendly gesture and flicked the cylinder open. He managed to push the ejector rod with one hand and six bullets bounced onto the bar. Slowly he placed the empty gun down. "See? No worries."

Red-cap nodded towards the blue-hatted elf, and they both placed their guns at the end of the bar. Knit-cap flipped the bar stool right-side-up with a scowl.

Mort levered himself back into a seat and nodded to the one beside him. He let himself relax a little as the elf dropped onto the stool. "Sorry about that. Let me get you a drink to make up for it."

"We're not here for a friendly visit." Red-cap was still glaring, although without the hat his elven features were more pronounced.

"Surely the Duke wouldn't begrudge you a few minutes to compose yourself before you brought me back." Mort smiled. "And if I have to go before a Duke, I need my courage." He waved to get Maddy's attention and pointed to his glass then the three of them.

"I dunno." Red-cap was staring over the bar with poorly hidden desire.

"Drink 'em or don't, I don't care. Just pay and get the hell out of my bar." Maddy slammed four glasses down.

Mort tossed her a coin which she caught without looking at him, then stormed off into the back. He was definitely getting pushed higher up in her bad list.

He lifted his glass. "Sorry for the trouble, gentlemen. Cheers."

"We aren't supposed to drink on the job." The one in the knit cap was staring down at the glasses.

"Seeing as you're about to take me to a very difficult conversation, I don't think the Duke would fault you for rewarding yourselves a little." Mort smiled. "And see, this is the good stuff."

"Don't need to tell me twice." Red-cap raised his glass. Mort leaned in to clink glasses, then they tilted their heads back.

"Feels like fire." The elf waved at his mouth as he sucked in air.

"That's a real drink, as my father used to say." Mort slammed his glass back down on the bar so hard it shattered on the bar top.

He was really going to owe Maddy an apology, but as long as no one actually died inside the bar Circe would forgive the damage. Probably.

He turned towards Red-cap. "My father also used to say it will make you tell your true name."

Red-cap started to rise, eyes wide, but Mort grabbed his wrist and slammed it against the bar. "None of you move."

The other two froze, staring at him, as Red-cap tried to pull his arm free.

"What's your name?"

The elf's face twisted like he was about to vomit, but finally he spat out the words through clenched teeth. "Sylvan Redleaf."

"Now let's talk," Mort said.

"Won't matter." Redleaf finally yanked his wrist free. "You can't do anything with just my name."

"Unless it's bound in iron and blood." In one motion Mort grabbed a bullet from the bar, a piece of his broken glass, and squeezed. Warm blood ran between his fingers.

Redleaf jumped to his feet so fast he flipped the bar stool over, but this time Mort was faster. His fingers traced a red symbol on the bar top, and he opened his hand to slam the iron bullet down against it, trying not to wince as the glass cut his palm again.

"Sylvan Redleaf, freeze."

The elf stopped like a statue, one hand stretched out towards the guns at the end of the bar.

"All of you, don't move," Mort said, "not if you want him to live."

Luckily neither of them looked likely to move, they were both just staring at their leader.

"Now," Mort grabbed a napkin to hold against his bleeding hand, "Who sent you?"

Redleaf spoke slowly. "Boss by the river says you got a stolen Heartstone, and he means to have it."

"That makes more sense." Mort shook his head. A low-level fae crime boss was a lot more logical than the Duke bothering with this. "Risky move, using the Duke's name like that."

"You're a traveler," Redleaf said. "We figured by the time word gets around you'd be long gone, and there'd be no one to say we did it."

Mort looked around, but Maddy was gone, and the bar was empty. Everyone else must have ducked out the back when the fight started.

"So, you thought it would be easy to rob a stranger and get the prize."

"It was ours!" The elf's face cleared from the compulsion as he spit the words at Mort. Clearly, he would have said this anyway. "Our people created those stones. They should be ours."

"Hundreds of years ago," Mort said. "You know the treaties; it doesn't matter who created them anymore."

"And you know the law." Redleaf was scowling again. "Any objects that powerful belong to the Duke. It shoulda been easy to take it from you."

"Time for you to get out of the bar." Maddy had reappeared from the back, shotgun still in her hands. "You three get moving." She nodded towards Mort. "You're paying for the damage, and then you're right behind them."

"I wouldn't dream of doing anything else." Mort stood straighter, trying to ignore the pain in his palm, and pointed his uninjured hand towards the door. "I release you. Leave this place, and never seek me out again."

Redleaf sprang into action, grabbing the arm of one of the others and hustling towards the door as fast as he could.

Knit-hat slowed down as they hit the doorway, and too late Mort realized there were three of them, but only two had left guns on the bar earlier. He turned to the whiskey glasses to see one still full.

"Maddy!" Mort yelled, but she'd already lowered her gun.

As the door slammed behind Redleaf and the other elf, Knit-hat spun and drew a pistol. He aimed it not at Mort, but at Maddy. "Put the shotgun down, Miss."

"You don't want to do this," Maddy said slowly. "Circe won't take it well."

"I'm not gonna hurt you unless you do anything stupid." He motioned down with the gun. "Drop it."

"It's ok," Mort said slowly. If bullets started flying in here Circe's opinion of him was going to change pretty fast. "I'll go with him."

Maddy slowly reached out and placed her shotgun on the bar. "You're gonna regret this."

"We'll see." The pistol swung to point at Mort. "Seems like you wouldn't have wasted your time questioning that idiot if you didn't know anything about the Heartstone. So, you're gonna come with me, and we're gonna go find where you left it. Let's go."

"Mind if I light a cigarette?" Mort asked. "I'm getting the feeling this is going to turn into a long walk."

"No smoking," Maddy called. It sounded like a reflex.

"I think Circe will forgive it, given the circumstances," Mort said.

Knit-hat waved the gun. "Just get going. And no sudden moves."

Mort drew the pack and lighter from his shirt pocket with a measured pace, placed one of the black cigarettes in his mouth, and lit it. He drew in just enough air to get it burning then walked towards the door. The elf pushed the door open, motioning Mort out with the gun barrel.

Mort sucked in a lungful of smoke and blew it out the door as hard as he could. "You should put the gun down," Mort said.

"What?" Before Knit-hat could move, hairy limbs burst through the doorway, encircling the elf. He tried to bring his pistol around, but it was already too late. He was sucked backwards into the darkness outside with a scream that cut off in an abrupt wet thud.

"You owe a whole cigarette to me." The words drifted back through the doorway and then the door swung closed.

"Oh damn, that was too close." Mort dropped the cigarette into the one full glass and collapsed onto a bar stool.

"Here." Maddy placed a clean towel on the bar. "Why do you hate elves so much, anyway?"

"It's a long story." Mort looked down to wrap the towel around his hand.

"Need a drink?"

"Several." He looked back up at her. "Sorry about all this."

"You're the one paying Circe back for the damages." She was smiling as she put down two new glasses and poured a generous shot of whiskey into both. "The guy out front won't bother himself for just anybody. But if you're moving a stolen elf stone through here, those guys had a point."

"I didn't steal anything." Mort picked up a glass and clinked it against hers. "And if something happened to be stolen before I got it, that's just business."

"Just business." She clinked her glass against his then tipped it back. Mort didn't waste any time following suit.

Maddy dropped her glass back on the bar. "So, what's your real name?"

Mort stared down at his empty glass, then back up at her face. "Oh, you're good."

Her smile dropped. "Tell me your name."

For the first time he noticed flecks of brighter purple in her brown eyes. The silver rings at the top of her ears were hiding sharper-than-human points. His hand jumped to the necklace under his shirt as he felt the words build up in his throat.

From the Author

When I was younger, I remember seeing my father with a whiskey cocktail one night at dinner, and asking him what it was. He told me that it was a strong drink, and his Great Aunt Gus always used to say "that stuff will make you tell your true name." That sentence bounced around in my head for years. Combined with the idea in folklore that knowing a fae creature's name would give you power over it, I knew there was a story idea I had to write.

Writing urban fantasy provides a lot of opportunities to combine the real and the fantastic. I like the idea of taking elves, traditionally the upper crust of fantasy society, and seeing what would happen if they weren't. I also think it's important for writing to address real issues, and fantasy allows that in a way that doesn't trivialize anyone's identity or demean anyone in the real world. I've also always had a soft spot for anti-heroes. It's a lot of fun to write someone who doesn't always do the right thing, but I also like showing that there are consequences to those actions.

I originally wrote "Tell Your True Name" in 2018, before I realized that there was no current market for urban fantasy short stories. I sent it out on a number of submissions, but it was never quite the right fit. When I saw the call for submissions to Particular Passages, it looked like the perfect spot for this story. I hope you enjoy reading it!

About the Author

Eric Fritz is a speculative fiction writer, web developer, and amateur bartender. His short fiction has appeared in *Every Day Fiction* and *Martian: The Magazine of Science Fiction Drabbles*. His awards include a Golden Cobra Award in 2020 for freeform LARP design. He is ambivalent towards our new robot overlords.

You can find him digitally at twitter.com/CommonHeresy and physically in Cambridge, where he lives with a plush cat named Will

Mama Said

by
John T. Biggs

Mama Said

Mama always said Oba would get himself into trouble—something she couldn't get him out of, something without a statute of limitations he could wait out in another jurisdiction. She was right, as usual.

He sopped up the grease from his last meal with a chunk of sour dough bread torn off the loaf. One male and one female guard stood outside the open door of his death row cell. They said they'd never seen a condemned man eat so much.

The male guard pointed his shock stick like a pretend rifle and summoned up a fake belch. His name was Anton Leemaster. Oba figured he was what the constitution had in mind when it mentioned cruel and unusual punishment.

The woman guard was different.

"Got to admire your appetite." Madeline was her name.

She was the prettiest woman Oba had seen in the ten years he was on the row, prettier than his court 'pointed attorneys, prettier than the newspaper women, even prettier than the death row groupies who sent him photographs.

"I brought that thing you asked me for, Oba." Madelaine didn't say *your last request*. She was still pretending he wasn't going to be put to death by the state of Oklahoma within the next hour. She stepped into his cell and fished a pair of panties out of the side pocket of her uniform.

"Hope these are what you had in mind." She dropped a skimpy pair of panties into his outstretched hand. She stared at Anton Leemaster, daring him to say something.

"A man needs a little compassion when he's facing ..." Madeline looked at Oba when she spoke. "You know." Her eyes explored his face, not like she was flirting though, more like she was curious.

"Wonderin' about my facial ink?" Oba was used to that. He was a walking billboard for the Arian Nation, had an 88 on his chin. Eight stood for the eighth letter of the alphabet—H times two.

"Means Heil Hitler." He scratched at the stubble that partly covered the white supremacist numerology.

"This one here . . ." He tapped at the number 83 on his forehead. "It means Heil Christ." It was the simplest way to keep Jesus on his mind.

Anton Leemaster's face was so red it looked like he might catch fire. Oba would love to see that before they put the needle in his arm and sent him on a one-way trip to a better place...

Another place, anyway. That's what Mama always said.

He wiped his mouth on Madeline's panties while she collected his dirty dishes.

"First meal the prison kitchen ever got exactly right," he said. Porterhouse steak, nearly burned. Fried potatoes, nearly burned. Chery pie with ice cream. All on the same plate, but with none of them touching.

"Cooked perfect. I take that as a sign." Not as good a sign as Madeline's panties, of course. He couldn't tell if she'd actually worn them, but he pictured it in his mind clear enough to make his execution almost worthwhile.

Madeline was sweet, and out of reach. Mama would say she was one of his childish ideas that never seemed to work out like Oba hoped. Santa Claus turned out to be his dad, who was a real son of a bitch; the GPS tracker on his stolen Lexus wasn't disabled by putting aluminum foil in the hubcaps; his Arian brothers rolled over on him just like any other inmates would have done.

Madeline was different. She carried a shock stick any time his door was open. That wasn't lost on Oba, but she didn't need it. He wouldn't hurt her even if he was absolutely sure he'd get away with it. In his mind, that was pretty much the same as love.

He waved her panties at Anton Leemaster like a flag and hummed the "Star Spangled Banner" in case the guard didn't get the point.

"Forty minutes, Taylor." Leemaster had his own special brand of ruining things.

The thought of execution exploded in Oba's mind like fireworks. It held his attention long enough to make him break into a cold sweat, and then it faded.

"Dying ain't so bad." He'd slide out of his body on a cocktail of lethal drugs, and his soul would go somewhere he wouldn't be troubled by Africans, or Mexicans, or Injuns, or any other mud people. His preacher had promised him that—not the prison chaplain, who was supposed to be in Oba's cell an hour before they took him down, but the leader of the Christian Identity Church in Elohim City.

Mama said mud people talk was another one of Oba's trouble-making ideas.

"Damn, she's a hard woman to please." He didn't mean to speak out loud, but there was no taking it back. Madeline looked at him like she might be glad her shock stick was handy. Anton Leemaster smirked and told him it wouldn't be much longer until he shook hands with the devil.

"Where's the god damned chaplain," Oba said. "Oklahoma can't kill a man until a civil service preacher prays for his soul."

Mama said prayer was a waste of time, for her boys at least. Nobody listened to Otto, Owen, and especially not Oba. God was no exception. She said they should probably pray anyway though, because at least they were killing time instead of people.

"Every minute that goes by without hurting someone is a plus," Oba told the guards. A psychologist gave him that piece of advice, or maybe it was a social worker.

The cherry pie stain on his panty napkin looked like one the Rorschach inkblots from his mental evaluations. It looked like his mother. All those inkblots looked like her a little, but this one was an especially good likeness.

"Pink is Mama's color," he said, just as Chaplain Ed Martin stepped in the door. The Preacher had his eyes on Madeline's panties.

"Sorry Rev, you'll have to find your own girl." That got a grunt from Anton Leemaster and a giggle from Madeline.

Oba fumbled with the garment label and saw the underwear had been inspected by number eight—like the number in his 88 tattoo. He felt the urge to explain that to the preacher but didn't want to waste his last half-hour of life in a religious discussion with a man who didn't have enough sense to believe in separation of the races.

"Thought you wasn't coming, Rev." It wasn't often a man on death row got to work a guilt trip. Oba made the most of it until he saw the chaplain glance at his watch.

"Eight thirty," the preacher said without being asked. "I meant to get here earlier but I stopped by to visit your family."

That would be Oba's Mama and his two brothers. His daddy was in a Supermax for killing an FBI agent, not on death row in Oklahoma, which went to prove there was no such thing as justice.

"Otto and Owen can't be here, Rev. They've got warrants. And Mama won't come because . . ." He didn't want to admit his mother didn't give a damn what happened to him, but that's the way things were. "She don't get too far from home." The place where she brought up her boys didn't have a regular name. People called it the patch.

"She sent something for you." The chaplain had an envelope in his hand. He offered it to Oba but kept it out of reach. The preacher nudged the trashcan with his foot. "After you toss the undergarment."

That's what Mama would have said, so Oba didn't waste time arguing. Everybody did what Mama wanted because she'd come for you if you didn't. He kissed Madeline's panties goodbye and gave them a toss. They caught on the rim, so he didn't get two points.

The envelope was smudged and wrinkled and had OBA printed on the outside in all caps.

"She ain't much for writing." Mama closed the envelope really well, though. It took him almost three minutes to tear it open and tease the paper out. He wasn't good with fractions, but he knew that was a tenth of the time he had left in the world.

"To whom it may concern." He read loud enough so Madeline and Anton Leemaster could hear it, and the preacher too.

"Please do your damnedest for my boy. He's got it coming. Sincerely, Mama Taylor."

The preacher looked like he didn't know what to make of that. Neither did the guards, but Anton Leemaster chuckled.

"People used to say the Taylor boys couldn't get into hell without a note from Mama," Oba said. "I reckon this is mine." His mother was complicated in her way. "She say anything more?"

"Not much," the preacher said. "Just that she always does for her boys."

"Well, that might mean I'm in trouble," Oba said.

Anton Leemaster laughed like that was the funniest thing he'd ever heard, but anyone who knew Mama Taylor would know it was no laughing matter.

"She does for her boys, all right," Oba said. "What she does don't look right to anyone outside the family, but nobody ever tried to stop her." He wadded the note into a tight little ball but didn't throw it away. He squeezed it in his right hand, the one with LOVE inked on the knuckles.

He tried to be good for her. He tried harder than he ever tried anything else in his whole life, but deep down he suspected it wouldn't make her like him any better even if he managed to pull it off.

"In the end, all a man has is his excuses," Oba said. And his excuses never satisfied Mama. "Come here and take your medicine. That's what she'd say." And she didn't mean a mix of IV drugs that would knock you out and kill you in your sleep—nothing as easy as that.

"If she started your way, it wouldn't take you long to regret it." Oba went quiet, like when he was a child, as if she would forget about him if he didn't make any noise.

"She remembers everything bad you ever did." That covered a lot of territory with the Taylor boys.

Somewhere on H-block a door opened. Footsteps moved along the corridor, three people taking their time. Oba didn't recognize the footfalls, but they scared him.

"The executioners' walk," the preacher said.

Oba was familiar with the ceremony. When a condemned man was put to death, his three volunteer executioners would stroll by his open cell door. They wore black hoods, like members of the Goth KKK. The hoods kept their identities secret, so family members of the man they killed wouldn't take revenge.

The three hooded figures stopped in front of Oba Taylor's open cell door and stared at him through the eye holes of their hoods.

One of them waved at him, and then they all moved on to the death chamber.

"Like performers in a medieval fair," the preacher said.

Oba had never been to one of those, but it sounded right. He stood from his seat on the death row bunk and walked as far as the cell door. Anton Leemaster held his shock stick like he was ready to put it to use, but Madeline told him to take it easy.

"One of them has a name belt." Oba strained to read it. "Had a fancy buckle," he said. "Like cowboys wear."

"Get back," Anton Leemaster said. "Don't make me tell you again."

Exactly what Mama used to say, so Oba did it.

"You see the belt, Rev?"

Instead of answering, the chaplain looked at his watch.

"Let me see that Rev." Oba reached for the preacher's hand, watched him jerk it back and then relax when he understood he wasn't being attacked.

"Time moves in a circle," Oba watched the second hand pass the numbers on the watch face. He still held the wadded-up note from his mother in his right hand. It was soggy from sweat, but he gave it a kiss as the second hand passed number twelve, and more kisses at numbers three, six, and nine. It felt like a magic ritual.

"People with you at the beginning are there at the end too," he told the chaplain. "Got to appreciate it, even if you don't like it very much."

He tossed the crumpled note into the air and caught it. "Gettin' philosophical in the final minutes, ain't I?"

Oba drummed his fingers on a bible donated by the Gideons. He picked it up and let it fall open. God would pick the most appropriate verse. He read a passage full of thees and thous and whosoevers.

"This crap don't make sense," he said. "Think you can tell me what it means?"

The chaplain looked at his watch again. "Eight forty-one," he said, as if that was everything God wanted him to know.

Madeline looked sad when she stepped into Oba's cell and told him it was time. Not sad enough to leave her shock stick behind, but he couldn't blame her for that.

"Sorry, big guy." She was a real heart breaker. "It's not a long walk, but the boys are afraid to leave you unrestrained."

The boys were Anton Leemaster and two other jittery male guards holding their shock sticks in white knuckle grips.

"Be brave." Madeline might have been talking to Oba or to Leemaster. He was the one with the shackles.

The preacher asked if he wanted to pray, but Oba didn't want to close his eyes.

"Chains make it real, don't they, Rev?" He kept hold of Mama's note, but offered Anton Leemaster both his hands and didn't flinch when the manacles snapped around his wrists and ankles. Shackles were a complicated bunch of chains and Leemaster struggled to get the loop around Oba's waist hooked up with his hand and leg restraints. He kept hold of his shock stick, which made it harder.

"Relax," Oba told him. "If I wanted you dead your buddies would already be mopping up your blood." He held that image in his mind to keep from thinking about the room next door. Mostly, it worked.

Anton Leemaster tugged on the chains to make certain they were secure and then he stepped hard on Oba Taylor's foot—shod in paper shoes since they moved him into the cell next to the execution chamber.

Madeline shoved Leemaster aside. "You're scum, Anton." She hooked her arm under Oba's and let him escort her like a bride down the four final yards to the place where things would end for him.

"Pretty goddamned good." He was probably the first person ever to take this walk with a smile on his face.

"Compartmentalization," he told Madeline, mostly because he wanted to show her he was smart enough to use big words. He'd heard that one during one of his psych evaluations, and he was finally figuring out what it meant. The shrink said compartmentalization had been one of the things that got him into trouble because he couldn't think of...

"Consequences." That was the other word the shrink used. Right then, compartmentalization felt pretty damned good until he remembered the consequences that lay on the other side of the execution room door.

"Damn." Thoughts of death danced through his mind like a naked woman twisting around a pole and Oba couldn't stop looking at her, not for a single second.

The death chamber door was stainless steel, not much different from ones on other cells, except it was bright yellow.

Oba heard there was a poison frog somewhere in South America that was yellow too. Best he could remember, the chaplain told him about them on one of his visits.

"Kill you in a minute," Oba said. Was the preacher thinking of poison frogs too?

"I'm here, Oba," the chaplain said. "It'll be all right."

It would be all right for everyone but Oba Taylor. He'd come out that yellow door in a body bag, wrapped in plastic like a cheap cut of meat on sale because it's started going bad.

Anton Leemaster looked over his shoulder as he worked the latch.

Oba sang a few lines from the Beatles' "Yellow Submarine" as Madeline escorted him over the threshold. The song came out of one of those psychology compartments that caused so much trouble. He stopped for a moment as they passed the witness room door, bolted from the inside and out. It was a solid piece of stainless steel, but he knew what was on the other side. Twelve seats, like a jury box, sat in front of a laminated safety glass window big enough for a department store. According to the preacher, a curtain would open when the warden gave the signal.

Oba reached for the outside bolt, but Anton Leemaster prodded him with the business end of the shock stick. No juice, but the feel of the electrodes was enough to get him moving.

He rattled the chains on his wrists so the witnesses could hear. "Hey there." Might as well give them a show. "This is the sound of a dead man walking."

The chamber was silent except for thumps and bumps from behind an angled partition where the executioners waited to push the buttons that would send the poison into his veins. The warden stood beside a wall mounted telephone, pretending the governor might have a last-minute change of heart. He gave Oba a friendly wave and nodded toward a table in the center of the room. It looked like a padded, horizontal version of a cross.

Madeline and two other guards moved aside and let Anton Leemaster take charge. She had lost her shock stick, Oba couldn't say when that happened, but the two men standing slightly behind her held theirs like they were expecting a fight.

The chaplain stood beside Leemaster, as if God was giving the guard his stamp of approval.

"I don't think the Lord likes assholes," Oba said. "How about you, preacher." He thought about how much of an asshole he'd been most of his life. Only stopped hurting people when he was in a single cell on death row.

The preacher said something, but there was no point in listening. If things went smooth, Oba Taylor would be inside a body bag in the next few minutes and his soul—if there was such a thing—would be wherever souls go, whether that was Aryan heaven or hell, where Oba would fit in just fine, or someplace else where he'd be an outcast.

"Be brave big guy," Madeline said. That made him hold out his hands to Anton Leemaster. The manacles snapped open, and the guard unwound the chains and let them drop on the floor.

"I'll get his ankles when he's on the table," Leemaster said.

The guard's fear made Oba smile.

Things were going better than anyone had a right to expect, and they would have kept on going that way if the state trained technician hadn't walked in, dressed in green scrubs with bleached splotches on the knees.

"The fuck . . ." Oba could see the shock on everybody's faces. People probably didn't cuss right before the state executed them.

"A colored man." Not the way an Aryan normally described an African American, but Oba Taylor tried to be polite for Madeline's sake, and that was as polite as he could manage.

The chaplain's hand touched his shoulder and pulled away like he'd been burned.

"Mama?" Oba was pretty sure she was around. His brothers were, for sure. He'd known that as soon as he saw the name belt. Maybe they were out of sight, ready to push the buttons that would start chemicals running into his blood, or maybe Mama had a plan. Either way, she wouldn't let strangers bring her boys to heel.

"Mama, it can't happen this way." Everybody thought this is what Oba Taylor looked like breaking down. Everybody but his brothers and Mama.

"This ain't right." He sounded angry but reasonable too, like a speeder arguing with a cop over a ticket.

Madeline moved in front of Oba, well out of his reach. "Don't make this harder than it needs to be." She edged toward the warden, away from the table. She whispered something to him, but he didn't react.

Oba's fists were clenched, his mother's note still in the right one. His eyes were locked on the African American technician who looked like he was searching for a back way out of the chamber.

Leemaster said, "Calm down, Taylor. We're on a tight schedule here." He held his shock stick like a baseball bat.

"A goddamned colored man is gonna put a killing needle in my arm?"

"Sorry, man." The tech hid his IV equipment behind his back. "If it wasn't me, it would be someone else."

Oba held his arms straight out. His left hand in a Nazi salute and his right one closed around Mama's note. Anton Leemaster grabbed one arm. A second guard took the other, but both of them together weren't strong enough.

Madeline and the remaining male guard stood behind the chaplain like they'd decided this was the perfect time to turn their lives over to a higher power. Leemaster and his brother guard needed to use their shock sticks, but Oba's muscles were pumped full of rage and they were afraid to let go.

"A little help," the warden said, as if rank would get the execution back on course.

Madeline stayed quiet but the male guard who wasn't holding one of Oba's arms said, "Preacher's in the way."

The chaplain started a half dozen sentences but didn't get past the first word in any of them. Finally, he just called for, "Help!"

Oba ended the small talk with a Rebel Yell.

The three hooded executioners stepped out of their cubicle. They moved toward Oba as if they meant to do something more than push anonymous buttons and collect a hundred dollars.

One of them held a belt in his hand, a wide belt with the fancy buckle that Oba noticed earlier. The name OTTO was hand tooled in the leather. Maybe not the best way to stay anonymous, but the belt could do a lot of damage. The name was special because it was the same forwards and backwards. Otto was Mama's favorite she gave him the best name of all her boys.

He said, "Hold on there, partner," as he swung the belt across Anton Leemaster's face. The guard pressed his hands over the mark left behind by Otto's attack. The crisp clear letters showed between his fingers.

Oba turned his full attention to the correctional officer, who was still hanging onto his outstretched arm. He lifted the man over his head and threw him into the witness room window. The guard smashed into the safety glass, left a body shaped spiderweb impression. He dropped to the floor and crawled toward the warden.

Oba dragged his chains past the preacher, snatched up another male guard and tossed him against the window too. This one made it through the glass as the curtain inside snapped open. The witnesses lost their taste for death after it was no longer certain who was going to die. They scrambled for the double-locked door that didn't seem like a safety feature anymore.

The warden punched numbers into the death chamber telephone but couldn't seem to get anyone to pick up. After several tries, he hung up and tried to convince Oba that his best move was to lay down on the table and take his needle like a man. "It's the law, Taylor." He looked to the preacher for support. "Tell him he's only making matters worse."

Anton Leemaster shook off the trauma of his belt-whipping. He found a shock stick on the floor and caught Oba in the groin with the business end of the electric prod. That bent him over and sent him shuffling into the three hooded figures.

"Stop this nonsense right now." A woman's voice, filtered through an executioner's hood, a voice made course by alcohol and tobacco, but a woman's voice none the less.

Oba would recognize it anywhere. Mama removed the hood, slowly, the way a magician might show off her final trick of the night.

"You're acting a fool." She pointed an accusing finger at Oba, who managed to stay on his feet, but only because Otto and Owen were holding him up.

"And you." She walked over to Anton Leemaster and slapped him hard across the Otto imprint. She took the shock stick from his hand and turned back to Oba.

"Time to take your medicine." She moved fast for a woman her size. She raised the shock stick, placed the electrodes against the 83 tattoo on his forehead, and pushed the button. The charge passed through Oba and into his brothers. It sent them all into a wild dance and left them sprawled on the floor. Owen and Otto were twitching. Oba wasn't.

"I see to my boys," Mama Taylor told the warden. She nudged Otto and Owen with her boot.

Goddamn it. Oba's soul drifted away from his body and floated a few inches below the ceiling of the execution chamber. He'd never seen things from that perspective. He wasn't sure he liked it, but there was definitely something to all the spirit talk he'd heard.

He looked down at his body on the chamber floor. His right hand had opened and the note from Mama rolled away. The colored technician checked Oba's pulse and asked, "Will I still get paid the regular amount?"

Madeline was crying. That was nice.

Anton Leemaster was crying too.

And Mama... She looked right at Oba's soul. Pointed at him, there was no denying it.

"Don't give me a reason to come over there," she said. "You know I will."

There was no getting away from Mama.

From the Author

I've never written a story to fit a suggested theme. I find characters who interest me and let the narratives build themselves around those individuals. Eventually an anthology or a magazine calls for submissions that match something in my inventory. Oba Taylor is a composite of inmates I met while working as a prison dentist at the Lexington Assessment and Reception Center in Oklahoma. Oba appeared in modified form in my short novel *Popsicle Styx*, which is about to be re-released by Oghma Creative Media.

Most of the death row rituals and procedures described in "Mama Said" were essentially accurate at the time I wrote the story. In case you haven't guessed, I am opposed to capital punishment even when guilt of the inmate is not in question. My concern is primarily for the potentially devastating effect of executions on death row staff who confine inmates for years and then assist in putting them to death.

About the Author

Don't bother trying to classify John T. Biggs' stories. They are a genre stew of speculative fiction, anthropology, mystery, and humor written in a mainstream literary style. Native Americans play a significant role in most of John's narratives. He reworks traditional Indian legends and sets them in modern times, the way oral historians always intended.

Eighty of John's short stories have been published in magazines and anthologies that vary from literary to young adult speculative fiction and everything in between. Some of these stories have won regional and national awards including Grand Prize in the Writers Digest 80th annual competition, third prize in the Lorian Hemingway short story contest, a *Storyteller Magazine's* Peoples Choice Award, and two OWFI Crème de la Crème awards.

John has published four novels: *Owl Dreams, Popsicle Styx* (Oklahoma Book Award Finalist), *Cherokee Ice* (Oklahoma Book Award Finalist & OWFI Best Published Fiction Book of 2015), and *Shiners* (OWFI Best Published Fiction Book 2017), as well as a linked short story collection, *Sacred Alarm Clock*, and *Clementine a song to end the world*, a series of post-apocalyptic novellas.

The best way to see what John is up to is on his FB page:

https://www.facebook.com/Johnbiggsoklahomawriter

Twitter: @biggspirit

Johnny's Ray Guns

by
J.T. Evans

Johnny's Ray Guns

*J*ohnny stared up at the opening to the barn's hay loft. "Melissa! I'm sorry!"

The young woman poked her head out of the window while buttoning up her blouse. "Go away, Johnny! I want nothing more to do with you."

Even though the gloom of the evening hid his features, Johnny refused to let his dismay show. "But why?"

Finished with her buttons, Melissa plucked a strand of straw from her hair and pointed it at Johnny. "Because you're nothing more than a boy. I need a man who will take me to the stars. You're stuck in a rut, just like your father."

Johnny ground his teeth together. He hated being called "boy." His nineteen years of working on the farm had pushed him to grow up tall and strong. He was a man now. He knew it. Unfortunately, he had yet to prove it beyond a few tumbles in the hay loft with local girls.

Melissa said, "Now go away. Maybe you can go over to the Carter Farm and have a toss with June again."

Her words about June, Johnny's father, and the path Johnny was on, hit home. With the nail of truth driven deep into his heart, Johnny bowed his head in defeat. He put his hat back on his straw-riddled hair and shuffled away into the darkening night.

Johnny hated his life on the farm. Nothing but dirt, cow patties, squawking chickens, kicked-over buckets of milk, and barely living crops filled his days. He started toiling for his family before the sun rose each morning and didn't stop until the sun kissed the horizon on the other side of the farm.

Nothing exciting ever happened like he dreamed it would. Cow rustlers were a thing of the past with the patrolling ships overhead keeping all of the chipped cows in the correct, laser-lined fences. Even his romps in the hay had grown boring. Those nights of heavy petting with June had ended two weeks ago, when she found out about Melissa. Now Melissa knew about June, and that was over as well.

Trudging a trench into the soft dirt as he walked, he thought over what Melissa had said. She'd been right about Johnny following in his father's path. It was unlikely he'd ever make it off this ball of brown dirt, and he'd probably never be able to take anyone with him.

Johnny wanted more out of each day. He *needed* to see the stars. He itched to board a star jumper to find another, less-backwater planet to explore. Now that his twin younger brothers were old enough to help out, he didn't feel tied to the farm like he once had.

He crested Cash Hill, at the edge of his farm, and stared down at the glittering lights of the spaceport. With a heavy sigh, Johnny sat down on a small boulder. He leaned his chin into the palms of his hands and allowed his eyes to lose focus. The vision of blurry lights, and the golden streamers tracing behind a launching shuttle, brought images of fame and fortune to his mind. The rumble of the earth couldn't be felt at this distance, but the shuttle's roar through the sky made a few of the cattle in the distance to bellow and snort.

When the shuttle lit its secondary engines, the shockwave rattled Johnny's bones. He raised his head and watched the shuttle leave behind a plume of smoke as it reached orbit. He dropped his chin back into his hands and desperately wanted to be on that shuttle, or any spacefaring ship for that matter.

With the certainty of a young man, he knew he was someone important who had yet to find his place or purpose. More waited for him in the galaxy than scraping a living out of the dirt like a beggar taking handouts from the planet. Unsure of what his ultimate fate was, but still knowing it waited for him out there somewhere, Johnny pressed himself to his feet with a heavy sigh. He trudged down the side of the hill nearest the farm and walked past the barn.

The dryness of the dirt, kicked into the air by the dragging of his boots, mixed with the smell of fresh cow manure and the pungent rankness of the chicken coop. Even though rocket fuel smelled of rotten eggs, Johnny figured it would be more pleasant than the stenches he'd grown up with. By the time he stomped up the sturdy steps to the porch and into the house, he'd made up his mind. He'd do his morning chores, hand the rest of the day to his brothers, and go into the spaceport in the afternoon. It'd been years since his last trip, and that had been with his father, who never let him stray from his grasp, let alone sight.

When Johnny entered the kitchen, his father looked up. "Where ya been?"

Johnny shrugged. "Cash Hill. Just thinkin'."

" 'Bout Melissa? Or is it June this time? You know you gotta watch yer tongue 'round all womenfolk. They chatter to each other like hens at feedin' time."

With a shake of his head, Johnny said, "Naw. Not girls, Pa. Just thinkin'." He paused, steeling himself for what he wanted to say next.

Pa took another sip of whiskey from his cracked glass. "Spit it out, Boy. Gettin' late."

The word "boy" rubbed Johnny the wrong way. At his age, no one should be called "boy" anymore. He knew he was a man already, even if he'd done nothing to prove it. Anger rose up from the bottom of his boots, and he found his nerve. "I'm goin' to the spaceport tomorrow, after mornin' chores."

Without looking up, Pa asked, "What fer? Need parts for the tractor? Didn't know it was broken again."

"It's not. I just wanna go down there to the 'port and walk around a bit."

With a smile into his whiskey, Pa said, " 'Bout time you got up the nerve to head down there on your own. I was startin' to think you'd end up like...." He trailed off and took a deep pull from the glass.

Johnny didn't probe into what his father was about to say. He already knew. Pa had always told his boys they should grow up to be better than him. He wanted more for them but didn't know how to provide it. Despite all of the back-breaking work, Pa couldn't quite move upward in society or expand the farm. He barely hung on as it was.

To break the silence, Johnny asked, "You okay with this?"

Pa didn't answer right away. He stared through the cracked glass into the amber liquid. With a small nod to himself, Pa downed the rest of the whiskey. Moving quickly, he snatched a black box from the chair next to him and pushed it across the table toward Johnny. "Take it. You'll need it. You've earned—" Pa's voice cracked before he could finish the last sentence.

Pretending he didn't hear the moment of weakness from his father, Johnny stared down at the box. It was a dusty, old box from the last time Pa had bought a pair of boots.

Pa snapped. "Dunno what yer waitin' fer. Open it up."

Johnny lifted the flimsy cardboard lid and set it aside. Someone had lined the interior of the box with felt, and two ray guns rested in holsters on the dark lining. The smell of fresh oil wafted up from the chrome weapons. Looking up at Pa, Johnny asked, "For me?"

Pa gave Johnny a hard look. "Yer man enough now. I bought those fer ya a few months back. Was gonna wait fer your birthday, but now's as good as then. Pulled them out of the back closet just before you got home."

Johnny looked back and forth between Pa and the ray guns. "Can I put them on?"

"You know how. I haven't left you all the way untrained, right?"

Johnny nodded. With ginger care he cradled the first ray gun into his hands and stared at it. The chrome surface gleamed in the dim light of the oil lamp hanging from the ceiling. The guns felt heavier than he remembered from when he fired Pa's guns at tin cans on the fence. A smile crawled its way onto Johnny's face as he hefted the weight, felt the gun's curves, and imagined it hanging from his belt. The smooth lines of the ray guns, with the shining barrels jutting just beyond the tip of the body, looked different from what his father carried. Johnny flipped the guns over with care and noticed the model number engraved next to the trigger guard. They weren't the latest model, but new enough.

Johnny wondered how much of the farm's profits went into this gift, but having his own guns made him feel less a boy and more a man.

Pa broke in. "Night's old. I'm gettin' older. Get to it."

With a curt nod, Johnny set to strapping the holsters at his hips with his belt. Once they hung there, Johnny looked to his father for approval.

Pa pointed at the ray guns. "They need to hang a little lower for a quicker draw. Not that I want you in a spot where you need to draw quick, but still. Never know what might happen at the 'port."

Under Pa's directions, Johnny eventually got the ray guns in their proper place. Making careful mental notes about how to hang the guns, he smiled at his father. "Thank you."

Returning the smile, Pa said, "One more thing. A man walks taller with some spendin' money in his pocket." Pa pulled a cred stick from his worn, dust-covered shirt and tossed it to Johnny.

With a deft catch, Johnny admired the stick.

Pa said, "Ain't much, but it's enough. Just don't spend it all in one place or on one woman. Got that?"

Johnny nodded. "Yes, sir. Thank you."

With a glance at his empty whiskey glass, Pa said, "Now get to bed. You gotta big day ahead of ya, once yer mornin' chores are done."

Johnny nodded again with a large grin on his face. "Yes, sir. G'night, Pa."

Pa waved toward the door. "G'night, Johnny."

Once he finished chores the next day, Johnny raced through a bath and threw on the cleanest, nicest clothes he had. He sat on the porch shining his boots even though the dust from the road between the farm and spaceport would ruin the shine. He felt like looking his best as he left the farm for the day.

A shadow fell across the boots and shining cloth in his lap.

Johnny squinted up at the person standing over him. "Hello, Ma." The sun behind her head haloed through a few wild hairs that had escaped her tight bun. For a moment, he thought of her as a beautiful angel, come down from the stars to bring him a gift or a message.

Ma asked, "What do you think you're doing?" She hitched her gray skirts up and squatted next to him. Knocking a patch of dust from one of her white sleeves, she peered deep into Johnny's eyes.

Johnny winced. He had hoped to avoid this conversation. He'd been taught the truth, no matter what it turned out to be, was the best course of action. "Pa said I could go to the 'port once morning chores were done. Peter and Michael can handle the rest."

"The 'port, huh?" Ma's gaze never wavered.

Johnny couldn't bear to continue matching his mother's gaze and lowered his eyes. "Yes'm."

Ma pulled a handkerchief from somewhere in her dress and spit into it. She smeared the cloth across Johnny's head. "Your hair's a fright. I know you bathed. I can smell the soap on you. It's like you don't even know how to comb your own hair. How are you going to get along in the 'port if you can't even comb your own hair?"

Johnny squirmed just enough to let his mother know he didn't like the treatment, but not enough to mess up the job she did on his hair. Even though he didn't like being treated as if he were still a child, he let Ma do her duty and fuss over him. "I'll get along fine. I'm just goin' for the day. I'll be back before morning chores tomorrow."

Finished with her ministrations on his hair, she stepped back and inspected him like she had when he ran off for the first day of school, so many years ago. "Fine." She slipped a cred stick from beneath the collar of her dress. "Get something nice for your brothers while you're at the 'port."

Johnny looked incredulously at the cred stick. "How did you? Where did—"

Ma stomped her foot. "Never you mind. None yer business. Just get the boys something they'd like."

Slipping his boots on, Johnny smiled at his mother. "I will."

Johnny stood up and the chromed ray guns glinted in the late morning sunlight.

She looked down at his hips with a frown. "What're you doing with those?"

With pride, Johnny smiled and patted the guns. "Pa gave them to me last night."

"He did, huh? I suppose you're man enough for them around the farm. Why take them to the 'port?"

Johnny shrugged. He didn't have a solid answer for the question. He finally mumbled, "Most men have 'em in the 'port."

"Most of those men with guns on their hips are outlaws, mercenaries, lawmen, and completely dangerous sorts. You're not any of those. Leave your guns at home, Johnny. Don't take your guns to 'port."

Standing a little taller and straighter, Johnny said, "I'm a man now. Pa's taught me well. I can shoot as quick and straight as anyone else. I'm not worried."

"Well, you may not be worried, but your poor mother sure is. Promise me something?"

Johnny nodded.

"Keep your hands off those guns. You won't need 'em if you don't draw 'em."

He reached out and gave her a strong hug which she returned with a slight sniffle. Johnny said, "I promise. I'll keep my hands away from the guns. I'll be back tomorrow."

As they ended their embrace, Ma placed a warm kiss on Johnny's cheek. "See that you do just that. I expect you back here tomorrow to help the boys finish off the chores."

Johnny pulled his hat on tight and made his way toward the road at the edge of the farm. With some luck, he might be able to hitch a ride with someone going to the spaceport. He crested the last hill between the farmhouse and the road and looked back. His parents stood in the front yard, arms around each other, watching him walk away. He waved at them and moved on over the hill.

Where their farm road ended, and the main way connected, Johnny found Mr. Tucker in a truck waiting for him. The man called out, "I saw you coming. Need a lift to the 'port?"

Smiling at his fortune, Johnny raised a hand in greeting. "Yes, sir! I most certainly do."

Mr. Tucker motioned to the bed of the truck. "My dogs ride up front with me. Sorry, but no room for you in the cab. You can sit on the bales of hay in the bed if you like."

Johnny leaped into the bed of the truck and settled himself on the offered hay. "Thank you. This'll do just fine."

The truck took off with a lurch and a slight grinding of gears. Johnny held onto the bed's edge for balance and enjoyed the bumpy ride into the spaceport. Dust and straws of hay filled the air as the wind whipped past the truck's load. Johnny pulled his handkerchief from a back pocket and covered his mouth. He found an old farmer's tune on his lips and sang to himself through the cloth to pass the time as they crossed the open lands between the farms and the spaceport.

The air under the cloth became cloying, but he didn't mind the annoyance because quick ride to the spaceport beat walking in the heat any day. Johnny spent the ride wondering who he could meet with and how the conversations would go. He played out several chats with spaceship captains and other spacefarers in his mind. At the end of each imagined conversation, he held an offer for a job as a hand on a ship.

An hour later, Mr. Tucker pulled his truck into a spot near a trading post. Johnny jumped from the back of the truck with a broad grin on his face and waved to his neighbor. "Thanks to you, sir."

The older man leaned out of the window of the truck. "You take care."

Johnny touched the brim of his hat. "Don't you worry none, Mister Tucker. I'll be careful."

The rotten smell of spilled rocket fuel mixed with the choking exhaust of ground vehicles. Because it was a different smell than the cow patties and chicken coop back home, Johnny smiled. Even though the sulfuric stench of the fuel made it difficult to breathe, Johnny enjoyed every new experience in the 'port.

While most everything on his farm was made of wood with some aluminum, the steel and concrete of the spaceport's buildings stood tall and proud. Johnny did his best to flow with the crowds as he admired the buildings. His farm was covered in the familiar dull dust of this world, but everything here in the 'port seemed to be covered with the black soot of burned fuel, hiding behind brilliant colors of holographic signs advertising food, drink, pleasure houses, star faring equipment, and so much more.

Johnny looked past the grit and grime of the place and saw nothing but shining promise and a hopeful future.

As he neared the launch facilities, he craned his neck for the job boards that advertised need of crewmen on ships. He'd heard, from June's older brother, about the boards. Even though the trip was only a day-long affair, Johnny hoped to make some connections with off-world traders. He thought that if he made enough friends in the spaceport, he could arrange for a trip to another planet, to start up his own future. He initially considered going to the pads where rockets landed and launched but decided against the idea. The rockets were too spread out. He'd have to spend most of his day walking between them instead of actually meeting people.

Johnny stood in the middle of the flow of foot traffic, blocking a good portion of the sidewalk while looking for the job board. People grumbled as they pressed past him, but he didn't notice the occasional jostle or harsh look until a woman muttered, "Get out of the way, you stupid boy."

Anger flared for a moment in Johnny at being called a boy, but he pressed it down because she was right. He'd been blocking the path. As he stepped to the edge of the sidewalk, the familiar rumble of a shuttle launch filled the air. This time, Johnny felt the earth shift and shake through the soles of his boots.

A goofy grin spread on his face as he imagined the upcoming roar and thunderous explosions of the secondary engines from this close.

He craned his neck around looking for where the shuttle was going to rise above the close-knit buildings. He didn't have to wait long before the sleek bulk of the shuttle rose overhead in a graceful arc trailing a plume of burnt fuel. The deafening thunder of the shuttle's engines rattled Johnny's bones to the core.

Within a few seconds, the clamor intensified when the shuttles secondary engines ignited and shot the craft toward space. Johnny clapped his hands to his ears to keep some of the tumultuous blast out of his head, but still had a smile on his face as he pictured being aboard the shuttle and flying into orbit, and beyond.

When the boom of the shuttle's engines finally faded, Johnny looked around. No one around him seemed to have noticed the launch or cared to stop and stare at it. Life had moved on during the wondrous event. With a shrug to what the others seemed to feel was a boring event, he spotted a holo-sign floating in front of a building across the street. It proclaimed, "Eddie's Corner Bar" in bright lettering. From the rumors he heard, he expected to find most of the rocket captains drinking inside. The job board could wait. He figured making personal connections with captains would be best.

Johnny pressed through the crowd to the edge of the sidewalk. A truck slipped past and the wind from the vehicle buffeted Johnny. He put a hand to his hat to keep it from blowing away. The startling incident brought Johnny's attention back to the area around him. He looked up and down the street and found it clear.

He jogged to the bar's entrance. Johnny walked into the bar and stopped. The clatter of clay chips being tossed into the pot in the middle of a poker game punctuated the steady hum of spaceship captains wheeling and dealing with each other. The occasional laugh broke over the waves of noise.

The sweet smell of vaporizers filled the air. The mist of the vaporized drugs formed low-hanging clouds in the big room. Johnny tried to not choke on the odd smells but failed. His coughing fit drew the attention of several of the men and women sitting around the vaporizer table with hoses hanging from their mouths.

Johnny smiled an apology at them, and the group turned back to what they were doing. Waving away the puffs of mist around his head, Johnny moved to the bar and found an empty spot near the middle.

Raucous laughter erupted from a nearby table, and Johnny turned to see what the uproar was about.

A man scooped a large pile of red, white, and blue chips into a smaller collection with a smile on his face. The man said, "I think I'll just count up Burt's chips later. I know this one came from you, though. I'll set the special one over here on the side." He plucked up one of the blue chips with a flourish and gingerly set it aside.

Another man with a red face full of anger growled, "You don't have to be an ass about it, Gerald."

The rest of the table laughed at the exchange, and after a moment Gerald and Burt joined in with the cat calls and throwing of insults.

Johnny's attention on the nearby poker game was so intense, he barely heard the bartender call out.

Blinking away visions of playing in such a game with his own credits, Johnny spun to face the bar. "Sorry. What was that?" While he waited, the man twirled the ends of his lengthy mustache into fine points. The bartender wore a reflective suit of foil, to ward off blasts from ray guns, and had a gun hanging low on his right hip.

Johnny swallowed hard when he realized that if the bartender needed consistent protection from ray gun shots, then this must be a rougher establishment than he'd originally imagined.

With a roll of his eyes, the bartender repeated, "What ya want?"

Johnny reached into his pants pocket for one of his cred sticks and brushed his hand against one of his chromed ray guns. His mother's words asking him to leave the guns at home echoed in his mind. Laying the stick on the bar, he pressed it forward. "Whiskey, please." Johnny figured a little liquid fire would help him raise the courage to talk to a captain.

The bartender gave the young man a look up and down before turning to the collection of bottles against the back mirror.

A sudden case of the nerves overpowered Johnny. He put his shaking hands into the polished surface of the bar to keep them still, but the quiver in his knees couldn't be stopped. He swallowed hard and thought about running out. "Too late," he thought, "I have to go through with this. I have to find a way off this world."

The bartender placed a shot glass full of a dark, amber liquid on the bar in front of Johnny and slipped away the cred stick. After waving it front of the register, the bartender returned the cred stick to its resting place.

With shaking hands, Johnny mumbled, "Time to become a man," before picking up the glass with as much care as he could.

Johnny raised the glass toward his lips. The harsh smell of the liquor made Johnny choke and splutter across the top of the shot glass. Droplets of whiskey spilled from the small glass as the shake in Johnny's hands returned with even more force. Taking a deep breath to calm his nerves, Johnny pursed his lips and tried again to bring the whiskey up.

A stranger next to him laughed and snorted. "You can barely hold the glass, boy. I don't think you can hold the liquor."

Rage burned in Johnny's chest. He railed against being called "boy." He'd suffered under that moniker for all his days, and felt it was time to bring a stop to being "just a boy." His father, Mellissa, June, the other kids at the country schoolhouse, and even his own mother considered him a boy.

His pulse pounded heat into his ears, and his face flushed with embarrassment. Johnny swallowed the bile that had risen into the back of his throat. Taking a deep breath to settle his hands, he gently placed the mostly full shot of whiskey back on the bar. Grinding his teeth together, Johnny turned to face the stranger. With the anger and hatred of being made fun of coursing through his veins, he didn't really see the man. Only a vague shape stood in front of him.

The man squared his shoulders and stood with a wide stance.

Johnny finally focused in on the stranger.

He wore a vacuum suit, common to most spaceship crew, with his helmet and gloves clipped on his left hip. A battered ray gun made of brass and steel hung low on the other hip. Wrinkles and burn marks scarred the man's face from years of exposure to space radiation.

"What ya gonna do, *boy*?" The last word came out dripping full of scorn.

He had to prove himself a man before this veteran. Johnny would show the spacefarer that no one could push around the boldest and bravest man any captain would be proud to have aboard. After today, no one would call Johnny a boy again.

Johnny threw back his leather coat and reached for the chromed surface of his ray guns.

But the stranger drew faster and fired.

Before the blast of the shot registered in Johnny's mind, he fell to the floor and slowly rolled over to his back. The hole running through Johnny's chest burned like liquid fire, but no blood poured from the cauterized wound. The ray guns he'd managed to draw, but not fire, clattered to the plasti-steel floorboards. He feebly reached his hand out to recover his precious ray guns but couldn't bear to move enough to lay more than a fingertip on one of them.

A crowd quickly gathered around Johnny.

He looked up at the collection of worried, curious, and amused faces. Through tears streaming from his eyes, he thought he saw the poker players. Burt nudged Gerald and said something, but through the pain in his chest, Johnny couldn't focus on the words.

The world became blurry and started to fade into darkness around Johnny's prone form. The pain in his chest subsided but breathing became harder.

One figure parted from the gathered crowd and grew close. The brilliant light from a nearby holo advertisement cascaded through golden locks as the figure leaned closer. The angelic appearance of the woman hovering over him reminded him of Ma.

The woman's lips moved, but Johnny couldn't make out the words through the searing pain in his chest. She was clearly concerned and asking a question, but Johnny made little sense of what she wanted.

After struggling for a final breath, Johnny opened his mouth and his Ma's words of wisdom rattled out.

"Don't take your ray guns to 'port."

From the Author

Anyone that is a fan of Johnny Cash's music will clearly recognize the storyline of his song "Don't Take Your Guns to Town" in this tale. However, I've set it on a backwater planet in a science fiction setting. If you're familiar with Cash's life and family, you may recognize some of the location and character names as well. If Johnny were still alive, I hope he would appreciate my retelling of his story.

I've listened to plenty of Johnny Cash over the decades (and I still do), and this particular song has always reached out to me as a cautionary tale about being young and hot-headed. The main reason this song touches my heart is that I was extremely hot-headed in my youth, and I'm amazed I came out alive. Perhaps the mother's words from the song echoed in my mind on those many occasions where losing my temper would be a poor life choice. My never-ending thanks go out to Johnny for sharing his stories and music with the world.

About the Author

J.T. Evans writes fantasy and urban fantasy novels. He'll dabble with sci-fi and horror in short form as well. He is the former president of the Colorado Springs Fiction Writers Group and Pikes Peak Writers. When not writing, he secures computers at the Day Job, home brews great beers, and plays way too many tabletop games. Despite having his right arm amputated and reattached after a nasty car crash, he types faster than the average bear. The first two novels in his Modern Mythology series, Griffin's Feather and Viper's Bane, are out now. He's hastily working on more right now, and you can find out more about him at www.jtevans.net.

Where Loyalties Lie
by
Andrea L. Staum

Where Loyalties Lie

*T*he thin soup sloshed against the side of the battered tin cup as Donoghue shifted the thick canvas out of his way to step into the earthen tunnel. He hadn't been this far down the support line before. There were whispers of private dugouts for officers, but he hadn't believed until he saw a second, wooden door at the end of the rough-cut corridor.

The guard at the door reached for his pistol, as it was too confined for the rifle leaning against the wall. The man relaxed when he saw the food in Donoghue's hand. " 'Course they'd feed him." Dropping his hand to his side, the guard's knuckles knocked against the door.

A crack of light appeared, the shadowed face of Captain Perkins peered out. "I said not to interrupt."

The guard grunted. "Galley rat's here."

Donoghue pressed his shoulders back, straightening himself at the comment. He had put in his time at the main fire trenches just like the rest of them. Doctor Hilmar had ordered him to be away from the main fire line, to "assist his nerves". Donoghue wasn't good at operating the equipment, so the communications posts weren't for him. This left him with supply duty, and he was to help with rations this week.

He'd tried to get back up front, but even his fellow soldiers were split on whether he was lucky for having survived not one but two trench collapses, or incredibly cursed for those around him. Before he let his anger speak for him, he looked down at the cup and saw a lump bob in the thin broth as his hand shook. Maybe that was what the guard meant; rations had become hard to come by the last few months and the only fresh meat was from the rats that infiltrated the trenches.

"Who brought it?" Perkins asked as he opened the door wider, the light invading the passageway more. "Donoghue, isn't it?"

He nodded. "Yes, sir."

"Good. Come in."

Donoghue felt his bad leg lock up as he tried to move forward. With effort, he bent his wounded left knee so he was almost marching to the room. The tunnel floor was the driest surface he had stepped on since returning from the hospital, but still, each step felt like muck and mud were trying to root him in place. It reminded him too much of forcing his way past fallen comrades after his first battle and the subsequent shell bombardment. The feeling continued as he got closer to the door.

"Hurry up," the guard grumbled.

"It's all right, Townsend," said Perkins as he stepped aside, allowing Donoghue his first glimpse of the other occupant of the room. "We should be all right here. Two others should be joining us shortly. It sounds as if the shelling has stopped, why don't you check on that?"

"Sir?" Townsend asked, his hand once more resting on his pistol.

Donoghue entered the room, brushing against Perkins in the tight quarters.

The captain scowled at him before snapping at the guard. "If you must guard us, then do so from outside."

The door was shut before the guard could reply.

Donoghue had heard about the prisoner through the rumors that lingered down the line, but that didn't prepare him to see the strange man hidden in the dugout. He had expected the man to be shackled or have some form of bindings on him, but he was sitting calmly beside a table drinking from a canteen.

"Sorry, sir," Donoghue started to Perkins. "I was only told to bring food for the prisoner. I din't grab anything for you."

Perkins and the prisoner laughed. "No, Donoghue, the meal is not for our guest. It is for you."

"I've 'ad my portion for the day, sir."

"Well, then you can have mine," the stranger commented. Setting the canteen down, he leaned back in the chair and crossed his legs. He rested pale hands on his ankle as if trying to keep the leg from straightening

Donoghue had heard the man had come before the stand-to order in the morning. He had walked across No Man's Land without a word. The sentries hadn't even called out to him in case he was a ploy for some sniper to pick them off in the predawn haze. Then he had jumped down into their listening hole and asked to be taken prisoner.

Donoghue hadn't believed them when they said the man was dressed as a gentleman about to go to the theater, but now he couldn't deny it. The man didn't show any sign of being a soldier. His hands were cleaner than an officer's, no dirt imbedded under the nails, no scrapes or scars from constantly shifting around the trenches. Even the cuffs of his herringbone tweed trousers were immaculate. No one could have gone through the mud and corpses of No Man's Land and come out unblemished, but here was this strange prisoner nearly glowing in the lantern light.

"Oh, I do love when their minds race," he said, gesturing to the chair beside him. "Now will you sit and eat?"

"It's alright Donoghue. Lord Alaric is a friend."

"Friend that came across the line," Donoghue muttered.

"There are things you need to better understand before you pass judgement," Perkins stated and, with a hand in the small of Donoghue's back, pushed him forward. "There should be a couple others joining us soon, and they are aware of your purpose. They were harder to pull away from their positions."

Donoghue's steps remained strained as he approached the prisoner. He pressed a hand to his forehead as an aura began to form at the corner of his sight, narrowing his vision. The headache he had been living with for the past few months intensified until he forced himself to the chair and leaned forward to let the nausea settle.

"He is recently back from hospital," Perkins stated, opening the door for two others to enter.

Donoghue looked up and recognized Farley, a telephone operator who had been complaining about a wire repair when he picked up rations that morning. The other was unfamiliar, but looking up to his shadowed eyes sent another wave of nausea through Donoghue.

He grabbed the soup cup hoping the liquid would help settle the nausea, but the chunk struck the back of his mouth and he spit it all back into the cup.

The prisoner pushed a canteen toward him without looking his direction.

"Lord Alaric," gasped the operator, and he fell to his knees with a bowed head.

"Get up Farley," Perkins ordered.

"Is it time?" asked the fourth man.

"After this evening's stand-to. Tonight will be different than the rest," Alaric replied. "That should give you enough time."

Donoghue forced himself to sit up in the chair. His hands shook as he took the canteen. His fingers refused to grip the cap, and he dropped it back to the tabletop. His heart pounded in his ears, and the pain hadn't subsided. The aura was replaced with a haze. With each blink he saw a different face showing from the other men in the room.

Except for the prisoner. While Alaric no longer looked as flawless as he had when Donoghue entered the room, he maintained his transformed appearance, unlike the others. The new sharp-edged jaw, with thin cheeks and black eyes set too close to his beak-like nose, was the same each time he looked at the man. The immaculate suit hung threadbare and limp from Alaric's shoulders and his collar bone was visible beneath the white dress shirt that had looked bleached and starched, but now showed stains from sweat and dirt.

"Perkins, I thought you said these were the chosen ones." Lord Alaric turned his gaze to Donoghue.

Unable to look away from Alaric's now orange-ringed pupils, Donoghue found his limbs tingling, and the pain eased. The pounding subsided to a dull ache behind his temple. He was able to look at Perkins. The captain had the same gaunt look the prisoner did now. The other two were worse, but they hadn't appeared in the best of health before as months in the trenches would do that to any man. Their thin frames cast twisted shadows behind them, and, if they hadn't blocked the only exit, he would have been on his way back to the mess.

"I received the list from the High Emissary himself," said Perkins.

Alaric pursed his thin lips, and cracks formed. "You three go ahead and spread the word to our brethren. I will confer with this confused foundling."

Farley was about to protest until Perkins shoved him toward the door. "I will explain it all to you. We have our orders."

Waiting until their voices faded beyond the outer canvas, Donoghue tensed his legs, ready to sprint out after them. Before he could raise himself from his seat more than an inch, he was pressed back into place. He hadn't seen Lord Alaric move, but the man now stood behind him with claw-like hands set upon his shoulders. There was no pressure bearing down on him, but he knew that if he tried to move, he could be easily broken.

"What is your name?" Alaric asked, his voice steady and compelling.

"Owen Donoghue."

"Wrong. What is your name?" he asked again, tapping his finger against Donoghue's temple.

There hadn't been much force, but stars speckled Donoghue's vision like he had been punched. He tried to focus on the question, and he heard a faint whisper of a memory calling out a name he did not recognize. He answered with what he felt was truth. "I told you, Owen Donoghue."

"Tsk, you're a stubborn one. Your mother must've forgotten where she left you," Alaric sighed. His finger tapped against Donoghue's temple three more times, each causing an increasingly jarring pain.

Donoghue tried to force himself from the chair to escape the pain, but the prisoner held him in place.

A memory skipped through. He was looking down at his crib, where a babe was wrapped tight. He was moving closer to the babe, and then he was lying on his back, looking up at a silver-haired woman who was not his mother. The babe shifted beside him a moment before the woman snatched it and was gone. When she was out of view, the memory was gone, and the pressure faded.

"Ah, I see. You were one of Zerelda's brood. A fine warrior she was. Fine and foolish. No wonder you don't remember who you are."

"I don't know what you're talkin' about," Donoghue spat as he tried to twist away from the creature's grip. He was sure now that some devil was in the room with him. It was the only possible reason for the impossible strength that held him in place.

Alaric laughed and switched so his left hand was on Donoghue's right shoulder before coming around to face him. He bowed at his waist so that he was looking into Donoghue's eyes. "No, sweet foundling, no devil be I. And no human be you. We are cut from the same cloth. If you'd only accept the truth of it."

Donoghue brought his arm up and tried to brush Alaric's arm away. "Get off me. I don't know what you are, but you and I are not alike."

The creature stepped back, his hands out to his sides, palms facing toward Donoghue. "Zerelda always knew where to put her brood for them to be raised stubborn. One of your kin nearly broke my arm before he saw the light."

"My mother's name was Katie Donoghue," Donoghue cried. Tears slid from his eyes as they refused to look away from the creature before him.

"Oh well, of course she was. That doesn't mean she birthed you." Alaric raised his right hand to stop any protest. "I'm sure Katie Donoghue had a strapping lad born January 23, 1896, but that boy was not you. You just saw when you replaced him. The real Owen Donoghue is likely a servant to the king by now, if he survived that is." Slowly, Lord Alaric brought his hand to the inside pocket of his coat and pulled a small, tattered book out. The pages were frayed and a few slipped from the binding as he paged through. "Yes, here we are. Oh. Sadly, he did not go past age five, when he got too close to a water sprite who wanted him for her own. It did not last long." He sucked air in through his front teeth in a hiss of disapproval. "Someone's nanny wasn't watching closely."

Donoghue shook his head, trying to shake the words he was hearing from his mind. Even unrestrained by Alaric, he found he could not move from the chair.

"No, you are really Emrik, son of Zerelda, the last great general of his highness's forces."

"There are no women generals."

"Not among these mortals, there certainly aren't, but haven't you figured it out foundling?"

"Stop callin' me that!" Donoghue finally found the strength to push himself up from the chair, but his legs were weak beneath him, and he only made it a couple steps before falling to his knees.

"Then I will call you my brother, even though only your mother grants you any respect from me. Haven't you figured it out? Haven't there been instances throughout your life you cannot explain? Times you should not have escaped unscathed, and yet, here you stand?"

"Well, they say the Irish are lucky."

"This isn't the luck o' the Irish you have, Brother. This is the power of the Fae."

"Fairy stories? You want me to believe fairy stories?"

"No stories are these, Brother. This is truth. This is your truth. Your Katie Donoghue—mum if you prefer—may have told you tales of a changeling taking your place if you didn't behave, but she didn't know she already had one on her lap."

Laughter rolled up from Donoghue's lungs like dry heaves. He hadn't heard anything so absurd in a long time, and there was very little to laugh at on the front lines. Mirth was foreign to his body, and he allowed the first ones to leave his lips.

Lord Alaric kicked him in the stomach to stop the laughter. "Do not make me out to be a fool, foundling. Whether you believe it or not, you are one of us, and you will fight by our side."

"I've been doin' my fightin'."

"Not against your proper enemy." He kicked out once more, but Donoghue twisted out of the way. "You clearly see the truth. The recognition was there when the glamor fell, Brother. Why then won't you understand who you are? What you are? You want to fight and die beside these inferior humans? We have an opportunity unlike any we have ever seen, foundling. This is what we have been waiting for."

"You want me to betray the men I've been fighting with?"

"It is your purpose! Why do you think we have been infiltrating their homes for centuries? Why else give our younglings to them to raise other than to lull them into false security? They have already torn themselves apart. How long have you been stuck in these godforsaken trenches with no movement and only a few shots fired for the sake of saying you did something with your day? Come, Brother, they have lined themselves up for the slaughter. Perkins and the others are already getting into position, and I assure you there are others of our kind on the other side doing the same. By midnight tonight we will have the greatest victory the Fae have seen in millennia, and it will hardly cost us because they will never expect it."

"And then what?"

Alaric crouched down before him. "Then we move on to the next front. The presumably lucky survivors of a desperate surge to break the stalemate will be dispersed to other companies, and again we will find our sleeping brethren and wake them to their potential. Once we conquer their ranks, we will turn them on themselves and return to the home front to finish off the humans."

"You're mad if you think you can get away with it," Donoghue said, reaching for the chair to balance himself.

"But we have, Emrik, we have. You are hardly the first one to find the truth hard to grasp. That's why I was sent. You gave Hilmar quite the trouble when he tried to trigger your abilities. It seems he only managed to give you a headache."

"Doctor Hilmar?" Donoghue had thought the headache was a result of the shelling and gunfire. He realized now that they had started shortly after he had arrived at the hospital. He remembered waking from strange dreams and finding Doctor Hilmar observing him from the foot of his bed. It had kept him from sleeping easily, and he saw that others received the same attention, but none of them seemed to have adverse reactions to any treatment. They had willingly gone back to their units whereas he had wanted more time to recover.

Alaric nodded. "We know our kind when we see them even when they don't know themselves. Sometimes they can be a liability in such a state. I can't have you warning those men out there, even if they would believe you. No, if I let you out there with this new knowledge, they will likely lock you up for your own good until they can send you back to hospital, or someone may shoot you to stop your madness."

"So, your goin' to keep me in here for the night?"

Alaric shook his head and pulled a matchbox from his pocket. "No, I'm taking you to your proper home. If you won't fight with us tonight, you will fight with us at the next battle. Once your memory is put to rights, of course." He drew out a single match.

"You say I'm the madman."

Alaric slid the match across the striking surface. A small flame jumped to life and the lantern dimmed in the dugout. Alaric drew a circle in the air with the flaming match, the smoke hanging long enough to show where its path had been traced. He traced a second circle, bigger than the first, and plunged his hand through the center to grab Donoghue's coat collar. He pulled Donoghue forward and the dugout fell away from them, and they now knelt in a wooded glen surround by stones.

There were other men, farther afield; the uniforms of several nations recognizable among the trees.

"You will fight for us because you are now a deserter of their army. If they see you without our protection, you will be court martialed and more than likely killed. I mean who would believe you were abducted by fairies?"

Before Donoghue could respond, he was alone in the center of the stone circle. He made his way from it to gain his bearings. The woods looked familiar to him, but the dulled tones made him feel as if he were walking with a veil over his eyes. He passed one man, in a French uniform, looking out from inside a hollowed tree with wide eyes. The man repeated himself over and over, but Donoghue couldn't understand his words. He had seen that stare among the shell-shocked patients at the hospital. This man was beyond any help Donoghue could give.

"Owen!"

Looking up, Donoghue saw a nearly recognizable face staring down at him from some upper branches of a young oak. "Seamus Walsh?"

"It *is* you," the man said and climbed down to the lower boughs. "Oh, it is good to see a familiar face for once."

"Seamus, I heard you were killed last month."

The joy of in Seamus' eyes flickered out and his tone was low when he next spoke. "A month? It's only been a month? It's felt like three at least. My poor mum must know by now then."

Donoghue nodded. "Mine was the one who wrote me about it."

Seamus jumped down to face him. "Well, then there's really no reason to protest if I'm already a dead man, is there?"

"What do you mean?"

As he looked, on Seamus's chin elongated as his cheeks hollowed. His eyes lost their brown hues for burnt orange. "Been fighting the change. Didn't want to believe it. Fight against those who raised us? Part of the fairy world?" he laughed. "Sounded loony. Then to see them actually do it. Take out the entire company so quickly. I wasn't going to be a part of it. Watched my captain get torn apart by a grogoch. Mum told me about them, but I didn't believe. Of all people we should've believed."

"Why? Because someone told us that's what we are?

"Makes sense though. Remember that time you fell from that cliff when we visited the beach as boys? You nearly got swept to sea."

"Yeah, but I've always been a good swimmer and the tide was with me."

"But it wasn't. You should've hit those rocks, but it was like you floated past them. You even said there was a woman in the clouds."

Donoghue stepped back from Seamus. He had forgotten about the shining woman with silver hair that seemed to sweep him past the rocks. He hadn't been afraid when she had appeared and wrapped him in her arms. She had whispered something to him that he had never understood. "You'll have your time soon enough, Emrik."

Seamus shuddered and fell to the ground. He convulsed as his body contorted, and the smoothness of his body sharpened, and he began to look more like Perkins and Farley had. "Yes!" he screamed. "I'll fight for my kind!"

Once the words left his cracked lips a shadow surrounded him, and he was gone from the woods.

Donoghue stared where his boyhood friend had been. They would have their soldiers, he realized. If he didn't go willingly, they would make sure he had no life to return to should he escape the glen. He had seen one way of escape was to relent, but if he were like them, couldn't he do as they did?

Pulling out his own matchbox he counted five sticks left. He didn't know fairy magic and had only witnessed it once, but if he were truly the son of a general, then he should be powerful. His mind thought of returning to his home but knew it would be short lived freedom as he would be considered a deserter, just as Alaric had said. No, there was only one place he needed to be. If he could get there, he would know they were telling him the truth, and the disfigurement wasn't some sort of ploy to trick humans to fight for them. If he returned, he could determine where his loyalties lay.

Donoghue struck the first match and drew the circle of smoke in the air along with the second. His mind focused on the dugout, and he could hear faint voices coming through the portal, but before he could try and step through the wind blew the ring away. Gritting his teeth and concentrating harder he struck the second match. A flicker of light came from the tunnel, and he saw a startled Perkins and Alaric through the opening. Perkins drew his pistol but before he could fire the wind destroyed the circle once more.

A hand covered his before he could strike the third one. Surprised, Donoghue looked up into the wide-eyed Frenchman's face, who shook his head emphatically. There were others surrounding him now. The lost souls that hadn't determined who they were meant to fight for.

"Not there." The words were not French or English and Donoghue realized those around him were all Fae, but not those like Alaric. These were the ones who had known what they were and still fought for the humans.

"Then where?"

"The High Emissary. He will tell you the proper path."

"He's the one who gave the list to Alaric."

"He is the one Alaric stole the list from. Alaric is forcing changelings to do his bidding instead of allowing them to come by it naturally," said one in a Russian uniform.

"Then you don't want war with humans?"

"Child, we are always at war with the humans," laughed the French fae. "We just prefer more finesse than a bloodbath in the trenches. Alaric has trapped us here to keep us from reporting him, but you can do what we can't. He didn't expect you to have real powers."

"I don't know where the High Emissary is."

"Yes, you do," replied the Russian. "How do you think the monarchy remains in place without a little glamour to aid it?"

"You mean the king wishes to eradicate his people?"

"Why else enter this war?" asked the French fae. "We don't need to do as Alaric says and destroy the men in the trenches, they'll do that themselves. We just need to be in the places of power for when they don't come back. Now think of the king and you will find the High Emissary."

His hands shook more as he drew the third match. It was harder to focus on someone that he had only seen in photographs. The portal glowed and he saw the king seated at his desk. A nod of approval toward Donoghue was followed by a gesture to come forward. The portal grew to the size of a door, and he stepped through.

"Welcome Emrik, son of Zerelda. I have been eagerly awaiting your return to us." The king stood.

Instinctively Donoghue kneeled. "You have?"

The king motioned for him to stand. "Of course. I've been waiting for my next general to come to power, and here you are before me."

Donoghue furrowed his brow as he stepped closer.

"Alaric's methods of accelerating this conflict prove that I need someone with a level head. Changelings of high-ranking Fae have been watched over by loyal subjects for many years. Your mother did so until her unfortunate demise, then the task went to others. Now you can assist me in ensuring our victory without the careless antics of Alaric. After all, you already enlisted in the fight before you knew the true purpose. We are here to win a war, not just a battle."

From the Author

What if the Fey were at war with mankind? How would they go about it? Would they wait out the shorter life span on humans or use mans' own bloodlust against them? If so, how?

Those questions led "Where Loyalties Lie." A hybrid strategy of infiltration and directing the course of history started to form. Then it evolved to even more questions. What if you don't know you're a soldier for the other side? Where do your loyalties lie? Is it with everything that you grew up with and know or do you accept what a captured officer tells you? Who is the real enemy? These are the answers Donoghue has to find while fighting in the trenches of the Great War.

About the Author

Andrea L. Staum is the author of *Rogue's Kiss*, the *Dragonchild Lore* series, *The Attic's Secret* novella, and *Scattered Dreams* short story collection. She's a mama, an amateur runner, and somehow manages to find time to write. She lives in south central Wisconsin with her husband, son, and their overlords...err...cats.

Facebook: https://www.facebook.com/AuthorAndreaLStaum

Twitter: @DragonchildLore

Website: https://dragonchildlore.wordpress.com/

The Killing Tree
by
Shannon Lawrence

The Killing Tree

*T*he bump and rumble of the wooden wagon wheels soothed Martha, even as the motion worked at her tailbone. After two months and eight days on the trail, she'd become accustomed to the wear on her bones. Ache was her permanent companion on this trek to a new life in the west. She'd heard rumors that women's lives were different in the west, that they could hold positions of power in the community. At the very least, there were ways for women to earn a living. In addition, she would not be judged for being a single mother, as for all they knew her husband had been lost on the trail, rather than the truth of his having abandoned her, pregnant and with a toddler.

It had cost her everything she owned, save her son and a milking cow, to purchase the wagon, supplies, and the two oxen currently pulling her wagon. The cow strolled behind the wagon, connected to it by a rope. Every once in a while, she lowed to make sure Martha knew she was still back there.

Little James sat beside her, large eyes taking in the landscape with a toddler's fascination. He babbled here and there, some words clear, others nonsense. Martha gathered the reins in one hand so she could caress his soft, sweet cheek. He smiled up at her.

Inside her, the child she was sure would turn out to be a younger sister for James, churned. Martha had cut things close but was determined to arrive in Cripple Creek before the baby came. Still three-and-a-half months out, she had time. The trek should only be another month or two, barring trouble on the trail.

A small creek meandered by the deeply embedded wagon ruts. With the sun getting low in the sky, Martha decided this was as good a time as any to stop. She pulled her team up at a spot several feet from a large tree, its weak, heat-dried leaves sparse on the many branches. The presence of the creek should have meant lush, green leaves.

When she roused James with a gentle nudge of his shoulder, he yawned with a squeak, stretched, and sat up. He'd lost some weight on their trek, but Martha knew baby fat went away in these early years, so she wasn't sure whether it was the usual weight loss of early childhood or if it was the strict rationing of their food. She'd certainly lost weight, but not an unreasonable amount. Her belly grew at a rapid rate now, heedless of the limited rations. She hadn't killed any game in over a week, and they were overdue for fresh meat. She'd need to hunt tomorrow, possibly remaining in this camping spot for another day to get the meat processed. It wouldn't hurt to wash and change out their clothing either.

Smoke rose in the distance, a dark column against a lightly blushing sky. A wagon train. She took a moment to wonder if this was one of the ones that had turned her down for being a woman alone. They'd told her it was inappropriate, that she needed a man to survive this trail. She looked forward to proving them wrong.

Martha put James to work finding the pans and preparing the fire. He couldn't light it, but he could gather kindling from nearby. She got the cow and the oxen ready for the night by tying them to the tree in a spot that would allow them to drink freely from the creek, then she checked the bucket hanging from the wagon. The butter inside looked ready. A quick stir with her finger showed it to be nice and thick. There'd be butter with dinner tonight.

The evening progressed well, and James went down for bed in the wagon without argument, much to Martha's relief. She doused the fire and snuggled up with him to keep them both warm. Luckily, he was still small enough his curled form fit above the bulk of her belly.

His soft breaths helped her relax, and she soon fell asleep beside him, rifle at her back.

Martha awakened, her bladder sending an urgent signal for relief. She unclasped James' hand from her nightgown with care and climbed ponderously from the wagon. Night bugs chirped around the camp, the creek chuckling beyond the oxen. Her footfalls were loud in the night, and she made haste toward the spot she'd marked out earlier.

Her back had cramped up, tweaking as she walked. She stopped to stretch. A series of pops brought a measure of relief. Nights like this, she pondered sleeping on the grass instead of in the wagon. There'd be rocks, but it had to be more comfortable than the hard, wooden surface. It always circled back to safety. At least in the wagon she had a measure of security and distance from the wildlife.

Something moved in the opposite direction of the animals. She felt the movement, heard a crackle in the grasses. The animals woke up and snorted, alerting her to their unease.

Martha backed toward the wagon, eyes straining against the darkness. The slivered moon shed only sparse light on her surroundings. Shadows moved but did not coalesce into anything recognizable.

Her back hit the sharp corner of the wagon. She gasped at the abrupt pain shooting through her shoulder blade like a bolt of lightning through her nerves. Freezing, she strained her ears for any sound.

Nothing stirred. Nothing made a sound. Even the crickets and other night insects had stopped their chirping.

Martha held her breath.

One of the oxen huffed, followed by a quiet snort.

Steps crackled through the grass, quickening, running.

Martha clasped her hands at her throat as the steps approached. She still couldn't make out anything useful in the dark.

The steps stopped.

Hairs on the back of Martha's neck stood up. Fear kept her glued to the spot. If she moved, it might pounce. Whatever *it* was.

She'd been warned of Indians on the plains. Newspaper articles spoke of savage men murdering settlers, stealing their goods. Sometimes even taking women and children captive. But a man she'd spoken to for advice had told her these reports were greatly exaggerated. While there was a possibility of danger, he'd said most of them wanted to be left alone and would, in turn, leave her alone. A single wagon held very little interest.

Maybe that man, as knowledgeable as he'd seemed with his sun-squinted eyes and rough skin, had been wrong. Maybe they'd circled her camp, intending to murder Martha and James in their sleep, and she'd ruined their plans by getting up to pee.

Gathering her courage, she moved sideways slowly, the cloth of her dress snagging along the rough wood of the wagon. Even with her back to its hard surface, she felt exposed. Anything could come at her from the front, the sides, or even underneath. Goosebumps spread up her legs at the thought of something grabbing her, and she picked up her pace, racing around to the back.

Getting inside proved to be a struggle. It was always hard with the orb of her stomach before her, but her panic didn't lend itself to graceful movement. She scrambled at the lip of the wagon. A fingernail ripped into the quick, followed by another, but she ignored the sharp flashes of pain and fought to get inside. The air at her back was a physical sensation of exposure to whatever might lurk in the dark.

Panting, she landed on the floor of the wagon, shielding her stomach and taking the brunt of the hit on her side. Her elbow smarted. She hurried to close the canvas cover, pulling the drawstrings and securing them. She crawled to her son, his soft breaths reassuring her that he still slept.

The footsteps began once more, this time coming all the way up to the wagon. Breaths puffed on the other side of the thick canvas from her. Had the canvas been lighter, she would have felt the air on her face. Something scratched at the wood in insistent repetition.

Martha's heart pounded in her chest. She fought to control her breaths, to silence them. Without conscious thought, she moved her hand over her mouth, breaths from her nose warming her index finger. She choked back the whimpers threatening to escape.

What do I do?

She couldn't leave. Without her oxen, the wagon was useless, a boulder on the prairie. The canvas wouldn't keep anyone or anything out for long. She grabbed her shotgun and pulled it toward her, the feel of the cool metal soothing against her palm.

The breathing moved away from her, toward the back of the wagon, the soft crackle of crushed grass accompanying it.

Darkness made everything worse. The sealed canvas kept even the scant moonlight out, and there was too little of that outside to cast a shadow so Martha could see what stalked her. She yearned for light. They already knew she was here, so the light shouldn't make it worse, and it would help to be able to see what she faced. She felt her way to the front where she kept the tinder box. It proved easy to find, her hand landing on the hard surface of the lid. The candle lantern stood beside it.

Martha pulled these to her and shifted to face the rear of the wagon, eyes glued to the canvas. It remained closed tight. For now.

Working quickly, her fingers accustomed to the motions and the items in the box, she took out her flint and steel. She opened the port of the lantern and struck steel against flint repeatedly. Each spark sent out a pallid light, exposing the back of the wagon. Martha switched her eyes between the lantern and the canvas, desperate for a spark to take.

The canvas bulged inward, something slim and dark extending through the slit.

Martha hurriedly struck the flint again, staring at the canvas. She couldn't tell what had been stuck through. A rifle? No, it appeared to come to a sharp point, closed and solid. It was rounded, so not a knife. It was dark and reflected each spark.

The candle took with a soft *puff*, the smell of fire and wax rising. Martha closed the glass and thrust the lantern toward the rear of the wagon.

The pointed object withdrew, as did the presence pressed against the outside. The canvas flattened.

Candle smoke drifted within the confines of the wagon, a pleasant smell now, but she knew it would become irritable to their lungs and eyes after a while. She had to figure out what was going on before then.

She considered her options. Without being able to see outside, she couldn't tell what time it was, or how long until morning. No one would be traveling at night, which meant no rescuers could happen across them. She was good with her weapons but had no clue how many awaited her out there. If she fired the gun, the camp she'd seen evidence of in the distance might be able to hear it, but she had no idea how likely they were to investigate, and they were too far to help her in time. As far as she could figure, her options were to try to wait them out or to go out blasting, but neither plan necessarily kept her and James alive until daylight.

Here she was assuming daylight meant safety, but she had no way to know for sure if that was a possibility. There might be more out there by daylight. The chances of anyone rolling up on them even then were spare, as she'd seen no nearby smoke back the way they'd come. They'd have daylight to work by, while she'd be trapped in the dark, vulnerable wagon.

Outside, one of the oxen snorted, huffing out a breath then lowing. The other two animals joined it, stamping their feet. The sounds became increasingly stressed and frantic. She couldn't let them kill the animals, or she and James would be stranded, which meant death just as surely as tangling with whatever stalked her outside this wagon.

The question remained what exactly awaited her out there. People or creatures. Surely, people would have spoken by now. Made some sort of sound. But she wasn't aware of a wild animal that would behave this way.

A meaty *thunk* sounded, followed by a horrendous high-pitched call from one of the animals.

A spike of adrenaline shot through her. Time to take action. If she stayed in here to wait things out, everything would be lost. She wrapped a leather thong around her upper arm and slid a knife through it, the cold of the metal radiating through her night dress. She maneuvered herself around James, still sleeping, bless him. She allowed herself a second to move a curl off his forehead.

James let out a small sigh and rolled onto his side, the curl flopping back onto his forehead.

The adrenaline had awakened the baby, and it kicked.

Her babies were depending upon her. Only her. No one would show up and save them. Through the difficulties of this journey, she had never felt as alone and frightened as she did now. If something happened to her, they would both die before they had a chance to live. Leaving James in the wagon would take all her strength, but it had to be done.

Strength flooded through her, and she moved to the back of the wagon with determination, dragging the lantern with her. She didn't need a husband or a wagon train. She'd never need a man again. This was her moment to prove she knew what she was doing and could take care of not only herself, but her babies, as well.

Loosening the tie of the wagon cover, she eased it open, taken aback by the bitter darkness outside. Her eyes had adjusted to the lantern light, rendering her blind to anything beyond the sallow light that now crept from the wagon. She climbed down as delicately as she could, set the rifle and the lantern at her feet, then tightened the cover as much as possible from the outside in hopes that James would remain safe inside.

Breathing became a struggle, her heart pounding against her ribs. The baby seemed to dance in rhythm with her pulse, kicking and rolling. Her stomach visibly shifted. Normally, she would have placed a hand on her belly to calm the baby, but one hand held the rifle, the other the lantern. She'd just have to do this with the tiny acrobat having her way.

Martha moved around the wagon, eyes straining into the darkness toward where the animals were tied. The cow moved at the edge of the light, and Martha set the lantern on the ground, figuring this was as good a place as any. Its light kept her eyes from adjusting all the way, and it was better as a beacon by the wagon than blocking her vision going forward, though she yearned to carry it with her, wooed by the false security its warm glow offered.

The crisp grass crunched under her feet. She stopped.

The sound continued, coming from all around her.

There arose a clicking from somewhere beyond the lantern's glow, and she stepped forward, ensuring the light stayed behind her. She could now make out the tree to which she'd tied the animals, its bare branches a looming threat in the dark.

The tree looked strange. Lumpy. Large shapes roosted around the branches. She took another step toward the animals, rifle held before her. The cow stared dumbly in her direction, eyes rolling. One of the oxen stumbled sideways, bumping its partner. Its mouth foamed, and it swayed. The other ox strained backward, pulling at the lead keeping it tied to the trunk.

"Shhh, it's okay," she whispered. "It's just me."

They all now faced the tree, yanking at the ropes. It didn't appear they'd even heard her voice. An ox pawed at the ground.

She continued forward until she stood among the frightened animals. The foaming ox's side shone, and she touched it. Her fingers came away dark and sticky with blood. She had no way to tell how bad the injury might be, but if the animal was still standing, she had to hope it could pull the wagon.

If she could get them untied and hooked up to the wagon, they could leave. At least they'd be moving targets. Speaking of which, where had the attackers gone? She stared up into the tree, but the shapes didn't move. They must be shadows or odd branches she hadn't noticed when it was still light out.

A twig broke with a snap, and she jerked around, the momentum of her belly taking her too far, almost making her fall. She corrected her position, sighting down the rifle, which she raked across the shadows. Light flashed near the wagon, reflecting off a moving surface until the figure disappeared under the wagon.

"Stay away from there!" she yelled. "Come this way."

But it was gone, swallowed by the darkness beyond the lantern's reach.

A branch creaked above her. She peered up, directly into a chitinous face, the features as black as the face itself. Three eyes clustered on the narrow face, which extended out on a long, slim neck that looked to be armored. The creature appeared to be nearly her height, with a hunched, rounded back. It had two legs firmly grasping the branch beneath it, with two more hanging limp at its belly. A long, scaly arm reached forward, a spike extended from a finger, elongating toward her. This was what she'd seen breaching the canvas of the wagon.

Repulsion filled her at the sight, an instinctual fear taking grip. She stepped backward, this time stumbling over a twisted root that had grown out of the hard-packed earth. Before hitting the ground, she dropped the gun and put her hands behind her, trying to cushion the fall. Even so, the impact rocketed up her spine, through her belly, and into her head.

Gasping, she looked up at the creature. The spike continued in her direction, even though the creature remained in the same position, the tip thinning from the initial width, just thicker than her thumb, down to maybe a pinkie's width. She scrambled away, but the spike moved faster. It reached her stomach, nudging against the bulge. She slapped at the spike, but it didn't budge, so she wrapped a hand around it and tried to push it sideways to no avail. It was hard and smooth, unbendable.

The baby kicked, raising her belly to the spike, impaling Martha's skin upon its tip for a second. A quick, hot pain shot from the cut, moving outward in a wave of dull, sick hurt. A dark stain appeared on the white of her sleep clothes, spreading slowly.

The spike withdrew.

She couldn't tell if it was the branch or the creature that creaked.

More creaking sounded, followed by clicking. The things in the tree stirred, shifting closer to the creature that had poked her. One leapt onto the same branch as the first and shot out its own spike.

This time she wouldn't allow it to get to her.

She grabbed the gun from the ground, pulled the right hammer back, and squeezed the forward trigger. The gun bucked against her shoulder, and the shot went wide. She pulled the left hammer back and squeezed the rear trigger, this time hitting the second creature. It screeched and dropped from the branch, making a sickening crunch upon impact with the ground. It didn't move.

The others moved faster now, this time away from her rather than toward her. They leapt higher into the tree, the branches bowing with their weight. Though thin, they had to weigh more than James.

With the gun now useless, she used it to help her stand. If the creatures stayed high in the tree long enough, she could get the animals loose. She pulled the knife from the thong and forced herself to go to the tree, where she rested the shotgun against the gnarled trunk. The knots came loose easily, but now she had to decide whether to keep the knife out and leave the shotgun against the tree or put the knife away and bring the shotgun with her, leaving her virtually unarmed.

The tree filled with chittering, high pitched and terrifying. She had the urge to cover her ears but resisted it.

Making the decision, she slid the knife back into the thong and grabbed the shotgun.

Eager to get away from the tree, the animals came with her easily. Every step she and the frightened animals took was loud, crackling thunder, covering up the possibility of hearing movement from the insect-like creatures hunting them.

She pulled them along rapidly, to the front of the wagon, hitching them as quickly as she could, despite the limited visibility. The lantern's light from beside the wagon caused dancing shadows to strain out ahead of the animals, their bodies blocking light from where her hands worked frantically. The chorus of cicada-like chittering assaulted her ears, forcing extra panic by virtue of the frantic sound. Her back itched with the feeling that at any moment one of the creatures might come up behind her.

Martha got the first ox hooked up with little trouble, but the hoop on the yoke of the second got caught. She struggled against it, panting with exertion, the baby shoving at her from the inside. Something crunched beyond the oxen, on the other side of the wagon, and she froze, though her stomach did not.

When there was no further movement, she continued, finally getting the hoop free to slide it up the yoke. She attached the yoke to the wagon tongue then checked both oxen to be sure they were tightly hooked up, all the while wondering when the creatures would attack.

Rather than take the extra step of bringing her cow to the rear of the wagon, she tied her to the front, hopeful the old girl would figure out how to stay out from under both the oxen and the wheels.

She grasped the gun with her left hand and pulled the knife out with her right before heading back toward the lantern and the rear of the wagon. Why the creatures hadn't left the tree yet was a mystery. Were they really that afraid of the gun? She could still make out the vague shadows at the edge of the lantern's light, chittering in the branches. Were there fewer now? She couldn't tell.

With her knife hand, she reached for the lantern, so close now to the rear of the wagon and possible safety. She needed to get inside the wagon to completely secure the rear in order to ensure none of the creatures climbed inside as she rode off. James would be back there, exposed and alone; she had to take precautions.

Just as her hand brushed the lantern, something cold and hard punctured the back of her ankle, sending her to her knees as sharp pain shot up her leg. The cold withdrew, but the pain increased, now burning white-hot.

Keenly aware of how vulnerable she was, Martha scrambled forward, once more trying to reach the lantern. Maybe it was the light keeping the creatures up in the tree instead of approaching her. Her middle finger hooked around the handle, her other fingers still clutching the knife. The lantern was heavy, pulling painfully at her finger.

Just as she got to her feet, it stabbed her once again, this time through the meat of her thigh. She didn't fall, instead yanking her leg sideways to disengage from the spike. She stumbled forward, leg and ankle holding, and broke into a sprint. Hot pain lanced across the skin of her back, but she didn't falter.

Her hands were full when she reached the back of the wagon. She set everything at her feet, the lantern warming her toes. It took a moment to get the back open, and there was her baby boy, still sleeping, just visible in the scant light the lantern provided. A moment's relief flooded through her at the sight of his chest moving peacefully up and down in the flicker of lamplight.

She squatted down to get the lantern and weapons. There, beneath the wagon, was the creature who had been stalking her, mere centimeters away. Their faces nearly touched, cold radiating from its body along with a vague, musty smell. Its glassy, black eyes stared back at her, empty and soulless, the lantern's glow reflecting off its dark shell of a body. Small mandibles opened, and it chittered, loud even against the racket of the others in the tree. When it stopped, they stopped, the prairie silent. The silence was stark and shocking after the constant sounds of before.

Martha held her breath, afraid to move. She stared back at it.

Neither of them moved.

She released her breath, fogging the shell. It jerked its face away from her. The spike appeared again out of the darkness, this time heading for her face. She rolled to her side, grabbing the knife as she went. Bringing her hand up as far as she could, she slammed it forward into the creature's head. The knife pierced with a crunch, and it shrieked, high pitched and frantic, disappearing under the wagon, the knife still stuck in its shell.

Martha grabbed the gun and stood up, throwing it into the wagon. It landed with a clunk, causing James to stir and whimper. There was nothing she could do about that now but hope he stayed asleep.

Off to her right, leaves rustled as if in a heavy wind, though no wind existed.

The chittering began again.

They were coming.

Desperate, Martha grabbed the lantern and ran in the direction of the tree. The lantern bounced with her steps, casting startling shadows. She slowed once the tree was in view. One of the creatures stood at the base. The others moved about over it, descending from the branches.

She threw the lantern, grunting with the effort. It arced though the air as she watched, heart in her throat, terrified it would miss entirely, that it would hit the creek and fizzle out. But her aim was true; it struck the ground in front of the creature standing there and shattered. At first, the darkness remained around the sickeningly small flame, which flickered, weak against the grass. Horror filled Martha as she saw it fading, sputtering, about to go out.

Then the flame caught the summer-parched grass and burst outward in a wave of heat and light, spreading rapidly. The creature lit up, looking almost humanoid in the sudden brightness. It reared back, standing on the rear set of legs, the others tucked at its sides. Its center mass was slim, surrounded by the larger, rounded shell and a plated armor of chitin that traced its torso and limbs. Shrieking as its cohort had, it ran in the direction opposite Martha. Flames licked up the tree trunk, climbing at a terrifying speed to where the others perched.

Martha didn't wait to see what happened. She turned and fled back to the wagon, climbing into the back. She closed it tight. Shrieks rent the air outside the wagon, slightly muffled by the fabric surrounding her. She took no pleasure in their pain.

With the creatures hopefully kept busy, she took the time to load the gun and strike her only other lantern, fearful that at any moment one of those spikes would pierce the canvas. The nerves around the injuries on her ankle and thigh were raw and screaming, the tacky blood covering her leg, but she had no time to tend to her wounds.

The baby's movements had become sluggish, and she patted her stomach, hoping this little one would fall asleep now, too. The calmer she was, the calmer it would be. The baby moved beneath her hand in a slow roll.

Outside, one of the oxen huffed in alarm. The wagon jerked then began to move. Perhaps the oxen were fleeing the fire. She could only hope that was it.

Stumbling, she worked her way forward. She hung the lantern on a hook just at the front entrance and leaned the gun there. Part of her wanted to remain inside the wagon and let the oxen continue forward, but the risks were too great. She had to go back out there to steer the team.

Martha took a deep breath and worked at the opening, afraid of what she might find on the other side.

Warm, orange light burst in as the cover opened to her. Climbing out was tricky with her swollen belly and the rickety motion of the wagon, but she got out onto the wooden bench and settled herself. Only then did she allow a glance back at the tree, now engulfed in flames. The fire had caught more of the grass and spread.

She took up the reins and urged the oxen forward. They could only go so fast in the dark, and the fire had them scared, but any additional speed she could get from them would be worth it. They shambled forward at a steady gait, the cow keeping up beside them.

Up ahead, a light bobbed in the air. She strained her eyes, trying to determine what it might be.

The light grew closer, changing shape.

One of the oxen let out a drawn-out moo. The other animals joined it with their own vocalizations and came to a sudden halt. The lantern behind her swayed, once again casting crazy shadows. Her own form bounced around before her in its frenzied light. She grabbed the gun and held it before her, aimed at the light that frightened her animals. It had to be the remaining creature, firelight bouncing off its reflective shell.

Squinting into the dark, Martha made out its form just before it leapt. It cleared the animals, chitinous body coming at her at a great speed. She pulled back the right hammer and pulled the front trigger without aiming. Ammunition met creature, and it jerked to a stop in mid-air, falling between the two oxen with a high-pitched, multi-toned squeal that sounded alien to Martha's ears. Slapping the reins, she urged the team forward and to the side. She heard and felt, more than saw, the still squealing creature being trampled beneath their hooves, its hard body crunching underfoot, the animals struggling over it. They let out frightened huffs, but continued forward, good, steady animals that they were.

The wagon bumped and heaved as one wheel ran over the body. The screams stopped. The only sounds were the huff of the oxen and the rumble of the wagon.

Looking behind her at her son, she saw he'd rolled to his side and put a thumb in his mouth, fully asleep.

Martha drove her team forward, ready to get to her new life and a safe bed. The ache of her bladder reminded her she'd never gotten the chance to pee. It could wait a bit longer. Though only as long as the baby slept.

From the Author

While I grew up on westerns, I'd never written one, and the idea of a woman alone, save a toddler, traveling across the country for the west, appealed to me. I wanted to play around with some of the aspects of various movie creatures I'd found memorable, including xenomorphs (*Alien*), the liquid terminator (*Terminator 2*), and the Garthim (*Dark Crystal*). I had fun researching things like yokes, lanterns, cow vocalizations, the animals accompanying wagon trains, and similar items for the story, too, falling down a few rabbit holes.

Ultimately, this ended up one of my most often shortlisted stories and got almost exclusively personal rejections saying they liked the story but just couldn't make it fit with others under consideration. It was just too different. I have a lot of affection for this story and Martha, the MC, and it broke my heart as the rejections piled up, no matter how nice the letters coming with the rejections were.

About the Author

Shannon Lawrence bounced between coasts before her family settled in Colorado when she was twelve, giving her a love of the mountains and red rocks, despite the yearning in her soul to be near bodies of water. The oldest of five kids, she spent a lot of time going for walks to get away from the racket, which ultimately led to the grown up version: hiking. Eventually, she started taking a camera on hikes with her, capturing the rugged beauty of Colorado. In her meanderings through the woods and trails, she's been inspired to write many a horror story.

Coveting the attention often denied to the oldest kids in big families, she struck out into the short story world, riding the roller coaster of rejections and acceptances. Now a mother, and with over forty short stories published in magazines and anthologies, she's jumped into releasing solo collections and leading workshops on writing and publishing short stories, which has led to her passion project, a book all about short stories: *The Business of Short Stories*.

With her publications not bringing her quite enough attention, and her ridiculous need to have too much to do, this extroverted introvert with ADHD formed the podcast *Mysteries, Monsters, & Mayhem* to talk about true crime, hauntings, and cryptids, which also feeds her incessant need for all things creepy. Find her and her stories at:

www.thewarriormuse.com

and

www.mysteriesmonstersmayhem.com.

Bittersweet

by
Peter Sartucci

Bittersweet

O *nly a little farther,* Susan Wooten thought as she panted. *Then I can rest.* Her joints creaked, but she ignored them to push her walker another step up the sidewalk. The hill of Denver's Overlook Park was neither high nor steep, unless you were a seventy-year-old woman with sciatica and a heart condition. She was glad there was no breeze. In late March, the wind-chill could be a fearsome thing.

A short distance ahead, her son John worked little Robin's wheelchair over a bump and then wedged it between two concrete benches against the curved sandstone wall of the old war memorial. He set the brakes and came back to help Susan over the last bump in the walk. She sank down onto the chair-cushion he positioned on the hard park bench and cuddled close to her granddaughter.

"You have everything you need?" John asked as he tucked a blanket around her and handed her a precious water bottle. "Should I leave you another blanket in case the wind comes up?" He glanced at the patchy clouds in the sky. Robin wore her snowsuit and had both of her lap robes tucked about her twisted legs; Susan thought it made the child look like a plush toy.

"I've got my long underwear on, and two pairs of pants. I'm fine," she told her son as she mustered a smile through the pain. "You get back to your wife and the boys. They shouldn't be left alone, even with your buddies to guard them."

He glanced down to the bottom of the hill where the group sheltered behind a stalled UPS van. Then he turned back and hugged her awkwardly.

"I love you, Mom." There were tears in his voice as well as his eyes.

"I know that, John, and I love you too. Now you take good care of the others," she ordered, using bossiness to help him hang onto his self-control. "And hug your daughter."

He did, and kissed Robin on the forehead. Susan noticed the girl's puzzlement, her damaged brain obviously struggling with the strange emotions. Susan pulled out Robin's favorite storybook and caught her attention with it as John turned away. He blew his nose into a hanky as he ran back to where Janet held his bike.

Susan peeked over her shoulder. Even from fifty yards away she could see how his buddies had made a guardian circle about their wives and kids. The men raised home-made spears to ward off any strangers who got too close. Her two teenaged grandsons yakked with the other kids, all excited and scared. Most had packs lashed to their bikes, but Janet towed the Burley where Robin usually rode. John's bike towed the bigger cart Susan had ridden to get here; the others put some of the sleeping bags and other bulky items into it. now that there was room.

Beyond them, little clots and pairs of other bike riders poured down the road, outbound from the city.

Robin fussed with her book. Her bent fingers struggled to turn the pages as she cooed the familiar words to herself. Susan turned back to her and separated a pair of stuck pages but couldn't resist one last peek at her son's shrunken family as they pedaled away. The group vanished behind an abandoned semi as they made for the highway.

If there's a God, I hope he's with you, John, she thought sadly. *I'm glad your father didn't live to see this day.*

"Gramma!" Robin tugged on her sleeve, and Susan turned back to her with a quiet sigh.

"Yes, dear?"

"Gramma, I'm hot." Robin pushed at the lap robes with her twisted fingers.

Susan peeled off the outer blanket and set it aside. "Is that better, dear?"

"Yes. Thank you, Gramma." Robin looked at her in transparent speculation and added: "Can I have a cookie now?"

"No dear, not until after lunch," Susan answered firmly. "I told you we would save our cookies for when the sun sets. Would you like to read another story, together this time?"

Robin beamed. "Yes."

"Yes what, dear?

"Yes please, Gramma. I'd like you to read me a story."

"That's better, dear. How about 'Franklin the Turtle and the Caterpillar'?"

"We already read that one at the house." Robin's lips pursed, and her voice started to whine. "I want something else."

"Okay, but no whining, dear. Big girls don't whine. Hmmm." Susan rummaged in the grocery-sack full of books John had duct-taped to Robin's chair. "Let's read about 'Arthur and the True Francine', honey."

"I like that one!" A beatific smile replaced the whine, to Susan's carefully concealed relief.

Susan read the story slowly and paused frequently to direct Robin's attention to the cartoon pictures. She thought nostalgically about the road trip to Massachusetts, back when John was a toddler. They'd driven through the town of Hingham, where the author of the 'Arthur' series lived. Many of the old colonial buildings played background to his tales. She remembered the gorgeous spring weather, azaleas and rhododendrons in bloom. Jeweled hummingbirds darted from blossom to blossom in beautifully landscaped yards, under the graceful fan shapes of old elm trees. It had been like a living museum cradling a genteel and elegant past...

Robin's voice pulled her back to the present with a start. "Gramma? We're done!"

"Oh, sorry dear, my thoughts were wandering. Would you like to read 'Arthur and the Lost Library Book'?"

"Yes! Please, yes, Gramma."

Susan handed it to Robin and glanced over her shoulder again. The crowds on the road had grown bigger as noon approached. Mostly she saw people on foot. Bikes were rarer now. Some pushed shopping carts loaded with possessions—many of those were women surrounded by men carrying rough weapons. Unshaven men, in dirty pants and jackets, nervously watched all around them. Frightened women stuck close to their sides and clutched children. Some of the groups had a predatory look; those swaggered and leered. She heard occasional screams back in the crowd, suddenly cut off.

Susan suppressed a shudder and turned her attention back to Robin. They read two more stories before they were distracted by a cheerful whistle and the tap of metal on pavement.

A dapper, brown-skinned man hobbled up the other side of the path. He wore a lined trench coat over a navy-blue suit at least two decades out of fashion, and leaned on a cane as he whistled; the hair under his fedora was curled silver, like steel wool. His eyes had been on the uneven concrete as he walked, but he glanced up to meet Susan's and smiled.

"Pardon me, ma'm, but would you mind if I sit with you and the little lady for a while?"

Susan caught a hint of Deep South in his generic Western accent. She admired his even white teeth, startling against that dark skin. She'd have suspected expensive dental work, but one had a visible filling.

"You're quite welcome to join us." Susan smiled and waved at the park bench on Robin's other side. *Nice looking fellow,* she thought. *Not that much older than me.*

"Thank you." He sat with a grunt and carefully set the cane aside, then made a little head-bow as he said, "My name is Paul Brown."

"I'm Susan Wooten, and this is my granddaughter, Robin Wooten. Say hello to the nice man, Robin."

Robin lifted her head from the storybook, studied the man, and said, "Hello. I am twelve years old today."

Paul blinked at her, nodded politely, and answered her like an adult.

"I am very pleased to meet you, Robin. Congratulations on your birthday—twelve is a very grown-up age to be."

"Gramma made me cookies!" Robin crowed. "Can we eat them now?"

"No dear, we haven't even had lunch yet."

"We ate left-overs for breakfast," Robin confided to Paul. "Mama said we had to eat what was left in the 'frige-er-a-tor, so I got to eat olives! And choc'late syrup on a tor-tee-ya too."

Paul smiled, the lines in his face growing deeper. "That sounds delicious, Robin."

"It was chewy," the little girl answered before her attention fell back into the story.

"Do you live close to the park, Paul?" Susan inquired as she helped turn a page.

"Right there." He pointed to a broad apartment building visible above the northern trees. "Sixth floor."

"Sixth floor?" Susan let her eyebrows rise. "You walked down five flights of stairs to take a walk in the park?"

Paul cleared his throat self-consciously, ducked his head a little. "Well, you see, I was looking out my window, and I saw you arrive. I've been alone since my wife died last year. My older brother George has been living with me the last three months, but he died the night—um, when that flash-thing happened. I think his pacemaker quit, and he had a coronary in his sleep. No power, no phones, I couldn't get a doctor or anyone to come, and staying there with his...well. I kinda hoped for some company before..." He cleared his throat again and met her eyes. "If you don't mind?"

Susan let her pleasure show in her smile. "I not only don't mind, I'd be delighted. Would you be willing to help me read stories? This chilly air's making me a little hoarse."

"I'd be honored." Paul turned to Robin and asked politely, "May I read you a story, Robin?"

Robin considered that for a moment and then smiled beatifically. "Yes please. I want a Winnie story."

Susan fished out a book and gave it to Paul. He had quite a good reading voice, clearly differentiating the characters with little changes of tone and accent and hand-motions; he even managed Piglet's stutter. Robin was enthralled.

Susan listened while she assembled lunch—a cup of yogurt mixed with a small can of cranberry-jelly leftover from Christmas. The result was a little watery, but the yogurt hadn't spoiled yet, and Robin liked cranberry. They only had two spoons, but she and Robin could share.

"Here." Paul interrupted his reading long enough to pluck two very ripe tangerines from a coat pocket and hand them to her, followed by a package of crackers. "I've got a can of ginger-ale too. I'm sorry I don't have more. George and I usually ate out, so I didn't keep much food in the apartment."

"It's wonderful," she assured him. The tangerine skins were a little tough, but she had a small paring-knife in her purse; it worked just right to peel them and cut up the fruit wedges. She still got quite a bit of juice on her fingers doing it. She was about to open one of Robin's wet-wipes to clean up, then decided to lick it off. The tart-sweet flavor was intense. She got the meal assembled just as Paul finished the story.

"Time for lunch, honey," she told Robin. "Let's put a towel in your lap while Gramma feeds you."

They juggled the tub, the crackers, the water bottle, and the soda-can, but managed to get all the meal eaten. From the eager way he gulped the food, Susan suspected that Paul hadn't had any breakfast, and probably not much for supper last night either. But he was conscientious about not taking more than one-third of the fruit-yogurt mix, and less than that of the crackers. Robin didn't like the ginger-ale, and it had never appealed to Susan either, so they split half the water bottle and left the soda to Paul.

"Where's Mommy and Daddy, Gramma?"

"On their way to your Uncle Marty's farm at Boyero, honey." Susan paused to pray the family would make it the hundred-fifty miles before snow came again. John had figured they ought to get there in three days. If the bikes held out, and if they found safe places to sleep at night, and if nothing else went wrong.

Nothing will go wrong, she told herself firmly. *The going-wrongness is here. They've got friends with them—nobody's going to bother twelve men with spears. Not until things get more desperate.*

"Where is Boy—boy—where's that?" Robin could get fixated on a question.

"A long way east of here, honey." Susan searched the bag for a book they hadn't read yet.

"I've been to Boyero," Paul volunteered.

"Really!?" Susan was astonished. "It's such a little nubbin of a place."

Paul nodded. "It was for a firemen's training event. A bunch of us, from Denver Fire, volunteered to teach some classes for the little volunteer fire districts out on the plains. It was fun meeting new folks, and, ah, breaking a few habits of thinking."

His brown face got a sly look. Susan chuckled.

"How long were you a fireman, Paul?"

"Thirty-seven years." He looked proud and sad at the same time.

"A long time. You must have liked it."

"That I did; but by the end I just couldn't pull my share anymore. It's a young man's profession, and I had to leave it to them." His eyes traveled to the pillars of smoke rising over many parts of the city. There were more today than yesterday, the wet-smoky stench getting stronger. His lips twisted. "Hard to let go, though. Harder still to watch everything I tried to protect—" He cut his words off.

"We lived too long in a garden," Susan remarked softly. "Forgetting the cruel world outside."

Paul glanced at her in surprise. "That's John Wyndham, isn't it? *Day of the Triffids*, maybe?"

"*Midwich Cuckoos*, the one about the alien children. You read science fiction?"

"Lots of it, in between calls at the station. In the slow times, there's only so much weightlifting and polishing the engines and shooting the sh—breeze, that a fireman can do. I liked reading, and the public library would let me check out a dozen books at once."

"I used to haunt that place when I was young," Susan shared. "After my little John came along, and I stopped working, I used to read bits of stories aloud to him. He read everything on the science fiction shelves in the library before he was sixteen—and ransacked the used bookstores too. That probably helped us both figure out what to do after the flash. John talked most of his friends, and some of our neighbors, into all heading out together; I think that'll help them a lot. Most people are probably going to wait around until it's too late. I told him not to do that."

There was a long pause while they both listened to the unnaturally quiet city. The usual noises were gone; no rumble of engines, no electric hum so omnipresent they'd long ago stopped noticing. She heard scattered shouts and screams, a faint smashing and hammering, and a soft crackling roar. The nasal bite of things not meant to burn competed with greening grass and the sap-smell of budding trees. Pigeons cooed mindlessly, a dog barked, and above them, on the monument, a crow croaked.

Robin patiently turned the pages in one of her books, one with only pictures and no words, ignoring the incomprehensible adult conversation.

"Speaking of stories about Alien visits, you think this might-a-been done by aliens?" Paul waved at the city around them, including the greater disaster by implication.

"I wish I knew." Susan opened her hands and poured out the unknowable. "One of Robert Heinlein's characters said, 'When you have no data, guessing is illogical.' "

"*Tunnel in the Sky*. I remember that one." Paul's smile flickered, and then sank into melancholy. "But they eventually found out what had happened to them."

"They were all young." Susan shrugged. "If there's anything beyond, maybe we'll find out what happened too. I didn't used to pray a lot, but I'm praying for that now."

"Know the feeling. I always went to church with Mayella while she was alive, but that was just to please her. Now . . . I don't know, maybe it'll help. Can't hurt, since my knees tell me I'm not gonna be riding no bike to Boyero, or anywheres else." He paused, looked at her, looked away.

Susan guessed the question in his mind. "John wanted to haul me along in a cart, but I said no. I don't want to die exhausted and frozen on some strange road; I want a familiar place around me. And Robin and I each need medicines that—anyway, I made them go without us, which his brain knew he should do. His heart; well, life goes on, and he's got the boys to think of."

Susan remembered the look on Janet's face when she'd made that announcement; half relieved and half guilty. At least her daughter-in-law had the good sense to keep quiet while Susan argued John into what had to be done.

There wasn't any happy solution, and she was smart enough to know it. She'll keep John focused until the memories fade.

Susan looked around at the greening grass, bobbing daffodils, the twists of tulip leaves poking through the ground, the hyacinths pushing up brighter green clubs, newly-burst into pink and purple clusters. "I always loved the view from this park."

Robin closed her book, looked up perkily. "Can we have cookies now, Gramma?"

Susan thought of the sunset—with the high clouds above the mountains and the half-moon, and the smoky haze, it ought to be spectacular. Now that she had somebody adult to sit and chat with it was easy to say: "No dear, not until it's time. Let's have another story, shall we?"

They read that one and two more; she and Paul alternated. The afternoon sun was warming nicely. The farther west it got, the more heat reflected off the sandstone monument behind them to make a little oasis of warmth. They set aside the blanket and lap robes, unzipped Robin's snowsuit, and Paul opened his trench coat.

Some pigeons pecked for food along the sidewalk at their feet. Paul looked at their bobbing gray-purple shapes and shook his head.

"Nope. I'm still not hungry enough to eat a pigeon," he told her sotto-voce.

"Ewww," Susan agreed. "I don't like to think about where their feet have been." A stray wisp of smoke made her eyes water, and all three of them sneezed. She hoped the breeze didn't start coming from the south, where several city blocks were burning. She groped for another book.

"How about 'Arthur and the New Puppy', honey?"

"I like that one! Can I have a doggie someday, Gramma?"

"I have a doggie on my keychain," Paul inserted helpfully. "Would you like to hold it while I read the story?"

"Oh yes!" Robin bounced a little in her seat as Paul brought out the cloisonné figurine and snapped it off the key ring; it was a Dalmatian inside a circle and had the initials 'DFD' on it in red and gold. Robin seized it eagerly and cooed as she stared at it, enraptured while they read.

A little later there was a loud clash of metal on metal and shrieks and screams came from the road below the park. Robin looked up in confusion, but Paul smoothly slipped another book in front of the girl and captured her attention again. Susan smiled at him in fresh gratitude and did her best to ignore the sound of the brawl. The noise faded away as they read another 'Arthur' book together, with Paul doing the boys' voices and herself handling the girls. Robin wiggled in delight.

Sneakered feet slapped the concrete walk amid gasped obscenities. A young man came around the monument and stopped. He leaned hands on his knees, panted and cursed. Blood splashed the sleeve of his sweatshirt, blood dripped from the knife he gripped in his right hand. Freckles showed stark on his pale face, and dirty hair stuck out every which-way; he stood up again and shook his head. He wore dirty jeans and an attitude that chilled Susan's heart.

Paul tensed, but Susan reached across Robin and laid a cautioning hand on his wrist, continued to read. "So, Arthur and his friends went to the Sugar Bowl for banana splits. The end. Did you like that story, honey?" Paul sat very still and watched the stranger intently while Susan thought hard at him: *Don't do anything stupid!*

Then she realized that Robin was also staring at the young man with the knife. His breath still heaved, and his eyes darted wildly.

"Hello," the girl said brightly. "My name's Robin. What's yours?"

The knifeman gaped at her, then looked away and twitched as fight/flight reactions still worked their way through him. Robin gazed at him expectantly, but he didn't respond. She tried offering him a sunny smile. "Did you hurt your hand?"

The knifeman suddenly remembered the blade in his hand. He stared at it, and his bloody knuckles, with wonder in his eyes, then a dark satisfaction that brought a smile to his face and a shiver to Susan's spine.

He never killed anyone with a knife before. But he liked it. She carefully let her breath out again and asked him politely, "Would you like a wet-wipe for your hand?" She fished through her purse, tugged one free and shook it open, held it out. *Please, God, please make him think of us as useful, non-threatening, not dangerous.*

The man stepped closer, grabbed the alcohol-soaked fabric and cleaned the knife and his hand. A harsh copper tang competed with the medicinal-alcohol smell of the wipe and the acrid smoke. She opened another wipe and handed that to him too, relieved that her own hands didn't tremble much.

Paul remained as still as a statue, his gaze almost as unblinking, while the man loomed over them. Robin looked puzzled.

The knifeman let the used-up wipes fall and tensed as another pair of running feet came up the hill behind the monument; but whoever it was curved away and the sound faded.

"It's my birthday," Robin added, still trying to chat. People were usually nice to her, and his silence upset her sense of how the world ought to be. "We're going to have cookies!"

"Cookies?" The knifeman had a gruff voice and a pinched look to his face, as if meals were a fading memory. "Gimme!"

Susan gulped; she'd made extras, but not a lot. She twitched the smaller package out of her walker-pouch and opened it, started to offer it. Paul tensed, but didn't move, possibly in answer to her prayer.

Knifeman snatched the baggie out of her hands and retreated a couple paces, looked all around as if to assure himself that nobody else was near enough to threaten his prize. He began to stuff the thick sandwich cookies into his mouth. They each had a gob of homemade icing between two Nilla wafers, with more icing slathered on top. She'd made them by hand last night, in the light of an old jar-candle that Joe had given her as an anniversary present. It had lasted just long enough to do the job, much like Joe.

Knifeman ate half the bag before he slowed down. The muscles in his jaws bulged; sugary cookies without water were heavy going. His eyes swept over the three of them before roving around the park again.

Susan said nothing, grappled with her fear and prayed. *Oh, please let him stay calm, please, please, please!*

Presently he stopped eating, stood quiet and blinked.

You're tired, she thought. *You just want to rest a little.*

The movements of his head got slower. He suddenly sat down on the edge of the grass. He blinked some more in a heavy-lidded way as his hands drifted to the ground for support. A couple of cookies spilled out onto the sidewalk and his knife scraped the concrete; he didn't seem to notice. At last, he sagged back into a flat sprawl and began to snore. His grip relaxed, and the knife dropped to the cement with a clatter.

Paul let his breath out, gave a soft snort. "Well. You think he'll stay asleep?"

"Should," Susan answered quietly. "I think he ate enough. Though he's young; his body might be able to absorb it."

Paul glanced at her wide-eyed, suddenly understanding. After a pause he said, "Should I maybe drag him around the corner?"

"I think that would be a good idea, Paul." Susan rubbed her trembling hands together and fought down the temptation to scream her relief. Will there be convulsions? The book said usually not, but she didn't know. "I don't want him in Robin's sight."

The girl's face had been running through a slow kaleidoscope of expressions as her brain fought to process it all. "Gramma, he took my cookies! And he didn't say please!"

"Not all of them, dear," Susan managed to answer as Paul got up and pocketed the knife. He gathered the fallen cookies into the baggie before he silently handed it back to her. Then he took the knifeman's limp hands and began to tug. Paul managed to drag him around the corner of the monument even though the younger man probably outweighed him by fifty pounds. Susan was relieved and impressed. It was several more minutes before the ragged snore suddenly stopped with a squelch. *That danger's over,* she thought while relief washed through her. *From the wait, I think Paul had to work himself up to do the deed. I'm glad of that.*

She soothed Robin. "We still have most of the cookies, dear. I'm sorry he was so rude, let's just ignore him and continue reading, shall we?"

Robin grumpily agreed and was soon enrapt in another book, the stranger forgotten.

Presently Paul came back. He limped now and collapsed on the bench next to her. "I think I just threw my back out, doing that," he winced. "And I used to haul hundred-pound hoses around, and bench-press two-fifty! Da—unh, I mean dang." His face had a harsh expression and he mumbled, "Too old."

Susan touched his arm. "Thank you very much for taking care of that for Robin and me," she told him, pouring as much warmth into her voice as she could.

The harshness faded from Paul's face, and after a moment he smiled at her. "Glad to help."

They read more stories to Robin and exhausted the selection just as the sun settled onto the mountain peaks. Clouds rapidly turned pink, and the air temperature began to drop. A chilly breeze parted the smoky air, a breath of freshness.

Susan zipped up the snowsuit and put Robin's lap robes back on her. She zipped up her own coat while Paul buttoned his trench coat.

"Would you like to share the blanket with me, Paul?"

His eyes met hers. "I'd like that very much—Susan." He switched to her bench and helped her spread the thick wool over both of their legs, so they shared the warmth.

Banners of gold and crimson spread across the sky.

"Beautiful," Paul remarked in a hoarse voice. "I should have come out here to watch the sunset more often. Lotta things I wish I'd done."

"No regrets," Susan answered firmly, ignoring the rasp in her own voice from the cold smoky air and too much story-reading; it would have been much worse without Paul to share the load. "We had our run, and it wasn't so bad. Maybe there'll be another one for us; sitting on clouds playing a harp always sounded boring to me. I'd rather be doing, or at least reading."

"Gramma, I'm hungry. Can we eat my cookies now?" Robin asked.

Susan considered; the temperature was dropping fast. "Yes, dear, I think it's time."

She took out the two packages, picked out the five special cookies with Robin's name on them in rather squashed red icing, and carefully set them on the girl's lap robe so they wouldn't fall off. She divided the remaining fourteen into two piles.

"I don't mean to pressure you, Paul, but we still have enough to share, if you want." She looked at him steadily, refusing to offer apology or excuse, only the fact.

He squirmed uneasily, looked away for a moment, then back.

"I'm not sure I should go barging into God's House uninvited," he said slowly. "Least . . . not after what I just done."

There were more screams from down on the road.

"I suspect," she told him, "that it will be set greatly to your credit in Heaven."

He met her eyes again and gave a slow nod. She handed over seven cookies in the baggie.

Robin greedily chewed and said she was thirsty; Susan gave her the last of the water-bottle to wash her cookies down. The thick sugar-frosting was studded with flaked baking chocolate, each bite both sweet and bitter. It hid the taste of the pills quite well. She had needed a whole hour to grind them in a mortar-and-pestle and longer to mix the result with leftover bits of chocolate, confectioner's sugar and water. Tenderly filling and icing the wafers had used the last light of Joe's candle.

"Gramma, I'm cold."

Susan took Robin's chilly little hand. "Do you mind if Mister Brown holds my other hand, Robin?"

"Okay." Robin bestowed one of her startling smiles on Paul as she drowsily told him, "Thank you for reading stories to me, Mister Brown."

His seamed face split in a gentle grin as he took Susan's other hand; his palm was dry with old callus. "Thank you for letting me do it, Robin." He turned his eyes to Susan and wordlessly added another thank you. "Let's just enjoy the pretty sunset together now, shall we?"

Susan leaned her head back against the still-warm sandstone behind the bench and admired the departure of warmth and light amidst purple spectacle. Denver burned around them and added drifting sparks to the show. Robin's head sagged forward loosely.

I'm glad Paul came out here to help me with Robin, Susan thought. She gave his hand a small squeeze and felt the answering pressure. *I'm glad we got to spend a little time together. I hope John and the others find some kind of safety.*

And, as her limbs went numb and the darkness closed in, *I wonder what will come after?*

From the Author

How do you react with love when the world shifts under your feet and suddenly you are not just superfluous, but actually a danger to the survival of people you care about? Or them to you? This is a story about one old woman's solution in the moment when there is no escape from the giant steamroller of the world that is grinding inexorably toward her.

About the Author

Peter Sartucci is a retired LARP producer and full-time dad who hides out in suburban Denver between a firehouse and a cemetery, where he enjoys the average noise level. He has written and published three alt-history books and four epic fantasy tomes, with a fifth on the way and more planned. He has occasionally conned people into reading his short stories too, and none of them have fled screaming yet! He hasn't the business sense that God (any god) gave to a mitochondria but has had the very good luck to be discovered by friends anyway. You can find him on Facebook—he's the only Peter Sartucci there.

From the Editor

Unlike most anthologies, the Particular Passages Anthologies are curated and edited with a light touch, so if you see a difference in grammar, punctuation, or spelling styles, that may be why. We are excited to give authors a chance to share a story they like, the way they like it.

Often, when submitting stories to anthologies, authors are required to fit a central theme somehow. But not all stories fit anthology themes. Not all stories fit what magazine editors want either. In fact, sometimes there are great stories that just don't fit in well anywhere else.

As an editor, I find it exhilarating to go through the stories and not have any idea what the next story will be. As a reader, I hope you found that kind of excitement in this anthology as well.

If you liked an author's story, reach out and let them know. The *best* way to make sure your favorite authors write more stories is to tell them you loved one of their stories. (Not to mention it will make their day!)

If you liked this kind of anthology, and would like to see more of them, please let us know. Comments to us, or to our authors, on our social media, our websites, or in an email all work. Tell us what you loved about it. That is the best way to make sure we do another one. The second-best way is to tell other people about the anthology, so that they buy the book, too. The third best way is to leave reviews. Not just at the place you bought the book, but anywhere you frequent online, including on your, and our, social media.

Seriously, that helps *a lot*.

In the spirit of these anthologies, in the search for great stories in unexpected places, I wish you great adventures in your searches, and I hope you find the best things that just don't quite fit in anywhere else.

Sam Knight
3/7/2022

Additional Copyright Information

www.ingramcontent.com/pod-product-compliance
Lightning Source LLC
Chambersburg PA
CBHW02082526O626
47169CB00003B/831